# FALLING ANGELS

Tracy Chevalier grew up in Washington, DC. She moved to England in 1984, and worked for several years as a reference book editor. In 1994 she graduated from the MA course in creative writing at the University of East Anglia. Her first novel, *The Virgin Blue*, was chosen by WH Smith for its Fresh Talent promotion in 1997. *Girl with a Pearl Earring* was longlisted for the Orange Prize in 2000. Tracy Chevalier lives in London with her husband and son.

To find out more about Tracy Chevalier visit www.tchevalier.com, and for exclusive updates visit www.AuthorTracker.co.uk.

Praise for *Girl with a Pearl Earring*:

'A portrait of radiance . . . Tracy Chevalier brings the real artist Vermeer and a fictional muse to life in a jewel of a novel.'                                                                         *Time*

'Beautifully written, mysterious and almost unbearably poignant − a magical experience.'     DEBORAH MOGGACH

'It has a slow, magical current of its own that picks you up and carries you stealthily along . . . a beautiful story, lovingly told by a very talented writer.'     *Daily Mail*

## Also by Tracy Chevalier

**GIRL WITH A PEARL EARRING**
**THE VIRGIN BLUE**
**THE LADY AND THE UNICORN**
**BURNING BRIGHT**

# FALLING ANGELS

## Tracy Chevalier

**HARPER**

This novel is entirely a work of fiction.
The names, characters and incidents portrayed in it are
the work of the author's imagination. Any resemblance to
actual persons, living or dead, events or localities is
entirely coincidental.

*Harper*
An imprint of HarperCollins*Publishers*
1 London Bridge Street
London SE1 9GF

www.harpercollins.co.uk

This paperback edition 2006

First published in Great Britain by
HarperCollins*Publishers* 2001

A catalogue record for this book is
available from the British Library

ISBN-13: 978 0 00 721723 6
ISBN-10: 0 00 721723 4

Set in PostScript Linotype Spectrum

Printed and bound by CPI Group (UK) Ltd, Croydon, CR0 4YY

For Jonathan, again

*January 1901*

# KITTY COLEMAN

I woke this morning with a stranger in my bed. The head of blond hair beside me was decidedly not my husband's. I did not know whether to be shocked or amused.

Well, I thought, here's a novel way to begin the new century.

Then I remembered the evening before and felt rather sick. I wondered where Richard was in this huge house and how we were meant to swap back. Everyone else here – the man beside me included – was far more experienced in the mechanics of these matters than I. Than we. Much as Richard bluffed last night, he was just as much in the dark as me, though he was more keen. Much more keen. It made me wonder.

I nudged the sleeper with my elbow, gently at first and then harder until at last he woke with a snort.

'Out you go,' I said. And he did, without a murmur. Thankfully he didn't try to kiss me. How I stood that beard last night I'll never remember – the claret helped, I suppose. My cheeks are red with scratches.

When Richard came in a few minutes later, clutching his clothes in a bundle, I could barely look at him. I was embarrassed, and angry too — angry that I should feel embarrassed and yet not expect him to feel so as well. It was all the more infuriating that he simply kissed me, said, 'Hello, darling,' and began to dress. I could smell her perfume on his neck.

Yet I could say nothing. As I myself have so often said, I am open-minded — I pride myself on it. Those words bite now.

I lay watching Richard dress, and found myself thinking of my brother. Harry always used to tease me for thinking too much — though he refused to concede that he was at all responsible for encouraging me. But all those evenings spent reviewing with me what his tutors had taught him in the morning — he said it was to help him remember it — what did that do but teach me to think and speak my mind? Perhaps he regretted it later. I shall never know now. I am only just out of mourning for him, but some days it feels as if I am still clutching that telegram.

Harry would be mortified to see where his teaching has led. Not that one has to be clever for this sort of thing — most of them downstairs are stupid as buckets of coal, my blond beard among them. Not one could I have a proper conversation with. I had to resort to the wine.

Frankly I'm relieved not to be of this set — to paddle in its shallows occasionally is quite enough for me. Richard, I suspect, feels differently, but he has married the wrong wife if he wanted that sort of life. Or perhaps it is I who chose badly — though I would never have thought so once, back when we were mad for each other.

I think Richard has made me do this to show me he is not as conventional as I feared. But it has had the opposite effect on me. He has become everything I had not thought he would when we married. He has become ordinary.

I feel so flat this morning. Daddy and Harry would have laughed at me, but I secretly hoped that the change in the century would bring a change in us all; that England would miraculously slough off her shabby black coat to reveal something glittering and new. It is only eleven hours into the twentieth century, but I know very well that nothing has changed but a number.

Enough. They are to ride today, which is not for me – I shall escape with my coffee to the library. It will undoubtedly be empty.

# RICHARD COLEMAN

I thought being with another woman would bring Kitty back, that jealousy would open her bedroom door to me again. Yet two weeks later she has not let me in any more than before.

I do not like to think that I am a desperate man, but I do not understand why my wife is being so difficult. I have provided a decent life for her and yet she is still unhappy, though she cannot – or will not – say why.

It is enough to drive any man to change wives, if only for a night.

# MAUDE COLEMAN

When Daddy saw the angel on the grave next to ours he cried, 'What the devil!'

Mummy just laughed.

I looked and looked until my neck ached. It hung above us, one foot forward, a hand pointing towards heaven. It was wearing a long robe with a square neck, and it had loose hair that flowed onto its wings. It was looking down towards me, but no matter how hard I stared it did not seem to see me.

Mummy and Daddy began to argue. Daddy does not like the angel. I don't know if Mummy likes it or not – she didn't say. I think the urn Daddy has had placed on our own grave bothers her more.

I wanted to sit down but didn't dare. It was very cold, too cold to sit on stone, and besides, the Queen is dead, which I think means no one can sit down, or play, or do anything comfortable.

I heard the bells ringing last night when I was in bed, and when Nanny came in this morning she told me the Queen died yesterday evening. I ate my porridge very slowly, to see if it tasted different from yesterday's, now that the

Queen is gone. But it tasted just the same — too salty. Mrs Baker always makes it that way.

Everyone we saw on our way to the cemetery was dressed in black. I wore a grey wool dress and a white pinafore, which I might have worn anyway but which Nanny said was fine for a girl to wear when someone died. Girls don't have to wear black. Nanny helped me to dress. She let me wear my black and white plaid coat and matching hat, but she wasn't sure about my rabbit's-fur muff, and I had to ask Mummy, who said it didn't matter what I wore. Mummy wore a blue silk dress and wrap, which did not please Daddy.

While they were arguing about the angel I buried my face in my muff. The fur is very soft. Then I heard a noise, like stone being tapped, and when I raised my head I saw a pair of blue eyes looking at me from over the headstone next to ours. I stared at them, and then the face of a boy appeared from behind the stone. His hair was full of mud, and his cheeks were dirty with it too. He winked at me, then disappeared behind the headstone.

I looked at Mummy and Daddy, who had walked a little way up the path to view the angel from another place. They had not seen the boy. I walked backwards between the graves, my eyes on them. When I was sure they were not looking I ducked behind the stone.

The boy was leaning against it, sitting on his heels.

'Why do you have mud in your hair?' I asked.

'Been down a grave,' he said.

I looked at him closely. There was mud on him everywhere — on his jacket, on his knees, on his shoes. There were even bits of it in his eyelashes.

'Can I touch the fur?' he asked.

'It's a muff,' I said. 'My muff.'

'Can I touch it?'

'No.' Then I felt bad saying that, so I held out the muff.

The boy spit on his fingers and wiped them on his jacket, then reached out and stroked the fur.

'What were you doing down a grave?' I asked.

'Helping our Pa.'

'What does your father do?'

'He digs the graves, of course. I helps him.'

Then we heard a sound, like a kitten mewing. We peeked over the headstone and a girl standing in the path looked straight into my eyes, just as I had with the boy. She was dressed all in black, and was very pretty, with bright brown eyes and long lashes and creamy skin. Her brown hair was long and curly and so much nicer than mine, which hangs flat like laundry and isn't one colour or another. Grandmother calls mine ditch-water blonde, which may be true but isn't very kind. Grandmother always speaks her mind.

The girl reminded me of my favourite chocolates, whipped hazelnut creams, and I knew just from looking at her that I wanted her for my best friend. I don't have a best friend, and have been praying for one. I have often wondered, as I sit in St Anne's getting colder and colder (why are churches always cold?), if prayers really work, but it seems this time God has answered them.

'Use your handkerchief, Livy dear, there's a darling.' The girl's mother was coming up the path, holding the hand of a younger girl. A tall man with a ginger beard followed them. The younger girl was not so pretty. Though she looked like the other girl, her chin was not so pointed, her hair not so curly, her lips not so big. Her eyes were hazel rather than brown, and she looked at everything as if nothing surprised her. She spotted the boy and me immediately.

'Lavinia,' the older girl said, shrugging her shoulders and tossing her head so that her curls bounced. 'Mama, I want you and Papa to call me Lavinia, not Livy.'

I decided then and there that I would never call her Livy.

'Don't be rude to your mother, Livy,' the man said. 'You're Livy to us and that's that. Livy is a fine name. When you're older we'll call you Lavinia.'

Lavinia frowned at the ground.

'Now stop all this crying,' he continued. 'She was a good queen and she lived a long life, but there's no need for a girl of five to weep quite so much. Besides, you'll frighten Ivy May.' He nodded at the sister.

I looked at Lavinia again. As far as I could see she was not crying at all, though she was twisting a handkerchief around her fingers. I waved at her to come.

Lavinia smiled. When her parents turned their backs she stepped off the path and behind the headstone.

'I'm five as well,' I said when she was standing next to us. 'Though I'll be six in March.'

'Is that so?' Lavinia said. 'I'll be six in February.'

'Why do you call your parents Mama and Papa? I call mine Mummy and Daddy.'

'Mama and Papa is much more elegant.' Lavinia stared at the boy, who was kneeling by the headstone. 'What is your name, please?'

'Maude,' I answered before I realised she was speaking to the boy.

'Simon.'

'You are a very dirty boy.'

'Stop,' I said.

Lavinia looked at me. 'Stop what?'

'He's a gravedigger, that's why he's muddy.'

Lavinia took a step backwards.

'An apprentice gravedigger,' Simon said. 'I was a mute for the undertakers first, but our Pa took me on once I could use a spade.'

'There were three mutes at my grandmother's funeral,' Lavinia said. 'One of them was whipped for laughing.'

'My mother says there are not so many funerals like that any more,' I said. 'She says they are too dear and the money should be spent on the living.'

'Our family always has mutes at its funerals. I shall have mutes at mine.'

'Are you dying, then?' Simon asked.

'Of course not!'

'Did you leave your nanny at home as well?' I asked, thinking we should talk about something else before Lavinia got upset and left.

She flushed. 'We don't have a nanny. Mama is perfectly able to look after us herself.'

I didn't know any children who didn't have a nanny.

Lavinia was looking at my muff. 'Do you like my angel, then?' she asked. 'My father let me choose it.'

'My father doesn't like it,' I declared, though I knew I shouldn't repeat what Daddy had said. 'He called it sentimental nonsense.'

Lavinia frowned. 'Well, Papa hates your urn. Anyway, what's wrong with my angel?'

'I like it,' the boy said.

'So do I,' I lied.

'I think it's lovely,' Lavinia sighed. 'When I go to heaven I want to be taken up by an angel just like that.'

'It's the nicest angel in the cemetery,' the boy said. 'And I know 'em all. There's thirty-one of 'em. D'you want me to show 'em to you?'

'Thirty-one is a prime number,' I said. 'It isn't divisible by anything except one and itself.' Daddy had just explained to me about prime numbers, though I hadn't understood it all.

Simon took a piece of coal from his pocket and began to draw on the back of the headstone. Soon he had drawn a skull and crossbones – round eyesockets, a black triangle for a nose, rows of square teeth, and a shadow scratched on one side of the face.

'Don't do that,' I said. He ignored me. 'You can't do that.'

'I have. Lots. Look at the stones all round us.'

I looked at our family grave. At the very bottom of the plinth that held the urn, a tiny skull and crossbones had been scratched. Daddy would be furious if he knew it were there. I saw then that every stone around us had a skull and crossbones on it. I had never seen them before.

'I'm going to draw one on every grave in the cemetery,' he continued.

'Why do you draw them?' I asked. 'Why a skull and crossbones?'

'Reminds you what's underneath, don't it? It's all bones down there, whatever you may put on the grave.'

'Naughty boy,' Lavinia said.

Simon stood up. 'I'll draw one for you,' he said. 'I'll draw one on the back of your angel.'

'Don't you dare,' Lavinia said.

Simon immediately dropped the piece of coal.

Lavinia looked around as if she were about to leave.

'I know a poem,' Simon said suddenly.

'What poem? Tennyson?'

'Dunno whose son. It's like this:

> 'There was a young man at Nunhead
> Who awoke in his coffin of lead;
>> "It is cosy enough,"
>> He remarked in a huff,
>> "But I wasn't aware I was dead."'

'Ugh! That's disgusting!' Lavinia cried. Simon and I laughed.

'Our Pa says lots of people've been buried alive,' Simon said. 'He says he's heard 'em, scrabbling inside their coffins as he's tossing dirt on 'em.'

'Really? Mummy's afraid of being buried alive,' I said.

'I can't bear to hear this,' Lavinia cried, covering her ears. 'I'm going back.' She went through the graves towards her parents. I wanted to follow her but Simon began talking again.

'Our Granpa's buried here in the meadow.'

'He never was.'

'He is.'

'Show me his grave.'

Simon pointed at a row of wooden crosses over the path from us. Paupers' graves – Mummy had told me about them, explaining that land had been set aside for people who had no money to pay for a proper plot.

'Which cross is his?' I asked.

'He don't have one. Cross don't last. We planted a rosebush, there, so we always know where he is. Stole it from one of the gardens down the bottom of the hill.'

I could see a stump of a bush, cut right back for the winter. We live at the bottom of the hill, and we have lots of roses at the front. Perhaps that rosebush was ours.

'He worked here too,' Simon said. 'Same as our Pa and me. Said it's the nicest cemetery in London. Wouldn't have wanted to be buried in any of t'others. He had stories to tell about t'others. Piles of bones everywhere. Bodies buried with just a sack of soil over 'em. Phew, the smell!' Simon waved his hand in front of his nose. 'And men snatching bodies in the night. Here he were at least safe and sound, with the boundary wall being so high, and the spikes on top.'

'I have to go now,' I said. I didn't want to look scared like Lavinia, but I didn't like hearing about the smell of bodies.

Simon shrugged. 'I could show you things.'

'Maybe another time.' I ran to catch up with our families, who were walking along together. Lavinia took my hand and squeezed it and I was so pleased I kissed her.

As we walked hand in hand up the hill I could see out of the corner of my eye a figure like a ghost jumping from stone to stone, following us and then running ahead. I wished we had not left him.

I nudged Lavinia. 'He's a funny boy, isn't he?' I said, nodding at his shadow as he went behind an obelisk.

'I like him,' Lavinia said, 'even if he talks about awful things.'

'Don't you wish we could run off the way he does?'

Lavinia smiled at me. 'Shall we follow him?'

I hadn't expected her to say that. I glanced at the others — only Lavinia's sister was looking at us. 'Let's,' I whispered. She squeezed my hand as we ran off to find him.

# KITTY COLEMAN

I don't dare tell anyone or I will be accused of treason, but I was terribly excited to hear the Queen is dead. The dullness I have felt since New Year's vanished, and I had to work very hard to appear appropriately sober. The turning of the century was merely a change in numbers, but now we shall have a true change in leadership, and I can't help thinking Edward is more truly representative of us than his mother.

For now, though, nothing has changed. We were expected to troop up to the cemetery and make a show of mourning, even though none of the Royal Family is buried there, nor is the Queen to be. Death is there, and that is enough, I suppose.

That blasted cemetery. I have never liked it.

To be fair, it is not the fault of the place itself, which has a lugubrious charm, with its banks of graves stacked on top of one another — granite headstones, Egyptian obelisks, gothic spires, plinths topped with columns, weeping ladies, angels, and of course, urns — winding up the hill to the glorious Lebanon Cedar at the top. I am even willing to overlook some of the more preposterous monuments —

ostentatious representations of a family's status. But the sentiments that the place encourages in mourners are too overblown for my taste. Moreover, it is the Colemans' cemetery, not my family's. I miss the little churchyard in Lincolnshire where Mummy and Daddy are buried and where there is now a stone for Harry, even if his body lies somewhere in southern Africa.

The excess of it all – which our own ridiculous urn now contributes to – is too much. How utterly out of scale it is to its surroundings! If only Richard had consulted me first. It was unlike him – for all his faults he is a rational man, and must have seen that the urn was too big. I suspect the hand of his mother in the choosing. Her taste has always been formidable.

It was amusing today to watch him splutter over the angel that has been erected on the grave next to the urn (far too close to it, as it happens – they look as if they may bash each other at any moment). It was all I could do to keep a straight face.

'How dare they inflict their taste on us,' he said. 'The thought of having to look at this sentimental nonsense every time we visit turns my stomach.'

'It is sentimental, but harmless,' I replied. 'At least the marble's Italian.'

'I don't give a hang about the marble! I don't want that angel next to our grave.'

'Have you thought that perhaps they're saying the same about the urn?'

'There's nothing wrong with our urn!'

'And they would say that there's nothing wrong with their angel.'

'The angel looks ridiculous next to the urn. It's far too close, for one thing.'

'Exactly,' I said. 'You didn't leave them room for anything.'

'Of course I did. Another urn would have looked fine. Perhaps a slightly smaller one.'

I raised my eyebrows the way I do when Maude has said something foolish. 'Or even the same size,' Richard conceded. 'Yes, that could have looked quite impressive, a pair of urns. Instead we have this nonsense.'

And on and on we went. While I don't think much of the blank-faced angels dotted around the cemetery, they bother me less than the urns, which seem a peculiar thing to put on a grave when one thinks that they were used by the Romans as receptacles for human ashes. A pagan symbol for a Christian society. But then, so is all the Egyptian symbolism one sees here as well. When I pointed this out to Richard he huffed and puffed but had no response other than to say, 'That urn adds dignity and grace to the Coleman grave.'

I don't know about that. Utter banality and misplaced symbolism are rather more like it. I had the sense not to say so.

He was still going on about the angel when who should appear but its owners, dressed in full mourning. Albert and Gertrude Waterhouse — no relation to the painter, they admitted. (Just as well — I want to scream when I see his overripe paintings at the Tate. The Lady of Shalott in her boat looks as if she has just taken opium.) We had never met them before, though they have owned their grave for several years. They are rather nondescript — he a gingerbearded, smiling type, she one of those short women whose waists have been ruined by children so that their dresses never fit properly. Her hair is crinkly rather than curly, and escapes its pins.

Her elder daughter, Lavinia, who looks to be Maude's age, has lovely hair, glossy brown and curly. She's a bossy, spoiled little thing – apparently her father bought the angel at her insistence. Richard nearly choked where he heard this. And she was wearing a black dress trimmed with crape – rather vulgar and unnecessary for a child that young.

Of course Maude has taken an instant liking to the girl. When we all took a turn around the cemetery together Lavinia kept dabbing at her eyes with a black-edged handkerchief, weeping as we passed the grave of a little boy dead fifty years. I just hope Maude doesn't begin copying her. I can't bear such nonsense. Maude is very sensible but I could see how attracted she was to the girl's behaviour. They disappeared off together – Lord knows what they got up to. They came back the best of friends.

I think it highly unlikely Gertrude Waterhouse and I would ever be the best of friends. When she said yet again how sad it was about the Queen, I couldn't help but comment that Lavinia seemed to be enjoying her mourning tremendously.

Gertrude Waterhouse said nothing for a moment, then remarked, 'That's a lovely dress. Such an unusual shade of blue.'

Richard snorted. We'd had a fierce argument about my dress. In truth I was now rather embarrassed about my choice – not one adult I'd seen since leaving the house was wearing anything but black. My dress was dark blue, but still I stood out far more than I'd intended.

I decided to be bold. 'Yes, I didn't think black quite the thing to wear for Queen Victoria,' I explained. 'Things are changing now. It will be different with her son. I'm sure Edward will make a fine king. He's been waiting long enough.'

'Too long, if you ask me,' Mr Waterhouse said. 'Poor chap, he's past his prime.' He looked abashed, as if surprised that he had voiced his opinion.

'Not with the ladies, apparently,' I said. I couldn't resist.

'Oh!' Gertrude Waterhouse looked horrified.

'For God's sake, Kitty!' Richard hissed. 'My wife is always saying things she shouldn't,' he said apologetically to Albert Waterhouse, who chuckled uneasily.

'Never mind, I'm sure she makes up for it in other ways,' he said.

There was a silence as we all took-in this remark. For one dizzy moment I wondered if he could possibly be referring to New Year's Eve. But of course he would know nothing about that – that is not his set. I myself have tried hard not to think about it. Richard has not mentioned it since, but I feel now that I died a little death that night, and nothing will ever be quite the same, new King or no.

Then the girls returned, all out of breath, providing a welcome distraction. The Waterhouses quickly made their excuses and left, which I think everyone was relieved about except the girls. Lavinia grew tearful, and I feared Maude would too. Afterwards she wouldn't stop talking about her new friend until at last I promised I would try to arrange for them to meet. I am hoping she will forget eventually, as the Waterhouses are just the kind of family who make me feel worse about myself.

# LAVINIA WATERHOUSE

I had an adventure at the cemetery today, with my new friend and a naughty boy. I've been to the cemetery many times before, but I've never been allowed out of Mama's sight. Today, though, Mama and Papa met the family that owns the grave next to ours, and while they were talking about the things grown-ups go on about, Maude and I went off with Simon, the boy who works at the cemetery. We ran up the Egyptian Avenue and all around the vaults circling the cedar of Lebanon. It is so delicious there, I almost fainted from excitement.

Then Simon took us on a tour of the angels. He showed us a wonderful child-angel near the Terrace Catacombs. I had never seen it before. It wore a little tunic and had short wings, and its head was turned away from us as if it were angry and had just stamped its foot. It is so lovely I almost wished I had chosen it for our grave. But it was not in the book of angels at the mason's yard. Anyway I am sure Mama and Papa agree that the one I chose for our grave is the best.

Simon took us to other angels close by and then he said he wanted to show us a grave he and his father had just dug. Well. I didn't want to see it but Maude said she did and I didn't want her to think I was afraid. So we went and looked down into it, and although it was frightening, I also got the strangest feeling that I wanted to lie down in that hole. Of course I didn't do such a thing, not in my lovely dress.

Then as we turned to go a horrid man appeared. He had a very red face and bristles on his cheeks, and he smelled of drink. I couldn't help but scream, even though I knew right away it was Simon's father as they have the same blue eyes like pieces of sky. He began shouting terrible things at Simon about where had he been and why were we there, and he used the most awful words. Papa would whip us if Ivy May or I were to use such words. And Papa is not a whipping man. That's how bad they were.

Then the man chased Simon round and round the grave until Simon jumped right into it! Well. I didn't wait to see more – Maude and I ran like fury all the way down the hill. Maude wondered if we shouldn't go back and see if Simon was all right but I refused, saying our parents would be worried about us. But really I didn't want to see that man again, as he frightened me. The naughty boy can take care of himself. I am sure he spends much of his time down graves.

So Maude is my new friend, and I hers – though I do not see why such a plain girl should have a beautiful muff, and a nanny too, neither of which I have. And a beautiful mother with such a tiny waist and big dark eyes. I could not look at Mama without feeling a little ashamed. It is really so unfair.

# GERTRUDE WATERHOUSE

Once we heard the news I lay awake all night, worrying about our clothes. Albert could wear his black work suit, with jet cufflinks and a black band for his hat. Mourning has always been easier for men. And Ivy May is too young for her clothes to be a concern.

But Livy and I were to be dressed properly for our Queen's passing. For myself I did not mind so much what I wore, but Livy is so very particular, and difficult if she doesn't get exactly what she wants. I do hate scenes with her – it is like being led in a dance where I know none of the steps and she all of them, so that I feel tripped up and foolish by the end. And yet she is only five years old! Albert says I am too soft with her, but then he bought her the angel she wanted for the grave when he knows how little money we have for that sort of thing, what with our saving to move house. Still, I can't fault him for it. It is so important that the grave be a proper reflection of the family's sentiments to our loved ones. Livy knows that very well, and she was right – the grave did need some attention, especially after that monstrous urn went up next to it.

I rose very early this morning and managed to find a bit of crape I had saved after my aunt's mourning. I had hidden it away because I was meant to have burned it and knew Livy would be horrified to see it in the house. There was not enough of it to trim both our dresses, so I did hers, with a bit left over for my hat. By the time I had finished sewing, Livy was up, and she was so delighted with the effect of the crape that she didn't ask where I'd got it from.

What with the little sleep and the waking early I was so tired by the time we reached the cemetery that I almost cried to see the blue silk Kitty Coleman was wearing. It was an affront to the eyes, like a peacock spreading its feathers at a funeral. It made me feel quite shabby and I was embarrassed even to stand next to her, as doing so begged comparisons and reminded me that my figure is not what it once was.

The one comfort I could take – and it is a shameful one that I shall ask God's forgiveness for – was that her daughter Maude is so plain. I feel proud to see Livy look so well next to drab little Maude.

I was of course as civil as I could be, but it was clear that Kitty Coleman was bored with me. And then she made cutting remarks about Livy, and said disrespectful things – not exactly about the Queen, but I couldn't help feeling that Victoria had in some way been slighted. And she made my poor Albert so tongue-tied he said something completely out of character. I could not bring myself even to ask him afterwards what he meant.

Never mind – she and I shall not have to see each other again. In all the years we have owned adjacent graves

at the cemetery, this is the first time we've met. With luck
it won't happen again, though I shall always worry that we
will. I shan't enjoy the cemetery so much now, I'm afraid.

# ALBERT WATERHOUSE

Damned good-looking woman. I don't know what I was thinking, saying what I said, though. Shall make it up to Trudy tomorrow by getting her some of her favourite violet sweeties.

I was glad to meet Richard Coleman, though, urn and all. (What's done is done, I say to Trudy. It's up and there's no use complaining now.) He's got a rather good position at a bank. They live down the bottom of the hill, and from what he says it could be just the place for us if we do decide to move from Islington. There's a good local cricket team he could introduce me to as well. Useful chap.

I don't envy him his wife, pretty as she is. More of a handful than I'd like. Livy is trouble enough.

# SIMON FIELD

I stay down the grave awhile after the girls have gone. There don't seem no reason to come out. Our Pa don't bother to come after me, or stand at the top of the hole and shout. He knows where he can get me when he wants. 'This cemetery has a high wall round it,' he always says. 'You can climb out but in the end you always come back through the front gate, feet first.'

The sky's pretty from eight feet down. It looks the colour of that girl's fur. Her muff, she called it. The fur was so soft. I wanted to put my face in it the way I saw her do.

I lie back on the ground and watch the sky. Sometimes a bird flies across, high above me. Bits of dirt from the sides of the hole crumble and fall on my face. I don't worry about the hole collapsing. For the deeper graves we use grave-boards to shore up the sides, but we don't bother with little ones like this. This one's in clay, good and damp so it holds up. It's happened before, the hole caving in, but mostly in sand, or when the clay's dried out. Men have got killed down graves. Our Pa always tells me to put a hand over my face and stick my other hand up if I'm down a grave and it falls in. Then I'll have an air hole through the dirt and they can see by my fingers where I am.

Someone comes then and looks into the grave. He's black against the light, so I can't see who it is. But I know it's not our Pa – he don't smell of the bottle.

'What are you doing down there, Simon?' the man says.

Then I know who it is. I jump to my feet and brush the dirt off my back and bum and legs.

'Just resting, sir.'

'You're not paid to rest.'

'I'm not paid nothing, sir,' I say before I can stop myself.

'Oh? I should think you earn plenty from all you learn here. You're learning a trade.'

'Learning don't feed me, sir.'

'Enough of your insolence, Simon. You are but a servant of the London Cemetery Company. There are plenty more waiting outside the gate who would gladly take your place. Don't you forget that. Now, have you finished that grave?'

'Yes, sir.'

'Then cover it over and go and find your father. He should be putting away the tools. God knows he needs the help. I don't know why I keep him on.'

I know why. Our Pa knows this place better'n anybody. He can take apart any grave, remember who's buried how far down and whether it's sand or clay. He learned it all from our Granpa. And he's fast digging when he wants to be. His arms are hard as rocks. He's best when he's had a bit of the bottle but not too much. Then he and Joe dig and laugh and I haul up and dump the bucket. But once he's had too much it's Joe and me does all the digging and dumping.

I look round for the long tree branch with the stumps on it what I use to climb out the little graves. Our Pa must've taken it out.

'Mr Jackson,' I call, but he's gone already. I shout again but he don't come back. Our Pa will think I've got out and covered the grave – he won't come back either.

I try to dig toeholds into the sides of the hole so I can climb out, but there's no spade, only my hands, and the ground's too hard. 'Sides, it's firm now but I don't know for sure it'll last. I don't want it to cave in on me.

It's cold in the hole now I'm stuck in it. I squat on my heels and wrap my arms round my legs. Every now and again I call out. There's four other graves being dug today and a couple of monuments going up, but none of them near me. Still, maybe a visitor will hear me, or one of them girls'll come back. Sometimes I hear voices and I call out 'Help! Help!' But no one comes. People stay away from graves just dug. They think something's going to pop out the hole and grab 'em.

The sky over me is going dark grey and I hear the bell ringing to tell visitors the cemetery's shutting. There's a boy goes round every day ringing it. I yell till my throat hurts but the bell drowns me out.

After a time the bell stops and after that it's dark. I jump up and down to get warm and then I crouch down again and hug my knees.

In the dark the hole starts to smell stronger of clay and wet things. There's an underground branch of the Fleet River runs through the cemetery. Feels close by.

The sky goes clear of clouds and I start to see little pricks of stars, more and more appearing till the patch of sky above me is full, like someone's sprinkled flour on the sky and is about to roll out dough on it.

I watch them stars all night. There's nothing else to do in the grave. I see things in 'em — a horse, a pickaxe, a spoon. Sometimes I look away and back again and they've moved a little. After a while the horse disappears off the edge of the sky, then the spoon. Once I see a star streak 'cross the sky. I wonder where it goes when it does that.

I think about them girls, the one with the muff and the one with the pretty face. They're tucked up in their beds, all toasty warm. I wish I was like them.

It's not so bad as long as I don't move. When I move it hurts like someone's hitting me with a plank of wood. After a time I can't move at all. My blood must be frozen.

The hardest part is towards the end of the night, when it might be getting light but it don't yet. Our Pa says that's when most people die 'cause they can't wait any longer for the day to start. I watch the stars. The pickaxe disappears and I cry a little bit and then I must fall asleep because when I look up again the stars are gone and it's light and the tears have frozen on my cheeks.

It gets lighter and lighter but no one comes. My mouth is stuck together I'm so thirsty.

Then I hear the hymn 'Holy, Holy, Holy,' which our Pa likes to whistle when he's working. It's funny 'cause he's not been inside a church in years. The whistling gets closer and closer and I try to call out but it hurts too much to make a noise.

I hear him walking round the hole, laying down boards and then the green carpets what look like grass, to make the ground round the grave look nice and neat. Then he lays the flat ropes across the hole that'll go under the coffin for lowering it, and then the two wooden bearers they lay the coffin on, one each end of the hole. He don't look down and see me. He's dug so many holes he don't need to look in 'em.

I try to open my mouth but can't. Then I hear the horses snorting and their halters creaking and the wheels crunching on the path and I know I have to get out or I never will. I straighten my legs, screaming from the pain 'cept there's no sound 'cause I still can't open my mouth. I manage to stagger to my feet and then I get my mouth working and call out, 'Pa! Pa!' I sound like one of them crows up in the trees. At first nothing happens. I call again and our Pa leans over the hole and squints at me.

'Jesus, boy! Wha're you doing there?'

'Get me out, our Pa! Get me out!'

Our Pa lays himself down the edge of the hole and holds out his arms. 'Hurry, boy! Take my hands.' But I can't reach him. Our Pa looks towards the sound of the horses and shakes his head. 'No time, boy. No time.' He jumps up and goes away and I yell again.

Our Pa comes back with Mr Jackson, who stares down at me with a terrible look on his face. He don't say nothing, but goes away while our Pa just stands there looking after him. Then Mr Jackson is back again and throws down the rope we use to measure how deep we've dug. There's a knot in it every foot. I grab a knot and hold on and he and our Pa pull me up out the hole so I land on the green carpet that's like grass. I jump up, though I hurt all over, and there I am, standing in front of the undertakers in their top hats and the boy mutes in their tiny black coats and the horses nodding so the black feathers strapped to their heads move. Behind the carriage holding the coffin are the mourners in black, all staring at me. I want to laugh at the looks they give me, but I see Mr Jackson's awful face and I run away.

Later, after our Pa's got rum down me and sat me by the fire with a blanket, he knocks me round the ears. 'Don't ever do that again, boy,' he says — like I planned to stay down the hole all night. 'I'll lose my job and then where'll we be?' Then Mr Jackson comes and whips me to make sure I've learned my lesson. I don't care, though, I hardly feel the whip. Nothing can ever hurt so bad as the cold down that grave.

*December 1901*

# RICHARD COLEMAN

I told Kitty we've been invited for New Year's by the same people as last year. She was quiet, looking at me with those dark brown eyes that seduced me years ago but now simply judge me. If she hadn't looked at me like that I might not have added what I did.

'I've already told them we've accepted,' I said, although I hadn't yet. 'With pleasure.'

We shall go on accepting their invitations every year until Kitty becomes my wife again.

*March 1903*

# LAVINIA WATERHOUSE

It was nothing short of a miracle. My best friend at the bottom of our garden! Can anything be more perfect than that?

I was feeling decidedly melancholy this morning as I brushed my hair, looking out of the window into our new garden. Although it is a sweet little patch, and Ivy May and I have a lovely bedroom looking out onto it, I couldn't help feeling a pang for our old house. It was smaller, and on a busy street, and not on the doorstep of a place as lovely as Hampstead Heath. But it was where I was born, and full of memories of my childhood. I wanted to take the bit of wallpaper in the hallway where Papa marked how tall Ivy May and I had grown every year, but he said I mustn't because it would damage the wall. I did cry as we left.

Then out of the corner of my eye I saw a fluttering, and when I looked over at the house backing onto ours, there was a girl hanging out of a window and waving! Well. I squinted and after a moment recognised her – it was Maude, the girl from the cemetery. I knew we had moved close to the cemetery but did not know she was here as well. I picked up my handkerchief and waved until my arm ached. Even

Ivy May, who never pays attention unless I pinch her (and not even then sometimes), got up from her bed to see what the fuss was about.

Maude called out something to me, but she was too far away and I couldn't hear. Then she pointed down at the fence separating our gardens and held up ten fingers. We are such kindred spirits that I understood immediately she meant we should meet there in ten minutes. I blew her a kiss and ducked inside to get dressed as quick as I could.

'Mama! Mama!' I shouted all the way down the stairs. Mama came running from the kitchen, thinking I was ill or had hurt myself. But when I told her about Maude she seemed not the least interested. She has not wanted me to see the Colemans, though she would never say why. Perhaps she has forgot them by now, but I have never forgot Maude, even after all this time. I knew we were destined to be together.

I ran outside and to the garden fence, which was too high to see over. I called to Maude and she answered, and after a moment her face appeared at the top of the fence.

'Oh! How did you get up there?' I cried.

'I'm standing on the birdbath,' said she, wobbling a bit. Then she managed to pull herself up, and before I knew it she'd tumbled over the fence and onto the ground! The poor dear was rather scratched by the rosebushes on the way down. I threw my arms around her and kissed her and brought her to Mama, who I am happy to say was very sweet to her and painted her scratches with iodine.

Then I took her up to my bedroom so that she could see my dollies.

'I didn't forget you,' I said. 'I've looked for you every time we've visited the cemetery, hoping to see you.'

'So have I,' she said.

'But I never did. Only that naughty boy now and then.'

'Simon. Digging with his father.'

'Now that I'm here we can go back together, and he can show us all the other angels. It will be lovely.'

'Yes.'

Then Ivy May tried to spoil it by knocking my dollies' heads together so hard I thought they might burst. I told her to leave but Maude said she didn't mind if Ivy May stayed with us as she didn't have a brother or sister to play with. Well. Ivy May looked pleased as Punch at that – as much as she looks pleased about anything.

Never mind. Then Maude had breakfast with us and we could not stop talking.

It is truly a miracle from heaven that the angels have led us to this house and me to my best friend.

# MAUDE COLEMAN

It is funny how things happen. Daddy always says that coincidences are usually nothing of the sort if only one studies them carefully enough. He proved his point today.

I was looking out of my window when I saw a girl standing in hers across the way, brushing her hair. I had never seen her there before; two spinsters used to live in that house but had moved out a few weeks before. Then she tossed her head and shrugged her shoulders, and I realised it was Lavinia. I was so surprised to see her that I simply stood and stared.

I hadn't seen her for so long – not since the Queen's death over two years ago. Although I had asked Mummy several times if we could meet, she always made an excuse. She did promise to ask at the cemetery for the Waterhouses' address, but I don't think she ever did. After a time I stopped asking because I knew it was her way of saying no. I didn't know why she didn't want me to have a best friend, but there was nothing I could do, except to hang about in the cemetery whenever we visited, hoping the Waterhouses would choose to visit then too. But they never did. I had given up on ever having a best friend. And I had not met

44

any other girls who would like to go around the cemetery with me the way Lavinia did.

Now here she was, just across the way. I began to wave, and when at last she saw me she waved too, frantically. It was very gratifying that she was so happy to see me. I signalled to her to meet me in the garden, then ran downstairs to tell my parents about the amazing coincidence.

Mummy and Daddy were already eating breakfast and reading the papers – Daddy the *Mail*, Mummy the *St Pancras Gazette*. When I told them who our new neighbours were, Daddy was not amazed at all but explained he'd told the Waterhouses about that house.

Mummy gave him a peculiar look. 'I didn't know you were so friendly with them,' she said.

'He contacted me at the bank,' Daddy said, 'quite some time ago. Said they were thinking of moving to the area and did I know of any property. When that house came up I told him about it.'

'So now we are to be neighbours in life as well as in death,' Mummy said. She cracked the shell of her egg very hard with a spoon.

'Apparently he's a fine batsman,' Daddy said. 'The team could do with one.'

When it became clear that there was no coincidence, that Daddy had led the Waterhouses here, I felt strangely let down. I wanted to believe in Fate, but Daddy has shown once again that there is no such thing.

# GERTRUDE WATERHOUSE

I would not dream of criticising Albert's judgement. He knows best in these matters, and to be sure I am very pleased with our new little house, a storey higher than our Islington house and with a garden full of roses rather than the neighbour's chickens scrabbling in the dirt.

But my heart did sink when I discovered that not only are we neighbours with the Colemans, but their house backs on to ours. And of course it is yet a storey higher than ours and has the most tremendous garden. When no one was about I stood on a chair and peeked over. There is a willow, and a pond, and a bank of rhododendrons, and a lovely long lawn which I am sure the girls will play croquet on all summer.

Kitty Coleman was working in the garden, planting out primroses. Her dress was of the same buttery colour, and she wore a lovely wide-brimmed hat tied on with a chiffon scarf. Even at her gardening she is so well dressed. She didn't see me, I am thankful to say, or I should have been so mortified I might have fallen from the chair. As it was I hopped down quickly and jarred my ankle.

I would not confess this to anyone, not even Albert, but

it irritates me that she keeps such a fine garden. It is south-facing and very sunny, which makes it easier. And she must have a man to help — at the very least with the lawn, which looks rolled. I shall do my best with our roses, but I do kill plants off so easily. I really am hopeless in the garden. It doesn't help that ours is north-facing. And we cannot manage any help with it at present. I hope she does not offer to send her man over — I wouldn't know what to do.

After Maude tumbled over the back fence I felt we should call round, if only to explain the scratches. The front of their house is so elegant — the garden is full of rosebushes, and the steps leading up to the door are tiled in black and white. (The door of our own house opens directly on to the pavement. But I must try not to compare.)

I was hoping just to leave my card, but Kitty Coleman received us very gracefully in her morning room. I blinked at the colours she'd had it done in — mustard yellow with a dark brown trim, which I suppose is fashionable now. She called them 'golden yellow' and 'chocolate brown', which sound much better than they looked. I prefer our own burgundy. There is nothing to compare with a simple burgundy parlour. Mind you, I don't have a morning room — perhaps if I did have such a light room as hers on the first floor I might paint it yellow as well.

But I doubt it.

Her taste is very refined — embroidered silk shawls over the sofas, potted ferns, vases of dried flowers, and a baby grand piano. I was rather shocked by the modern coffee set, which has a pattern of tiny black and yellow checks that made me feel dizzy. I myself prefer a simple rose pattern. But *chacun à son goût*. Oh! I made the mistake of saying so out loud, and she replied in French. I understood not a word of it! It was my own silly fault for trying to show off.

I came away with one secret comfort. No, two. The girls at least are delighted with each other, and Livy could do with a sensible friend. At least Maude will be a steadying influence, unless she too succumbs to Livy's spell as the rest of us have – all but dear Ivy May, who is impervious to her sister's excesses. I am always surprised by her. Quiet as she is, she does not let Livy get the upper hand.

And the other comfort: Kitty Coleman's At Homes are Tuesday afternoons, just as mine are. When we discovered this, she smiled a little and said, 'Oh dear, that is a pity.' I will not switch mine, however – some traditions I will not tamper with. And I know she will not switch hers. In this way we shall be able to avoid that social occasion, at least.

I can't say exactly why I don't like her. She is perfectly civil and has good manners and is lovely to look at. She has a fine house and a handsome husband and a clever daughter. But I would not be her. A vein of discontent runs through her that disturbs everything around her. And I know it is uncharitable of me to think it, but I do doubt her Christian commitment. She thinks too much and prays too little, I suspect. But they are the only people we know close by, and the girls are already so fond of each other, and so I am afraid we are bound to see a great deal of each other.

When we got home and were sitting in our back parlour, I couldn't help but look out of the window at their grand house in the distance. It will always be there to remind me of their superior position. I found this so upsetting that I let my teacup crash into its saucer, and the dear thing cracked. I did weep then, and even Ivy May's arms around my neck (she does not like hugs, as a rule) did little to comfort me.

*June* 1903

June 1993

# MAUDE COLEMAN

Lavinia and I are desperate to get to the cemetery. Now that we can go together it will be so much more fun than before. But since the Waterhouses have moved to the house at the bottom of the garden, we have not managed to go, what with one thing and another: we went to Auntie Sarah's in the country at Easter, and then Lavinia was ill, and then Mummy or Mrs Waterhouse had a visit to make or an errand to run. What a bother — we live so close yet cannot get anyone to take us and are not allowed to go there on our own. It is a shame Nanny left to look after her old mother, or she could have taken us.

Yesterday I asked Mummy if she would go with us.

'I'm too busy,' she said. She didn't seem busy to me — she was just reading a book. I did not say so, however. She is meant to be looking after me now that Nanny has gone. But mostly I end up with Jenny and Mrs Baker.

I asked her if Jenny could take Lavinia and me.

'Jenny has far too much to do to be dragging you up there.'

'Oh, please, Mummy. Just for a little while.'

'Don't use that wheedling tone with me. You've learned it from Lavinia and it doesn't suit you.'

'Sorry. But perhaps – perhaps Jenny has an errand to run for you up in the Village. Then she could take us.'

'Haven't you lessons to prepare for?'

'Finished them.'

Mummy sighed. 'It's just as well you're going to school in the autumn. Your tutor can't keep up with you.'

I tried to be helpful. 'Perhaps you have books that need returning to the library?'

'I do, in fact. Oh, all right, go and tell Jenny to come here. And she can see if the fabric I've ordered has arrived while she's in the Village.'

Lavinia and I raced up the hill, pulling Jenny with us. She complained the whole way, and was quite puffed at the top, though if she hadn't used her breath for complaining she might have been all right. All our hurrying didn't make any difference anyway – Ivy May refused to run, and Jenny made Lavinia go back and get her. At times it can be a trial having Ivy May with us, but Mrs Waterhouse insisted upon it. Once we got to the cemetery, though, Jenny let us do whatever we liked, as long as we kept Ivy May with us. We immediately ran off to find Simon.

It was such a treat to be in the cemetery without anyone to look after us. Whenever I go with Mummy and Daddy or Grandmother I feel I have to be very quiet and solemn, when really what I want to do is just what Lavinia and I did – rush about and explore. As we looked for Simon we played all sorts of games: jumping from grave to grave without touching the ground (which is not difficult, as the graves are so packed in); taking a side each of a path and scoring points for seeing an obelisk, or a woman leaning on an urn, or an animal; playing tag around the Circle of Lebanon. Lavinia does shriek when she's being chased, and some grown-ups told us to hush and mind our manners. After that we tried to be quiet but we had such fun playing that it was hard.

At last we found Simon, right up the top of the cemetery not far from the north gate. We didn't see him at first, but his Pa was standing next to a new grave, pulling a bucket of soil up using a rope and pulley on a frame set over the hole. He dumped it into what looked like a big wooden box on wheels, several feet high and heaped with soil.

We crept closer and hid behind a headstone, not wanting Simon's Pa to see us, for he is dirty and red-faced and whiskery, and we could smell the drink on him even from where we were. Lavinia says he's just like a character out of Dickens. I suppose all gravediggers are.

We could hear Simon singing in the grave, a song Jenny sometimes sings along with the crowds on the Heath on a Bank Holiday Monday:

> 'Now if you want a 'igh old time
> Just take the tip from me,
> Why 'Ampstead, 'appy 'Ampstead is
> The place to 'ave a spree.'

Simon's Pa wasn't even looking at us, but somehow he knew we were there, for he called out, 'Well, little missies, wha're you wanting?'

Simon stopped singing. His Pa said, 'Come out from there, all three of youse.'

Lavinia and I looked at each other, but before we could

decide what to do, Ivy May had stepped out from behind the headstone, and we had no choice but to follow.

'Please, sir, we want to see Simon.' I was surprised that I called him sir.

He seemed surprised too, looking at us as if he couldn't believe we were there. Then he suddenly shouted into the hole, 'Boy, you got visitors!'

After a moment Simon's head popped out of the grave. He stared at us.

'Well, naughty boy,' Lavinia said, 'aren't you going to say anything?'

'Can we switch places for a bit, our Pa?' he said.

''Tain't much room down there for me and Joe,' Simon's Pa said. Simon didn't say anything, and his Pa chuckled. 'Oh well, then, go on there with your girlies.'

Simon climbed out and his Pa climbed in, grinning at us before disappearing into the grave. Simon pulled the bucket up and dumped it into the wooden box. He was very muddy.

'What's that?' I asked, pointing at the box.

'Lamb's box,' Simon said. 'You put what you've dug in it, then when the coffin's in the hole you roll it up and open the side – see, it's got a hinge – and let the dirt go straight into the grave. So as you don't make a mess round the grave, see. There's two more over there, already full.' He waved at the other boxes, pulled up against the boundary wall. 'You just leave a little pile of dirt at the end of the grave for the mourners to drop in.'

'Can we look in the grave?'

Simon nodded and we edged up to the hole. It was deeper than I'd expected. Simon's Pa was at the bottom with another man. I could only see the tops of their heads – Simon's Pa's like steel wool, the other man's completely bald. They were hacking at the sides of the hole with spades. There was hardly room for them to turn around. The bald man looked up at us. He had a long face and a nose like a sausage. He and Simon's Pa seemed to be digging partners, with Simon helping.

Simon hauled up another bucket full of clumps of clay. I could see a worm wriggling on top.

'Do you ever find anything while you're digging?' I asked, 'besides worms?'

Simon dumped the clay into the Lamb's box and lowered the bucket back into the grave. 'Pieces of china. Some fountain pens. A spinning top. This were school grounds before it were a cemetery. And before that it were the gardens of a big house.'

Simon's Pa looked up. 'Need more shoring down here, boy.'

Simon began handing down planks of wood from a pile. I noticed then that wood had been pushed in at regular intervals around the edges of the hole.

'How deep is it?' I asked.

'Twelve feet so far,' Simon said. 'We're going down to seventeen, ain't we, our Pa?'

I stared down. 'That deep?'

'Lots of people to bury over the years. Coffin's eighteen inches, plus a foot 'tween each coffin, makes space for six coffins. That's a family.'

I added it in my head – it was like a puzzle my tutor would give me. 'Seven coffins.'

'No, you leave a bit more than a foot at the top.'

'Of course. Six feet under.'

'Not really,' Simon said. 'That's just a saying. We just leave two feet atop the last coffin.'

'What on earth are you two going on about?' Lavinia said.

Simon's Pa began hammering on a piece of wood with a mallet.

'Are they safe down there?' I asked.

Simon shrugged. 'Safe enough. The wood shores up the grave. And it's clay, so it's not likely to cave in. Holds itself up. It's sand you got to watch out for. Sand's easier to dig but it don't hold. Sand's deadly.'

'Oh, do stop talking about such tedious things!' Lavinia cried. 'We want you to show us some angels.'

'Leave him alone, Lavinia,' I said. 'Can't you see he's working?' While I love Lavinia – she is my best friend, after all – she is rarely interested in what I am. She never wants to look through the telescope Daddy sets up in the garden, for instance, or dig about in the *Encyclopaedia Britannica* at the library. I wanted to ask Simon more about the graves and the digging but Lavinia wouldn't let me.

'Maybe later, when this is done,' Simon said.

'We only have half an hour,' I explained. 'Jenny said.'

'Who's Jenny?'

'Our maid.'

'Where's she now?'

'Up in the Village. We left her by the gate.'

'She met a man,' Ivy May said.

Simon looked at her. 'Who's this, then?'

'Ivy May. My little sister,' Lavinia said. 'But she's wrong. You didn't see any man, did you, Maude?'

I shook my head, but I wasn't sure.

'He had a wheelbarrow and she followed him into the cemetery,' Ivy May insisted.

'Did he have red hair?' Simon asked.

Ivy May nodded.

'Oh, him. He'll be knocking her, then.'

'What, someone's hitting Jenny?' I cried. 'Then we must go and rescue her!'

'Nah, not hitting,' Simon said. 'It's –' He looked at me and Lavinia and stopped. 'Never mind. 'Tis nothing.'

Simon's Pa laughed from down the hole. 'Got yourself all tangled up there, boy! Forgot who you was talking to. Got to be careful what you say if you're going to mix with them girls!'

'Hush, our Pa.'

'We'd best go,' I said, uneasy now about Jenny. 'I'm sure half an hour's gone now. Which is the quickest path back to the main gate?'

Simon pointed at a statue of a horse a little way away. 'Take the path by the horse and follow it down.'

'Not that way!' Lavinia cried. 'That's straight through the Dissenters!'

'So?' Simon said. 'They won't bite you. They're dead.'

The Dissenters' section is where all the people who are not Church of England are buried – Catholics, mostly, as well as Baptists and Methodists and other sorts. I've heard suicides are buried back there, though I didn't say that to Lavinia. I've only walked through it twice. It wasn't so different from the rest of the cemetery, but I did feel peculiar, as if I were in a foreign country. 'Come, Lavinia,' I said, not wanting Simon to think we were judging the Dissenters, 'it doesn't matter. Besides, wasn't your mother Catholic before she married your father?' I'd found a rosary under a cushion at Lavinia's house recently and their char, Elizabeth, had told me.

Lavinia flushed. 'No! And what would it matter if she were?'

'It doesn't matter — that's just what I'm saying.'

'I know,' Simon interrupted. 'If you want you can go back by the sleeping angel. Have you seen it? It's on the main path, not in the Dissenters.'

We shook our heads.

'I'll show you — it's not far. I'm just off for a tick, our Pa,' he called down into the hole.

Simon's Pa grunted.

'C'mon, quick.' Simon ran down the path and we hurried after him. This time even Ivy May ran.

We had never seen the angel he showed us. All the other angels in the cemetery are walking or flying or pointing or at least standing and bowing their heads. This one was lying on its side, wings tucked under it, fast asleep. I didn't know angels needed sleep as humans do.

Lavinia adored it, of course. I preferred to talk more about grave-digging, but when I turned to ask Simon something about the Lamb's box, he was gone. He had run back to his grave without saying goodbye.

At last I managed to drag Lavinia away from the angel, but when we got back to the main gate, Jenny wasn't there. I still didn't understand what Simon had meant about her and the man, and was a little worried. Lavinia wasn't bothered, though.

'Let's go to the mason's yard next door and look at the angels,' she said. 'Just for a minute.'

I had never been to the yard before. It was full of all sorts of stone, big blocks and slabs, blank headstones, plinths, even a stack of obelisks leaning against one another in a corner. It was very dusty and the ground gritty. Everywhere we could hear the 'tink tink tink' of men chipping stone.

Lavinia led the way into the shop. 'May we look at the book of angels, please?' she said to the man behind the counter. I thought she was very bold.

He didn't seem at all surprised, however. He pulled from the shelf behind him a large, dusty book and laid it on the counter.

'This is what we chose our angel from,' Lavinia explained. 'I love to look in it. It's got hundreds of angels. Aren't they lovely?' She began turning the pages. There were drawings of all sorts of angels – standing, kneeling, looking up, looking down, eyes closed, holding wreaths, trumpets, folds of cloth. There were baby angels and twin angels and cherubim and little angel heads with wings.

'They're – nice,' I said. I don't know why, exactly, but I don't much like the cemetery angels. They are very smooth and regular, and their eyes are so blank – even when I stand in their line of sight they never seem to look at me. What is the good of a messenger who doesn't even notice you?

Daddy hates angels because he says they are sentimental. Mummy calls them vapid. I had to look up the word – it means that something is dull or flat or empty. I think she is right. That is certainly what their eyes are like. Mummy says angels get more attention than they deserve. When there is an angel on a grave in the cemetery, everyone looks at it rather than the other monuments around it, but there is really nothing to see.

'Why do you like angels so much?' I asked Lavinia.

She laughed. 'Who couldn't like them? They are God's messengers and they bring love. Whenever I look in their gentle faces they make me feel peaceful and secure.'

That, I suspect, is an example of what Daddy calls sentimental thinking.

'Where is God, exactly?' I asked, thinking about angels flying between us and Him.

Lavinia looked shocked and stopped turning pages. 'Why, up there, of course.' She pointed at the sky outside. 'Don't you listen at Sunday school?'

'But there are stars and planets up there,' I said. 'I know – I've seen them through Daddy's telescope.'

'You watch out, Maude Coleman,' Lavinia said, 'or you'll commit blasphemy.'

'But –'

'Don't!' Lavinia covered her ears. 'I can't bear to listen!'

Ivy May giggled.

I gave up. 'Let's go back to Jenny.'

This time Jenny was waiting for us at the main gate, red and breathless as if she'd just climbed the hill again, but unhurt, I was glad to see.

'Where've you girls been?' she cried. 'I've been worried silly!'

We were all just starting down the hill when I asked her if she'd checked on the fabric for Mummy.

'The book!' she shrieked, and ran back into the cemetery to fetch it. I hate to think where she left it.

# JENNY WHITBY

I were none too pleased to be running errands for the missus, I can tell you. She knows very well how busy I am. Six in the blooming morning till nine at night – later if they've a supper party. One day's holiday a year apart from Christmas and Boxing Day. And she wants me to take back books and pick up fabric – things she can very well do herself. Books I've no time to read myself, even if I wanted to – which I don't.

Still, it were a lovely sunny day, and I'll admit 'twas nice to get out, though I don't much like that hill up to the Village. We got to the cemetery and I were going to leave the girls there and nip up to the shops and back. Then I saw him, on his own, pushing a wheelbarrow across the courtyard with a little skip in his step. He looked back at me and smiled, and I thought, Hang on a tick.

So I went in with the girls and told 'em to do what they liked for half an hour, no more. They was wanting to find a little boy they play with, and I said to be careful and not to let him get cheeky. And to keep an eye on the little girl, Ivy May. She's of the habit of getting left behind, it seems – though I bet she likes it that way. I made 'em all hold hands. So they run off one way, and I t'other.

*November 1903*

# KITTY COLEMAN

Tonight we went with the Waterhouses to a bonfire on the Heath. The girls wanted to, and the men get on well enough (though Richard privately mocks Albert Waterhouse as a buffoon), and it's left to Gertrude Waterhouse and me to smile and bear each other's company as best we can. We stood around an enormous bonfire on Parliament Hill, clutching our sausages and baked potatoes, and marvelling that we were gathered on the very hill where Guy Fawkes waited to see Parliament burn. I watched as people moved closer to or farther away from the heat of the flames, trying to find a spot where they were comfortable. But even if our faces were hot, our backs were cold – like the potatoes, charred on the outside, raw inside.

My threshold to heat is much higher than Richard's or Maude's – or most people's, for that matter. I stepped closer and closer until my cheeks flamed. When I looked around, the ring of people was far behind me – I stood alone by the edge of the fire.

Richard wasn't even looking at the fire, but up at the clear sky. That is just like him – his love is not heat, but the cold distance of the universe. When we were first courting he would take me, with Harry as chaperone, to observation parties to look at the stars. I thought it most romantic then. Tonight, though, when I followed his gaze up to the starry sky all I felt was the blank space between those pinpricks and me, and it was like a heavy blanket waiting to drop on me. It was almost as suffocating as my fear of being buried alive.

I cannot see what he sees in the stars – he and now Maude, for he has begun taking her with him when he goes out to the Heath at night with his telescope. I haven't said anything, because there is nothing I can truly complain of, and Maude clearly thrives on his attention. But it brings me low, for I can see him fostering in her the same cold rationality that I discovered in him once we were married.

I am being ridiculous, of course. I too was brought up by my father to be logical, and I despise the sentimentality of the age, as embodied to perfection by the Waterhouses. But I'm secretly glad Maude and Lavinia are friends. Irritating and melodramatic as Lavinia is, she is not cold, and she counterbalances the icy hand of astronomy.

I stood by the fire, everyone around me so cheerful, and thought what an odd creature I am – even I know that. Too much space and I'm frightened, too little and I'm frightened. There is indeed no comfortable place for me – I am too near the fire or too far away.

Behind me, Gertrude Waterhouse stood with an arm around each daughter. Maude stood next to Lavinia, and they were all laughing about something – Maude a little shyly, as if she was not sure she should be sharing the laughter with them. I felt a pang for her.

At times it is painful to be with the Waterhouses. Lavinia

may be bossy with her mother, but there is clearly an affection between them that I cannot muster with Maude. After a few hours with them I come away resolved to link my arm with Maude's when we walk, as Gertrude does with Lavinia. And to be with her more – read to her, help her with her sewing, bring her into the garden with me, take her into town.

It has never been like that with her. Maude's birth was a shock from which I have not recovered. When I came to from the ether and first held her in my arms I felt as if I were nailed to the bed, trapped by her mouth at my breast. Of course I loved her – love her – but my life as I had imagined it ended on that day. It fed a low feeling in me that resurfaces with increasing frequency.

At least I was lucky in my doctor. When he came to see me a few days after the birth I sent the nurse from the room and told him I wanted no more babies. He took pity on me and explained the timing and the signs to look for, and what I might say to my husband to keep him away during those times. It does not work for every woman, but it has for me, and Richard has never guessed – not that he is often in my bed these days. I had to pay the doctor, of course, an ironic fee – 'to make certain you've understood my lesson' was how he put it – just the once when my body had recovered. I kept my eyes closed and it wasn't so bad. It did occur to me that he could use it against me, blackmail me for further payments in the flesh, but he never did. For that and his biology lesson I have always been grateful. I even shed a tear when I later heard he had died. An understanding doctor can come in handy at times.

To be fair to Maude, that trapped feeling had emerged

well before her birth. I first felt it one morning when Richard and I were just back from our honeymoon and newly installed in our London house. He kissed me goodbye in my new morning room – which I had chosen to be at the front of the house, overlooking the street rather than the garden, so that I could keep an eye on the world outside – and left to catch his train to work. I watched from the window as he walked away, and felt the same jealousy I had suffered when seeing my brother go off to school. When he had gone round the corner, I turned and looked at the still, quiet room, just on the edge of the city that is the centre of the world, and I began to cry. I was twenty years old, and my life had settled into a long, slow course over which I had no control.

I recovered, of course. I knew very well that I was lucky in many things: to have had an education and a liberal father, to have a husband who is handsome and well enough off that we can afford a cook as well as a live-in maid, and who does not discourage me from bettering myself, even if he is unable to give me the larger world I long for. I dried my tears that morning, grateful that at least my mother-in-law had not been there to see me cry. Small mercies – I thank my God for them.

My marriage is no longer what it once was. Now I dread Richard's announcement about New Year's Eve. I do not know that he really takes pleasure from the experience itself. Rather he is doing it to punish me. But I do not think I am capable of being what he wants me to be, of becoming once more the lively wife who thinks the world a reasonable place and he a reasonable man.

If I could do that, or even pretend to, we could spend our New Year's at home. But I can't do it.

I tried tonight to quell my black feelings and at least not neglect Maude. As we were leaving the bonfire I went up to her, took her hand and slipped it into the crook of my elbow. Maude jumped as if I had bitten her, then looked guilty for having such a response. She held onto me rather awkwardly, but we managed to remain like that for several minutes before she made an excuse and ran to catch up with her friend. To my shame, I was relieved.

*May 1904*

# MAUDE COLEMAN

I know I shouldn't say this, but Grandmother always manages to ruin our day when she visits, even before she arrives. Until her letter came yesterday we were having such a lovely time, sitting around the table on the patio and reading out bits from the papers to each other. That is my favourite time with Mummy and Daddy. It was a warm spring day, the flowers in Mummy's garden were just beginning to bloom, and Mummy for once seemed happy.

Daddy was reading little snippets out from the *Mail*, and Mummy from the local paper all the crimes committed that week – fraud, wife-beating, and petty theft the most common. She loves the crimes page.

'Listen to this,' she said. '"James Smithson has appeared before the court charged with stealing his neighbour's cat. In his defence Mr Smithson said the puss had made off with the Sunday joint and he was only reclaiming his property, now inside the cat."'

We all three laughed, but when Jenny arrived with the letter Mummy stopped smiling.

'What on earth am I going to do with her for the day?' she said when she had finished the letter.

Daddy didn't answer, but frowned and kept reading his paper.

That was when I suggested visiting the columbarium. I was not entirely certain what a columbarium was, but one had opened at the cemetery, and it sounded grand enough for Grandmother.

'Good idea, Maude,' Mummy said. 'If she'll agree.'

Daddy looked up from the *Mail*. 'I would be very surprised if she agreed to see such an unsavoury thing.'

'Oh, I don't know,' Mummy said. 'I think it's rather a clever idea. I'm surprised you don't, given how much you like urns.'

When I heard the word urn, I knew they would argue, so I ran down to the bottom of the garden to tell Lavinia that we might go to the cemetery the next day. Daddy and Mr Waterhouse have put up ladders so that we can climb the fence more easily, after I sprained my wrist once from falling.

I am rather frightened of Grandmother. She looks as if she has swallowed a fishbone and can't get it out, and she says things that I would be punished for saying. Today when she arrived she looked at me and said, 'Lord, child, you are plain. No one would guess you were Kitty's daughter. Or my granddaughter, for that matter.' She always likes to remind everyone that she was a beauty when she was younger.

We went up to the morning room, and Grandmother said once again that she did not approve of the colours Mummy had done the room in. I rather like them. They remind me of the workman's café Jenny sometimes takes me to as a treat, where there is a pot of mustard and a bottle of brown sauce on each table. Perhaps Mummy saw them there and decided to use them in her morning room – though it is hard to imagine Mummy in a workman's café, with all the smoke and grease and the men who have not shaved. Mummy has always said she prefers a man with smooth skin like Daddy's.

Mummy ignored Grandmother's remarks. 'Coffee, please, Jenny,' she ordered.

'Not for me,' Grandmother said. 'Just a cup of hot water and a slice of lemon.'

I stood behind them by the window so that I could look out through the venetian blinds. It was dusty outside, what with all the activity in the street – horses pulling carts loaded with milk, coal, ice, the baker's boy going door to door with his basket of bread, boys bringing letters, maids running errands. Jenny always says she is at war with dust and is losing the battle.

I liked looking out. When I turned back to the room, where dust floated in a shaft of sunlight, it seemed very still.

'Why are you lurking back there?' Grandmother said. 'Come out so we can see you. Play us something on the piano.'

I looked at Mummy, horrified. She knew I hated playing.

She was no help. 'Go on, Maude,' she said. 'Play us something from your last lesson.'

I sat down at the piano and wiped my hands on my pinafore. I knew Grandmother would prefer a hymn to Mozart, so I began to play 'Abide with me', which I know Mummy hates. After a few bars Grandmother said, 'Gracious, child, that's terrible. Can't you play better than that?'

I stopped and stared down at the keys; my hands were trembling. I hated Grandmother's visits.

'Come, now, Mother Coleman, she's nine years old,' Mummy at last defended me. 'She hasn't been taking lessons for long.'

'A girl needs to learn these things. How's her sewing?'

'Not good,' Mummy answered frankly. 'She's inherited that from me. But she reads very well. She's reading *Sense and Sensibility*, aren't you, Maude?'

I nodded. 'And *Through the Looking-Glass* again. Daddy and I have been recreating the chess game from it.'

'Reading,' Grandmother said, her fishbone look even stronger. 'That won't get a girl anywhere. It'll just put ideas in her head. Especially rubbish like those Alice books.'

Mummy sat up a little straighter. She read all the time. 'What's the matter with a girl having ideas, Mother Coleman?'

'She won't be satisfied with her life if she has ideas,' Grandmother said. 'Like you. I always said to my son that you wouldn't be happy. "Marry her if you must," I said, "but she'll never be satisfied." I was right. You always want something more, but all your ideas don't tell you what.'

Mummy didn't say anything, but sat with her hands clasped so tightly in her lap I could see the whites of her knuckles.

'But *I* know what you need.'

Mummy glanced at me, then shook her head at Grandmother, which meant Grandmother was about to say something I should not hear. 'You should have more children,' she said, ignoring Mummy. She always ignores Mummy. 'The doctor said there's no physical reason why you can't. You'd like a brother or sister, wouldn't you, Maude?'

I looked from Grandmother to Mummy. 'Yes,' I said, to punish Mummy for making me play the piano. I felt bad the moment I said it, but it was true, after all. I am often jealous of Lavinia because she has Ivy May, even though Ivy May can be a nuisance when she has to come everywhere with us.

Just then Jenny arrived with a tray, and we were all relieved to see her. When she had served them I managed to slip out after her as she left. Mummy was saying something about the Summer Exhibition at the Royal Academy. 'It's sure to be rubbish,' Grandmother was saying as I shut the door.

'*Rubbish*,' Jenny repeated when we were in the kitchen, her head shaking and her nose wrinkling. She sounded so much like Grandmother that I laughed till my stomach hurt.

I sometimes wonder why Grandmother bothers to visit. She and Mummy disagree on almost everything, and Grandmother is not very polite about it. It is always left to Mummy to smooth things over. 'The privilege of age,' Daddy says whenever Mummy complains.

For a moment I felt bad about abandoning Mummy upstairs, but I was still angry that she said my sewing was as bad as my piano. So I stayed in the kitchen and helped Mrs Baker with lunch. We were to have cold cow's tongue and salad, and lady's fingers for pudding. Lunches with Grandmother are never very interesting.

When Jenny came down with the coffee tray she said she

had overheard Grandmother say she does want to visit the columbarium, 'even though it is for *heathens*.' I didn't wait for her to finish, but ran to get Lavinia.

# KITTY COLEMAN

Frankly I was surprised that Mrs Coleman was so keen on seeing the columbarium. I expect the idea appeals to her sense of tidiness and economy, though she made it clear it would never be appropriate for Christians.

At any rate I was relieved to have something to do with her. I always dread her visits, though it is easier than when I was first married. It has taken these ten years of marriage to learn to handle her – like a horse, except that I have never managed a horse – they are so big and clumsy.

But handle her I have. The portraits, for example. As a wedding present she gave us several dark oil portraits of various Colemans from the last century or so, all with the same dour expression that she wears as well – which is remarkable given that she married into the family rather than inheriting the look.

They are dreary things, but Mrs Coleman insisted they be hung in the hallway where every visitor could see and admire them; and Richard did nothing to dissuade her. It is rare he will cross her. His one rebellious act has been to marry a doctor's daughter from Lincolnshire, and he will probably spend the rest of his days avoiding other conflicts.

So up went the portraits. After six months I found some botanical watercolours exactly the same size, and hung them instead, replacing them with the portraits whenever Mrs Coleman came to call. Luckily she is not the kind of woman to pay surprise visits – she always announces her arrival the day before, giving me plenty of time to switch paintings.

After several years of swapping I grew more confident, and at last felt able to leave up the watercolours. Of course on arrival she noticed them first thing, before she had even unbuttoned her coat. 'Where are the family portraits?' she demanded. 'Why are they not in their places?'

Luckily I was prepared. 'Oh, Mother Coleman' (how it grates to call her that – she is no mother to me), 'I was concerned that the draughts from the door might damage them, and so I had them rehung in Richard's study, where he can take comfort from his ancestors' presence.'

Her response was typical. 'I myself don't know why you've left them there all that time. I should like to have said something, but this is your home, after all, and far be it from me to tell you how to run it.'

Jenny almost dropped Mrs Coleman's coat on the floor from giggling – she knew all too well the palaver that had gone on over the pictures, for it had been she who'd helped me switch the paintings each time.

I did have one victory over Mrs Coleman early on, and it has seen me through many a grinding afternoon with her when afterwards I have had to lie down with a dose of Beecham's. Mrs Baker was my triumph. I chose her as our cook because of her name – the frivolity of the reason was irresistible. And I could not help it – I told Mrs Coleman as well.

When she heard she spat out her tea, appalled. 'Chosen for her name? Don't be ridiculous! What way is that to run a household?'

To my immense satisfaction, Mrs Baker — a small, self-contained woman who reminds me of a bundle of twigs — has turned out to be a gem, a thrifty, able cook who instinctively understands certain things so that I do not need to spell them out. When I tell her Mrs Coleman is coming for lunch, for example, she serves bouillon rather than mulligatawny, a poached egg rather than an omelette. Yes, she is a gem.

Jenny has been more of a trial, but I like her better than Mrs Baker, who has a way of looking at everyone sideways and so appearing constantly suspicious. Jenny has a big mouth and wide cheeks — a face made for laughing. She is always going about her work with a smirk on her face, as if she is about to burst with some great joke. And she does, too — I can hear her laugh all the way up from the kitchen. I try not to think it but I can't help wondering if the laughter is ever directed at me. I am sure it is.

Mrs Coleman says she is not to be trusted, of course. I suspect she may be right. There is something restless about Jenny that suggests one day she will crash, and we will all suffer the consequences. But I am determined to keep her on, if only to annoy Mrs Coleman.

And she has been good for Maude — she is a warm girl. (Mrs Baker is cold like pewter.) Since Maude's nanny left and I am meant to be looking after her, Jenny has become indispensable in keeping an eye on her. She often takes her to the cemetery — a whim of Lavinia's that Maude has unfortunately adopted and which I did not nip in the bud as I ought to have done. Jenny doesn't complain much — I suspect she welcomes the chance for a rest. She always leaves for the cemetery in high spirits.

Maude said the Waterhouses would like to come along to see the columbarium too, which was just as well. I suspected that Gertrude Waterhouse is, if not the class of woman Mrs Coleman would have had her son marry (not that I was either), then at least more compatible with her. They could talk about their mutual adoration of the late Queen, if nothing else.

The columbarium is housed in one of the vaults in the Circle of Lebanon, where a sort of channel has been dug round a big Lebanon cedar and lined with a double row of family vaults. To get to it one walks up the Egyptian Avenue, a gloomy row of vaults overhung with rhododendrons, the entrance done in the Egyptian style, with elaborate columns decorated with lotus flowers. The whole thing is rather theatrical – I am sure it was very stylish back in the 1840s, and now it makes me want to laugh. The tree is lovely, at least, its branches crooked and almost horizontally spread, like an umbrella of blue-green needles. With the blue sky behind it like today it can make the heart soar.

Perhaps I should have prepared the girls more for what they were about to see. Maude is quite phlegmatic and robust, and Ivy May, the younger Waterhouse girl with the big hazel eyes, keeps her thoughts to herself. But Lavinia is the kind of girl who will find any excuse to fall into a faint, which she promptly did the moment she peered through the iron grillwork into the columbarium. Not that there is much to see, really – it is a small, high vault lined with cubicles of about one foot by eighteen inches. They are all empty except for two quite high up which have been covered over with stone plaques, and another with an urn sitting in it, with no plaque as of yet. Given that there are urns everywhere on graves here, it is hard to see what Lavinia made such a fuss about.

It was secretly gratifying too, I must confess, for up until that moment Gertrude Waterhouse and Mrs Coleman had been getting on very well. I would never say I was jealous, but it did make me feel rather inadequate. However, when Gertrude had to attend to her prone daughter, waving smelling salts under her nose while Ivy May fanned her with a handkerchief, Mrs Coleman grew more disapproving. 'What's wrong with the girl?' she barked.

'She's a bit sensitive, I'm afraid,' poor Gertrude replied. 'She's not meant to see such sights.'

Mrs Coleman humphed. Her humphs are often more damaging than her words.

While we waited for Lavinia to revive, Maude asked me why it was called a columbarium.

'That's Latin for dovecote, where birds live.'

'But birds don't live there.'

'No. The little cubbyholes are for urns, as you can see, like what we have on our grave except much smaller.'

'But why do they keep urns there?'

'Most people when they die are buried in coffins. But some people choose to be burned. The urns hold their ashes and this is where you can put them.'

'Burned?' Maude looked a bit shocked.

'Cremated is the word, actually,' I said. 'There's nothing wrong with it. In a way it's less frightening than being buried. Much quicker, at least. It's becoming a little more popular now. Perhaps I'd like to be cremated.' I threw out the last comment rather flippantly, as I had never really considered it before. But now, staring at the urn in one of the cubby-holes, it began to appeal – though I should not want my ashes placed in an urn. Rather they be scattered somewhere, to help the flowers grow.

'Rubbish!' Mrs Coleman interrupted. 'And it's entirely inappropriate for a girl of Maude's age to be told about such things.' Having said that, however, she couldn't resist continuing. 'Besides, it's un-Christian and illegal. I wonder if it is even legal to build such a thing –' she waved at the columbarium – 'if it encourages criminal activity.'

As she was speaking a man came trotting down the steps next to the columbarium that led from the upper to the lower level of the Circle. He stopped abruptly when he heard her. 'Pardon me, madam,' he said, bowing to Mrs Coleman. 'I couldn't help overhearing your comment. Indeed, crem-ation is not illegal. It has never been illegal in England – it's simply been disapproved of by society, and so it has not been carried out. But there have been crematoria for many years – the first was built at Woking in 1885.'

'Who are you?' Mrs Coleman demanded. 'And what business is it of yours what I say?'

'Pardon me, madam,' the man repeated, with another bow. 'I am Mr Jackson, the superintendent of the cemetery. I simply wished to set you straight on the facts of cremation because I wanted to reassure you that there is nothing illegal about the columbarium. The Cremation Act passed two years ago regulates the procedures and practice throughout all of Britain. The cemetery is simply responding to the public's demand, and reflecting public opinion on the matter.'

'You are certainly not reflecting *my* opinion on the matter, young man,' Mrs Coleman huffed, 'and I am a grave owner here – have been for almost fifty years.'

I smiled at her idea of a young man – he looked to be forty at least, with grey hairs in his rather bushy moustache. He was quite tall, and wore a dark suit with a bowler hat. If he had not introduced himself I would have thought he was a mourner. I had probably seen him before, but could not remember him.

'I am not saying that cremation should never be practised,' Mrs Coleman went on. 'For non-Christians it can be an option: the Hindu and the Jew, atheists and suicides, those sorts who don't care about their souls. But I am truly shocked to see such a thing sited on consecrated ground. It should have been placed in the Dissenters' section, where the ground is not blessed. Here it is an offence to Christianity.'

'Those whose remains lie in the columbarium were certainly Christian, madam,' Mr Jackson said.

'But what about reassembly? How can the body and soul be reunited on the Day of Resurrection if the body has been –' Mrs Coleman did not complete her sentence, but waved a hand at the cubicles.

'Burned to a crisp,' Maude finished for her. I stifled a giggle.

Rather than wilting under her onslaught, Mr Jackson seemed to grow from it. He stood quite calmly, hands clasped behind his back, as if he were discussing a mathematical equation rather than a sticky question of theology. Maude and I, and the Waterhouses – Lavinia having recovered by this time – all stared at him, waiting for him to speak.

'Surely there is no difference between the decomposed

remains of a buried body and the ashes of a burned one,' he said.

'There is all the difference!' Mrs Coleman sputtered. 'But this is a most distasteful argument, especially in front of our girls here, one of whom has just recovered from a fit.'

Mr Jackson looked around as if he were just seeing the rest of us. 'My apologies, ladies,' he bowed (again). 'I did not mean to offend.' But then he did not leave the argument, as Mrs Coleman clearly wanted him to. 'I would simply say that God is capable of all things, and nothing we do with our remains will stop Him if he wishes to reunite our souls with our bodies.'

There was a little silence then, punctuated by a tiny gasp from Gertrude Waterhouse. The implication behind his words – that with her argument Mrs Coleman might be doubting the power of God Himself – was not lost on her. Nor on Mrs Coleman, who, for the first time since I have known her, seemed at a loss for words. It was not a long moment, of course, but it was an immensely satisfying one.

'Young man,' Mrs Coleman said finally, 'if God wanted us to burn our dead he would have said so in the Bible. Come, Maude,' she said, turning her back on him, 'it is time we paid a visit to our grave.'

As she led away a reluctant Maude, Mr Jackson glanced at me and I smiled at him. He bowed for the fourth time, muttered something about having a great deal to do, and rushed off, quite red in the face.

Well, I thought. Well.

# LAVINIA WATERHOUSE

I didn't mean to faint, really I didn't. I know Maude thinks I bring it on deliberately, but I didn't – not this time. It was just that when I looked into the columbarium, I was sure I saw a little movement. I thought it might be the ghost of one of the poor souls with their ashes in there, hovering about in search of its body. Then I felt something touch the back of my neck and I knew it must be a ghost, and I fainted.

When I told Maude afterwards what had happened she said it was probably the shadow from the cedar against the back wall of the columbarium. But I know what I saw, and it was not of this world.

Afterwards I felt quite wretched, but no one paid any attention to me, not even to get me a glass of water – they were all agog at that man talking about burning and whatnot. I could not follow what he said at all, it was so tedious.

Then Maude's grandmother dragged her off, and our mothers began to follow, and only Ivy May waited for me. She can be a dear sometimes. I got to my feet and was brushing off my dress when I heard a noise above me and looked up to see Simon on the roof of the columbarium! I couldn't help but scream, what with the ghost and all. I don't think anyone but Ivy May heard me – no one came back to see what was wrong.

When I had recovered I said, 'What are you doing up there, naughty boy?'

'Looking at you,' he said cheekily.

'Do you like me, then?' I asked.

'Sure.'

'Better than Maude? I'm prettier.'

'Her mum's the prettiest of all,' he said.

I frowned. That was not at all what I'd wanted him to say. 'Come, Ivy May,' I said, 'we must find the others.' I held out my hand to her, but she would not take it. She just looked up at Simon, her hands clasped behind her as if she were inspecting something.

'Ivy May don't say much, do she?' he said.

'No, she doesn't.'

'Sometimes I do,' she said.

'There you go,' Simon nodded. He smiled at her, and to my surprise Ivy May smiled back.

That was when the man came back – Mr Jackson, the one who talked about all the burning. He rushed round the corner, saw Simon and me and stopped.

'What are you doing here, Simon? You're meant to be helping your father. And what are you doing with these girls? They're not for the likes of you. Has he been bothering you, young lady?' he said to me.

'Oh, yes, he's been bothering me awfully,' I said.

'Simon! I'll have your father's job for this. Go and tell him to stop digging. That's the end of you, lad.'

I wasn't sure if he was bluffing. But Simon scrambled to his feet and stared at the man. He looked as if he wanted to say something, but he glanced at me and didn't. Then suddenly he took a few steps back and before I knew it he'd jumped clear over our heads from the roof of the columbarium to the Circle with the cedar in it. I was so surprised I just stood there with my mouth open. He must have jumped ten feet.

'Simon!' the man shouted again. Simon scrambled up the cedar and began creeping out along one of the branches. When he was quite a long way up he stopped and sat on the branch with his back to us, swinging his legs. He wore no shoes.

'She was lying. He wasn't bothering us.'

Ivy May often chooses to speak just when I don't want her to. I felt like pinching her.

Mr Jackson raised his eyebrows. 'What was he doing?'

I couldn't think what to say, and looked at Ivy May.

'He was showing us where to go,' Ivy May said.

I nodded. 'We were lost, you see.'

Mr Jackson sighed. His jaw moved about as if he were chewing something. 'Why don't I escort you two young ladies to your mother. Do you know where she is?'

'At our grave,' I said.

'And what is your name?'

'Lavinia Ermyntrude Waterhouse.'

'Ah, in the meadow, with an angel on it.'

'Yes. I chose that angel, you know.'

'Come with me, then.'

As we turned to follow him I did give Ivy May a great

pinch, but it was not very satisfying because she did not cry out. I suppose she thought she had used her mouth enough for one day.

# EDITH COLEMAN

I cut short my visit. I had planned to stay to supper and to see Richard, but found the trip to the cemetery so trying that when we returned to my son's house I asked the maid to fetch me a cab. The girl was standing in the hallway with a dose of Beecham's on a tray – the only time she has ever had the sense to anticipate anyone's needs. She had flavoured it with lime water, which was entirely unnecessary, and I told her so, at which point she giggled. Insolent girl. I would have shown her the door in an instant, but Kitty didn't seem to notice.

It was most annoying that Kitty didn't tell me who the Waterhouses were – then I would have avoided an unfortunate moment. (I can't help wondering if she did it deliberately.) When we visited our grave I remarked on the angel on the next grave. Richard has indicated for some time that he intends to ask the grave owners to replace the angel with an urn to match ours. I merely asked Gertrude Waterhouse her opinion – neglecting as I did so to note the name on the grave. I was as surprised to discover it is their angel as she was to find we do not like it. In the interest of getting the truth out into the open – someone must, after all, and these things always seem to come down to me – I set aside any social embarrassment I felt and explained that everyone would prefer the graves to have matching urns. But then Kitty undermined my argument by saying she rather liked the angel now, while at the same time Gertrude Waterhouse confessed they did not at all like our urn. (Fancy that!)

Then that tiresome Waterhouse girl piped up, saying that if the graves had matching urns people would think the two families were related. That remark gave me pause, I must say. I don't think such an association with the Waterhouses would be beneficial to the Colemans in the least.

And I don't think much of the Waterhouse girl's influence over my granddaughter – she has no sense of proportion, and she may well ruin Maude's. Maude could do much better for a friend.

I wash my hands of the affair of the angel and the urn. I have tried, but it is for the men to sort out, while we women bear the consequences. It is unlikely that Richard will do anything now, as it has been over three years since the angel was erected, and apparently he and Albert Waterhouse are quite friendly on the cricket team.

It was all very awkward, and I was furious with Kitty for making it so. It is just like her to embarrass me. She has never been easy, but I was more inclined to be tolerant of her when she and Richard were first married, as I knew she made him happy. These past few years, however, they have clearly been at odds. I could never speak to Richard of it, of course, but frankly I am sure she does not welcome him into her bed – otherwise they would have more children and Richard would not look so grim. I can do nothing but hint to Kitty that things ought to be otherwise, but it has no effect — she no longer makes Richard happy, and she seems unlikely to make me a grandmother again.

Now, to smooth things over with Gertrude Waterhouse, I changed the subject to the upkeep of the cemetery, about which I was sure we would all be in agreement. When my husband and I were married he brought me to the cemetery to show me the Coleman family grave, and I was all the more certain that I had chosen well in a husband. It looked to be a solid, safe and orderly place: the boundary walls were high, the flowerbeds and paths well-tended, the staff unobtrusive and professional. The much-praised landscape design did not interest me, and I didn't care for the excesses of the Egyptian Avenue and Circle of Lebanon, but I recognised them as features that have established the reputation of the cemetery as the preferred burial place of our class. Far be it from me to complain.

Now, however, standards are slipping. Today I saw dead tulips in the flowerbeds. That would never have happened thirty years ago — then a flower was replaced the moment it passed its prime. And it is not just the management. Some grave owners are even choosing to plant wild flowers around their graves! Next they'll bring in a cow to munch the buttercups.

As an example of lowered standards I pointed out some ivy from an adjacent grave (not the Waterhouses') that was creeping up the side of ours. If nothing is done it will soon cover the urn and topple it. Kitty made to pull it off, but I stopped her, saying it was for the cemetery management to make sure other people's ivy doesn't grow onto our property. I insisted that she leave the ivy as evidence, and that the superintendent himself be alerted to the situation.

To my surprise Kitty went off then and there to find the superintendent, leaving Gertrude Waterhouse and me to make awkward conversation until she reappeared — which was a very long time indeed. She must have taken a turn around the entire cemetery.

To be fair, Gertrude Waterhouse is pleasant enough. What she needs is more backbone. She should take some from my daughter-in-law, who has far more than is good for her.

# SIMON FIELD

I like it up the tree. You can see all over the cemetery, and down to town. You can sit up there all peaceful and no one else sees you. One of them big black crows comes and sits on the branch near me. I don't throw nothing or yell at it. I let it sit with me.

I don't stay long, though. When the girls are gone a few minutes I climb down to find 'em. I'm running down the main path when I see Mr Jackson coming the other way and I have to dive behind a grave.

He's talking to one of the gardeners. 'Who is that woman with the girls?' he says. 'The one wearing the apple-green dress?'

'Tha's Mrs Coleman, guv. Kitty Coleman. You know that grave down by the paupers with the big urn? Tha's theirs.'

'Yes, of course. The urn and the angel, too close together.'

'Tha's it. She's a looker, ain't she?'

'Watch yourself, man.'

The gardener chuckled. 'Sure, guv. Sure I'll watch myself.'

When they've passed I go down to the graves. I have to hide from the gardeners working in the meadow. It's tidy here, all the grass clipped and the weeds pulled and the paths raked. Some places in the cemetery they don't bother with so much now, but in the meadow there's always someone doing something. Mr Jackson says it has to look good for the visitors, else they won't buy plots and there'll be no money to pay us. Our Pa says that's rubbish – people die every day and need a place to be buried, and they'll pay whether the grass is cut or no. He says all that matters is a grave well dug.

I crouch down behind the grave with the angel on it. Livy's grave. There still ain't no skull 'n' crossbones marked on it, though it makes my fingers itch to see it blank like that. I kept my word.

The ladies are standing in front of the two graves talking, and Livy and Maude are sitting in the grass, making chains out of little daisies. I peek out now and then but they don't see me. Only Ivy May does. She stares straight at me with big greeny-brown eyes like a cat that freezes when it sees you and waits to see what you're going to do – kick it or pat it. She don't say nothing and I put my finger on my mouth to go shhh. I owe her for saving our Pa's job.

Then I hear the lady in the green dress say, 'I'll go and find the superintendent, Mr Jackson. He may be able to get someone to look after things here.'

'It won't make any difference,' the old lady says. 'It's the attitude that's changed. The attitude of this new age which doesn't respect the dead.'

'Nevertheless, he can at least have someone remove the ivy since you won't allow me to,' the lady in green says. She kicks at her skirts. I like it when she does that. It's like she's trying to kick 'em off. 'I'll just go and find him. Won't be a minute.' She goes up the path and I slip from grave to grave, following her.

I'd like to tell her where Mr Jackson is now but I don't know myself. There's three graves being dug today, and four funerals. There's a column being put up near the monkey puzzle tree, and there's some new graves sunk and need more dirt on 'em. Mr Jackson could be any of them places, overseeing the men. Or he could be having a cuppa down the lodge, or selling someone a grave. She don't know that, though.

On the main path she almost gets run down by a team of horses pulling a slab of granite. She jumps back, but she don't shriek like lots of ladies would. She just stands there, all white, and I have to hide behind a yew tree while she takes out a handkerchief and presses it to her forehead and neck.

Near the Egyptian Avenue another lot of diggers comes down towards her with spades over their shoulders. They're hard men – our Pa and me stay away from 'em. But when she stops 'em and says something they look at the ground, both of 'em, like they're under a spell. One points up the path and over to the right and she thanks 'em and walks the way he pointed. When she's past they look at each other and one says something I can't hear and they both laugh.

They don't see me following her. I jump from grave to grave, ducking behind the tombstones. The granite slabs on the graves are warm under my feet where they've been in the sun. Sometimes I just stand still for a minute to feel that warmth. Then I run to catch up with her. Her back from behind looks like an hour-glass. We got hour-glasses on graves here with wings on 'em. Time flies, our Pa says they mean. You think you got long in this world but you don't.

She turns down the path by the horse statue into the Dissenters, and then I remember they're trimming branches off the horse chestnuts back there. We go round a corner and there's Mr Jackson with four gardeners – two on the ground and two who have climbed a big chestnut tree. One of 'em straddles a branch and shinnies out along it, holding tight with his legs. A gardener on the ground makes a joke about the branch being a woman, and everybody laughs 'cept Mr Jackson and the lady, who nobody knows is there yet. She smiles, though.

They've tied ropes round the branch and the two men up the tree are pulling back and forth on a two-man saw. They stop to wipe the sweat off their faces, and to unstick the saw when it gets caught.

Some of the men see the lady in the green dress. They nudge each other but nobody tells Mr Jackson. She looks happier watching the men in the tree than when she was with the other ladies. Her eyes are dark, like there's coal smudged round them, and little bits of her hair are coming out of their pins.

Suddenly there's a crack, and the branch breaks where they're sawing it. The lady cries out, and Mr Jackson turns round and sees her. The men let the branch down with the ropes and when it's on the ground they start sawing it to pieces.

Mr Jackson comes over to the lady. He's red in the face like it's him been sawing the branch all this time instead of telling others what to do.

'I'm sorry, Mrs Coleman, I didn't see you. Have you been here long?'

'Long enough to hear a tree branch compared to a woman.'

Mr Jackson sputters like his beer's gone down the wrong way.

Mrs Coleman laughs. 'That's all right,' she says. 'It was quite refreshing, actually.'

Mr Jackson don't seem to know what to say. Lucky for him one of the men in the tree shouts down, 'Any other branches to cut here, guv?'

'No, just take this one down to the bonfire area. Then we're finished here.'

'Do you have fires here?' Mrs C. asks.

'At night, yes, to burn wood and leaves and other refuse. Now, madam, how may I be of service?'

'I wanted to thank you for speaking to my mother-in-law about cremation,' she says. 'It was very instructive, though I expect she was rather taken aback to be answered so forthrightly.'

'Those with firm opinions must be dealt with firmly.'

'Whom are you quoting?'

'Myself.'

'Oh.'

They don't say nothing for a minute. Then she says, 'I think I should like to be cremated, now that I know it will be no more of a challenge to God than interment.'

'It is something you must consider carefully and decide for yourself, madam. It is not a decision to be taken lightly.'

'I don't know about that,' she says. 'Sometimes I think it

matters not a jot what I do or don't do, or what is done to me.'

He looks at her shocked, like she's just cursed. Then one of the gatekeepers comes running up the path and says, 'Guv, the Anderson procession's at the bottom of Swain's Lane.'

'Already?' Mr Jackson says. He pulls his watch from his pocket. 'Blast, they're early. Send a boy over to the grave to tell the diggers to stand by. I'll be down in a moment.'

'Right, guv.' The man runs back down the path.

'Is it always this busy?' Mrs C. says. 'So much activity doesn't encourage quiet contemplation. Though I suppose it is a little quieter here in the Dissenters.'

'A cemetery is a business, like any other,' Mr Jackson says. 'People tend to forget that. Today in fact is relatively quiet for burials. But I'm afraid we can't guarantee peace and quiet, except on Sundays. It's the nature of the work — it's impossible to predict when people will pass on. We must be prepared to act swiftly — nothing can be planned in advance. We have had twenty funerals in one day. Other days we've had none. Now, madam, was there something else you wanted? I'm afraid I must be getting on.'

'Oh, it seems so trivial now, compared to all this.' She waves her hand round her. I'll have to ask our Pa what trivial means.

'Nothing is trivial here. What is it?'

'It's about our grave down in the meadow. Some ivy from another grave is growing up the side of it. Though I believe it is our responsibility to cut it, it's rather upset my mother-in-law, who feels the cemetery should complain to the neighbouring grave owner.'

Now I understand what trivial means.

Mr Jackson smiles a smile you only see when he's with visitors, like he's got a pain in his back and is trying to hide it. Mrs C. looks embarrassed.

'I'll have someone remove it at once,' he says, 'and I shall have a word with the other owners.' He looks round as if he's looking for a boy to give orders to, so I step out from the stone I was standing behind. It's risky 'cause I know he's still mad at me for hanging round Livy and Ivy May rather'n working. But I want Mrs C. to see me.

'I'll do it, sir,' I say.

Mr Jackson looks surprised. 'Simon, what are you doing here? Have you been harassing Mrs Coleman?'

'I don't know what harassing means, sir, but I ain't been doing it. I'm just offering to clear off that ivy.'

Mr Jackson is about to say something but Mrs C. interrupts. 'Thank you, Simon. That would be very kind of you.' And she smiles at me.

No lady's ever said such a nice thing to me, nor smiled at me. I can't move, staring at her smile.

'Go, boy. Go,' Mr Jackson says quietly.

I smile back at her. Then I go.

*January 1905*

# JENNY WHITBY

It were a right nuisance, that was sure. We'd got into a routine, he and I. Everyone was happy – the missus, the girls, him and me. (I always come last on the list.) I'd take the girls up the hill once a week or so. I'd my bit of fun, they'd theirs, and her ladyship didn't have to do nothing but sit at home and read.

But then she got it into her head to take them to the cemetery herself. In the summer she started going up there two, three times a week. The girls were in heaven, but me, I were in hell.

Then she stopped, and started sending me again, and I thought: It's back on. But now it's winter the girls don't go so much, and when they do she wants to take them again. Sometimes she even takes them when they ain't so keen on going. It's cold there, with all that stone round the place. They have to run to keep warm. Me, I know how to keep warm when I'm there.

Once or twice I've convinced the missus that I should go instead of her. Rest of the time I've to sneak out of an afternoon. He ain't there evenings. Gardeners work shorter hours than maids, I like to remind him.

'Yep, an' we get paid twice as much,' he said. 'It's a dog's life, innit?'

I asked him what it is with the missus — what she goes to the cemetery so much for.

'Maybe the same reason as you,' he said.

'She never!' I laughed. 'Who would she go for, anyhow — a gravedigger?'

'The guvnor, more like,' he said.

I laughed again, but he were serious — said everyone saw 'em together, talking over in the Dissenters.

'Just talking?'

'Yep, just like us,' he said. 'Fact is, we talk too much, you an' me. Just shut your mouth an' open your legs, now.'

Cheeky sod.

*October 1905*

# GERTRUDE WATERHOUSE

I do like to make an effort with my At Homes. I always have them in the front parlour, and use the rose-pattern tea set, and Elizabeth bakes a cake – lemon this week.

Albert asks sometimes if we oughtn't use the front parlour as the dining room instead, rather than eating in the back parlour, which is a bit cramped when the table is pulled out. Now Albert is right in most things, but when it comes to running a household I do get my way. I always feel better having a 'best' room to show visitors to, even if it's only used once or twice a week. Thus I have insisted that we leave the rooms as they are, though I admit it is a bit inconvenient to fold the table back three times a day.

It is very silly too, and I will never tell Albert, but I also prefer to have my At Homes in the front parlour because it is out of view of the Colemans' house. This is very silly because for one thing, according to Livy, who has been to them a few times with Maude (I have never gone, of course), Kitty Coleman has her At Homes in her morning room, which is on the other side of the house, overlooking the street rather than us. And even if it were on this side, she would hardly have the time to look out of her window over at us. But just the same I do not like to think of her presence at my back, judging what I do. It would make me nervous and unable to attend to my visitors.

I am always a little anxious when Lavinia goes to Kitty Coleman's At Homes, which I'm relieved to say is not very often. Indeed, more often than not the girls come here after school. Maude says it's much more snug here, which on reflection I think is intended as a compliment rather than a comment on the lack of space. At any rate I have decided to take it as such. She is a dear girl and I do try to see her as separate from her mother.

I am quietly pleased that, for all the space and elegance of the Colemans' house, it is here that the girls prefer to be. Livy says their house gets very cold and draughty except in the kitchen, and she fears she'll catch a chill – though really apart from her fainting, she has a robust constitution and a healthy appetite. She also says she prefers our comfortable dark sofas and chairs and the velvet curtains to Kitty Coleman's taste for rattan furniture and Venetian blinds.

Until the girls arrive back from school, Ivy May helps me with the At Homes, passing round the cake and taking the teapot back to the kitchen for Elizabeth to fill. The ladies who come – neighbours from the street and from church, and stalwart friends who make the journey from Islington to see me, bless them – all smile at her, though they are often puzzled by her as well.

She is indeed a funny little thing. At first her refusal to speak very often did upset me, but over time I've grown used to it and now love her the better for it. Ivy May's silence can be a great comfort after Livy's dramas and tears. And there is nothing the matter with her head – she reads and writes well enough for a girl of seven, and her numbers are good. In a year I will send her to school with Livy and Maude, and then it may be harder for her — her teachers may not be so patient with her as we are.

I asked her once why she said so little, and the dear replied, 'When I do speak, you listen.' It is surprising that someone so young should have worked that out for herself. I could have done with the lesson — I do go on and on, from nerves and to fill the silence. Sometimes in front of Kitty Coleman I could just sink into the ground from hearing myself chatter like a performing monkey. Kitty Coleman just smiles as if she's terribly bored but hiding it so civilly.

When the girls get home Livy immediately takes over the passing out of the cake to the ladies and little Ivy May sits quietly in the corner. It breaks my heart sometimes. Still, I am glad to have the girls around me, and I try to make things as comfortable as possible. Here at least I can have some influence over them. I don't know what Kitty Coleman gets up to when they are at Maude's. Mostly she ignores them, according to Livy.

They like to come here, but they love best of all to go to the cemetery. I have had to limit how often Livy may go — else she'd be up there every day. As it is, I do believe she lies to me about it. A neighbour said she thought she saw Livy and Maude running among the graves with a boy one day when she was meant to be playing at Maude's, but when I questioned her she denied it, saying the neighbour must need new spectacles! I did not look convinced, and Livy began to cry to think I suspected her of lying. So really I do not know what to think.

I wanted to have a word with Kitty Coleman about the

frequency of their visits – it being she who most often takes them. What an awkward conversation it was! She does make me feel such a fool. When I suggested that it was perhaps unhealthy for them to visit the cemetery so often, she replied, 'Oh, the girls are getting plenty of fresh air, which is very healthy for them. But really if they want to go there, we have Queen Victoria to blame for it, elevating mourning to such ridiculous heights that girls with romantic notions grow drunk from it.'

Well! I was mortified, and not a little angry too. Apart from the slight on Livy, Kitty Coleman knows how dear the late Queen still is to me, God bless her soul. There is no need to go criticising the dead. I told Kitty Coleman so, straight to her face.

She just smiled and said, 'If we can't criticise her now, when can we? Do so when she was alive and we'd likely have been tried for treason.'

'The monarchy is above criticism,' I responded with as much dignity as I could muster. 'They are our sovereign representatives, and we do well to look up to them or it reflects poorly on us.'

Soon after I made my excuses and left, still furious with her. It was only afterwards that I remembered I had not properly spoken to her about curtailing Livy's cemetery visits. She is impossible – I shall never understand her. If I am honest, nor do I wish to.

*February 1906*

# MAUDE COLEMAN

I know every inch of the cemetery now. I know it better than my own garden. Mummy does take us there all the time, even after school in winter when it is already getting dark and we have not asked to go.

Of course it is great fun playing there. We find Simon first, and if he is free he comes with us for a bit. We play hide and seek, and tour the angels (there are two new ones), and sometimes we sit at our graves and Lavinia tells stories about the people buried in the cemetery. She has an old guide to the cemetery that she likes to read from, about the girl whose dress caught fire, or the lieutenant-colonel killed in the Boer War described as 'brave and kind-hearted', or the man who died in a railway accident. Or she simply makes up stories, which I find rather tedious but which Simon likes. I haven't the imagination she has. I am more interested in the plants and trees, or the kind of stone used for the memorials; or, if Ivy May is with is, I test her reading using words on the graves.

I do not know what Mummy does while we play. She wanders off and I rarely see her until she comes looking for us when it is time to go. She says it is good for us to take the air, and I suppose she is right, but I am sometimes cold and, I admit, a little weary of the place. It is funny to think how desperate I used to be to get to the cemetery when I wasn't allowed to, and yet now that I go there all the time, it is no longer quite so special.

# KITTY COLEMAN

He will not have me. I am mad for him but he will not have me.

For almost two years I have visited the cemetery solely for the purpose of seeing him. And yet he will not take me.

I was careful at first — although I sought him out I did not want it to appear so. I always took the girls with me, then let them go off to play and pretended to be looking for them when really I was looking for him. I have paced up and down its paths, appearing to be fascinated by the merits of Roman versus plain crosses, or obelisks in Portland stone versus granite, or the names on graves chiselled into the stone versus fastened on with metal letters. I do not know what the workers there think of me, but they have grown used to my presence, and always nod respectfully.

I have learned a great deal about the cemetery that I did not know before. I know where they dump the extra soil displaced by coffins, and where the timber is kept for shoring up the deep graves, and the green rugs they place round freshly dug graves to look like grass. I know which grave-diggers sing as they work, and where they hide their bottles of spirits. I have seen the ledgers and the detailed maps, each plot numbered, used to record graves. I have grown used to the horses pulling stones about the place. I have come to know the cemetery as an industry rather than as a place of spiritual contemplation.

He runs it as if it were an immaculate passenger ship crossing the ocean. He can be hard and brutal if necessary with the staff — some of the men are very rough indeed. But I think he is fair, too, and he respects good work.

Above all, he is kind to me without making me feel a lesser person.

We talk about all sorts of things — about the world and how it works, and about God and how He works. He asks my opinions, and does not laugh at them, but considers them. He is how I had always hoped Richard would turn out to be. But I made the mistake of thinking my husband would change when we married; instead he became more entrenched.

John Jackson is not a handsome man. He is not a prosperous man, though he is not poor either. He is not from a good family. He does not attend supper parties or the theatre or openings to exhibitions. He is not an educated man, though he is learned; when he showed me Michael Faraday's grave in the Dissenters he was able to explain his experiments with magnetic fields far better than Richard or even my brother could have.

He is a truthful man, a religious man, a principled man, a moral man. It is those last qualities that have undone me.

I am not accustomed to being turned down. Not that I have offered myself as such before, but I enjoy flirting and expect a response, else I would not do it. But he does not flirt. When I tried to with him, early on, he said he does not like coquettes, that he only wants the truth, and I stopped. And so over several months – constantly interrupted by his cemetery duties – I told him what little there is to tell of my small life: of how much I miss my late parents and brother, of my dull despair, of my impossible search for a place by the fire that is neither too hot nor too cold. (Only a few things I have kept from him – my knowledge of how to avoid having a baby, my cold bed, the New Year's Eve Richard insists upon. He would be disgusted by the last. Myself, I am not disgusted so much as resigned.)

When, at last, in the autumn after a summer of what felt like a courtship, I told him in clear terms what I was prepared to do, he said no.

I stopped going to the cemetery for a time then, sending Jenny with the girls when they wanted to go. But I could not keep away. And so for this past year we have again seen each other, but not as often and without the heightened expectations. It is painful, but he has upheld his principles, and I have come to accept that they are more important than me.

So we meet, and he speaks kindly to me. Today he said to me that he has always wanted a sister and now he has one. I did not reply that I have already had a brother and don't want another.

*April 1906*

April 1906

# LAVINIA WATERHOUSE

It is so nice to have someone to mourn properly. And now I am eleven and old enough to wear a proper mourning dress, it is even better. Dear Auntie would have been so touched to see me dressed like this, and Papa got tears in his eyes when he saw me 'looking so much like my dear sister'.

I have studied *The Queen* and *Cassell's* very carefully so that I will not make any mistakes, and I have even written my own manual to help out other girls in my position who may have questions about the correct etiquette for mourning. I asked Maude to help me but she was not interested. Sometimes she will go on about constellations, or planets, or stones she has found in the Heath, or plants in her mother's garden, until I just want to scream.

So I have had to do it all myself. I think it has turned out very well – at least Mama says so. I have written it in my best script on black-edged paper, and I got Ivy May to draw an angel on the cover. Her drawing is quite good, and the book looks very handsome. I am going to copy the text below so that I shall always have it.

## The Complete Guide to Mourning Etiquette
## by Miss Lavinia Ermyntrude Waterhouse

It is a very sad thing when someone dies. We mark the occasion with mourning. We wear special black clothes and black jewellery, we use special stationery for letters, and we do not go to parties or concerts.

Mourning lasts different lengths of time depending upon the loved one who has died.

The Widow mourns the longest because she is the saddest. What a terrible thing it is to lose a husband! She mourns for 2 years – 18 months full mourning, 6 months half-mourning. Some ladies mourn for longer. Our own late Queen wore mourning for her husband Albert for the rest of her life – forty years!

How sad it is for a mother to lose her child, or a child her mother. They mourn for 1 year.

For brothers and sisters – 6 months
For grandparents – 6 months
Uncles and aunts – 2 months
Great-uncles and great-aunts – 6 weeks
First cousins – 4 weeks
Second cousins – 3 weeks

## Clothing

It is very important to obtain proper mourning clothes. They must be new, and they must be burned after mourning, because it is bad luck to keep them in the house.

Jay's on Regent Street is where all good London families buy their mourning clothes.

Ladies wear dresses made of best paramatta silk and trimmed with crape for full mourning of their husbands, parents, or children. For grandparents and brothers and sisters, ladies wear plain black silk trimmed with crape. For everyone else ladies wear black with no crape.

Ladies wear black gloves and carry white handkerchiefs edged with black.

After a time they can take off the crape. This is called 'slighting' the mourning.

Then there is half-mourning. Ladies wear grey or lavender or violet, or black and white stripes. Their gloves are grey as well.

## Jewellery

During full mourning ladies may wear jet brooches and earrings. The brooches may be adorned with the hair of the loved one. In half-mourning ladies may wear a little gold, silver, and pearls and diamonds.

## Stationery

Paper for writing must have a black edge. It is very important that the edge should be wide enough to honour the loved one, but not so wide as to be vulgar.

## Gentlemen

Gentlemen wear what they normally wear to work but also wear black hatbands, black cravats, and black gloves. They do not wear jewellery.

## Children (under ten)

Children may wear black if they wish, but most often they wear white dresses, and sometimes lavender or mauve or grey. They may wear gloves. Children over ten should wear full mourning.

# MAUDE COLEMAN

When we went up to the cemetery today they were taking apart the Waterhouse grave. I knew the funeral for Lavinia's aunt was the next day, but I had thought they would be digging the grave later in the day. It was strange to see Simon and his Pa working on one of our graves rather than a stranger's. I had always thought of our graves as solid and indestructible, but now I know that you can take a crowbar to them and pull them apart, and even knock down an angel in the process.

Lavinia took my arm when she saw the group of men around the grave, and I wondered if she was going to make a scene. I was rather weary of her, I must confess. Since her aunt died she has talked of nothing but black clothes and when she can begin wearing jewellery again – even though she is hardly allowed to wear any anyway! The mourning rules of conduct are quite ferocious, from what she says. I don't think I would be very good at it. I would break rules all the time without even knowing it.

Then Mummy suddenly shouted 'John!' I have never heard her shout so loudly. We all jumped, and next thing I knew Simon's Pa had shoved Mr Jackson and sent him flying. And then the Waterhouse angel hit the ground.

It was all very strange. For the longest time I couldn't connect any of the things I saw. I did not understand why Simon's Pa pushed Mr Jackson and why Mr Jackson, looking very pale, then thanked him for it. I did not understand why the angel had fallen. And I did not understand why Mummy knew Mr Jackson's Christian name.

When I saw that the angel's head had broken from its body I found it hard not to laugh. Lavinia fainted, of course. Then Simon ran off with the angel's head under his arm and I did laugh – it made me think of the poem about Isabella burying her lover's head in the pot of basil.

Luckily Lavinia didn't hear me laugh – she had woken up and was busy being sick. Mummy made a surprising fuss over her, putting her arm round her and handing her a handkerchief.

Lavinia stared at Mummy's handkerchief. 'Oh no, I must use my own mourning handkerchief,' she said.

'It doesn't matter,' Mummy said. 'Really it doesn't.'

'Are you sure?'

'God won't strike you dead for using a plain handkerchief.'

'But it's not to do with God,' Lavinia said very earnestly. 'It's about respecting the dead. My auntie would be so hurt if she thought I wasn't thinking of her in everything I do.'

'I shouldn't think your auntie would want to be thought of while you're wiping your mouth after being sick.'

Ivy May giggled. Lavinia frowned at her.

'Things are changing,' Mummy said. 'No one expects you or your father or mother to go through full mourning any longer. You may not remember this, but King Edward limited the mourning period for his mother to three months.'

'I remember. But my mother wore black for longer than anyone else. And I would feel ashamed if I didn't wear black for my auntie.'

'May I be of assistance, madam?' Mr Jackson asked, standing over them.

'Could you order a cab to take us home, please,' Mummy said without looking at him.

Mr Jackson went off to whistle for a cab. By the time he had returned Lavinia was standing, but she was still very pale and shaken.

'Shall we bring her down to the courtyard?' Mr Jackson asked. 'Can you walk, young lady, or would you like me to carry you?'

'I can walk,' Lavinia said. She took a few wobbly steps.

Mummy slipped her arm round Lavinia's shoulders and Mr Jackson took her elbow. They began to go slowly down the path towards the entrance. As Ivy May and I trailed after them, I noticed that Mummy's and Mr Jackson's hands seemed to be touching under Lavinia's upper arm. I wasn't entirely sure, and I thought for a moment of asking Ivy May what she saw, but then decided against it.

Mr Jackson had to carry Lavinia down the steps to the courtyard, and then she insisted she was well enough to walk on her own. When we got to the front gate a hansom was waiting for us, which was not very big for four people, even if three of us were girls. I suppose it was the first cab to be found. Mr Jackson handed Lavinia in – really he had to lift her, she was so weak. Then he turned and handed me in, and then Ivy May. Ivy May sat on my lap so that there would be room for Mummy. She sat very still, without wriggling. She is a solid little bundle, but I liked having her there, and put my arms round her to keep her steady. It made me wish I had a brother or sister to sit on my lap from time to time.

Mr Jackson handed my mother in and shut the door for her. She opened the window, and he leaned in for a moment to say, 'Goodbye, young ladies. I do hope you feel better, miss,' he added, nodding at Lavinia. 'We'll have your angel up again in no time.'

Lavinia hardly looked at him, but leaned back and closed her eyes.

Then, as the wheels began to turn, I heard someone say in a low voice, 'Tomorrow.' I thought it must be Mr Jackson adding that the angel would be ready in time for the funeral the next day.

Mummy must have heard it too, for she sat up suddenly as if Miss Linden at school had come around with her ruler and prodded her in the side the way she does to us during comportment lessons.

Then we were whizzing down the hill, and I spotted Simon coming out of the mason's yard, without the angel's head. He saw us too, and from the corner of my eye I watched him sprint alongside the hansom until he could not keep up any longer.

# SIMON FIELD

This is what happens. I see it all.

When we slide the marble slab off the Waterhouse grave, we has to pry it loose from the base of the plinth where the angel stands. Joe and I are doing it, with our Pa and Mr Jackson watching. Mr Jackson's giving advice the way he likes to do. I want to tell him we knows what we're doing, but he's the guvnor – he can say what he likes.

Joe's working at the slab with a crowbar and he leans against the plinth to put his weight behind the bar. Now Joe's a big strong man and his back's pushing that plinth, and before you know it the plinth starts moving. Them masons must've made a mess of the foundation when they put it in for that to happen. I been digging at the cemetery six years and never seen one shift so.

Worse'n that, the mortar holding the angel to the base of the plinth ain't strong. I see the angel wobble back and forth.

'Joe,' I says, 'stop.'

Joe stops with the crowbar but he's still leaning against the plinth, and the angel wobbles again. I can see the crack in the mortar now, but before I can say something the angel starts·to topple. I hear a woman shout just as the angel falls sideways and hits the Coleman urn. The head cracks right off, and it falls one way and the body the other. In fact the body falls right where Mr Jackson's standing, 'cept he ain't there now 'cause our Pa's knocked him right out the way.

It all happens slow and fast too. Then Kitty Coleman and the girls run up to us. Livy takes one look at the headless angel and shrieks and faints, which is nothing new. Mrs C. helps up Mr Jackson – his face is all pale and sweaty. He's breathing heavy and he takes out a kerchief and wipes his face. Then he looks at the base of the plinth and the cracked mortar, clears his throat and says, 'I'm going to strangle that mason with my bare hands.'

I know what he means.

Then he says, 'Thank you, Paul,' real quiet and solemn to our Pa. It sounds funny 'cause he never calls our Pa by his name.

Our Pa just shrugs. 'Dunno what they need an angel up there for anyways,' he says. 'Urns and angels and columns and whatnot. Bloody nonsense. When you're dead you're dead. You don't need an angel to tell you that. Give me a pauper's grave any day.' Our Pa taps one of the paupers' wood crosses. 'My Pa were buried in one and that'll suit me too.'

'Just as well,' Mr Jackson says, 'for that's where you're likely to end up.'

You might think our Pa would be offended, but something in the way Mr Jackson says it makes our Pa smile. The guvnor smiles too, and it's a funny sight, given he's just almost been struck down dead. It's like they're mates sitting over a jar in the pub, laughing at a joke.

'Anyhows, best see to the girlie,' our Pa says then, nodding at Livy. Maude's crouching by her, and Mrs C. goes over to her too. Livy sits up. She's all right – she always is.

Ivy May's standing next to me. 'You should have marked that angel,' she says.

Takes me a minute to work out she means the skull 'n' crossbones. 'Can't,' I say. 'Livy won't let me.'

Ivy May shakes her head and I feel bad, like I let her down. No time to say more, though, 'cause Mr Jackson says to me, 'Simon, run to the mason's yard and tell Mr Watson he's wanted here immediately. If he complains, give him this.' He hands me the angel's head, whose nose is broke off. It's heavy and I almost drop it, which makes Livy shriek again. I tuck it under my arm and run.

# JENNY WHITBY

I were in the garden beating carpets when he came tumbling over the fence and fell right at my feet. 'Ow!' I shouted. 'What's this boy doing here? You muddy little rascal, jumping the fence like you own the place. Don't you come tracking that mud from the grave into this garden!'

Cheeky boy just grinned at me. 'Why not?' he said. 'You track enough of it here yourself on the bottom of your skirts. Though we ain't seen much of you these days up at the cemetery.'

'Shut your trap,' I said. Oh, he were cheeky, all right. Simon, he's called. Never said much to him at the cemetery but the girls talk about him all the time. He's the brother Maude never had, I always think.

I seen him creeping behind graves to have a look when I been busy with that gardener. He thought he were hidden, but I seen him. Wanted to see the business. I didn't care — I thought it was funny. Not now, though. Gardener don't want no more to do with me. Bastard.

'I never thought much of him,' Simon said now, like he knew exactly what I was thinking. 'You're well clear of him, I'd say.'

'Shut it,' I said. 'No one asked you.' But I weren't really mad at the boy. Talking to him gave me a chance to rest my back – these days beating rugs is a killer. 'Anyways, what you come here for?'

'Want to see where the girls live.'

'How'd you find it?'

'Ran after their cab. Lost it for a bit, so I just walked round till I saw it again, leaving Maude and her mum here. Must've already let out Livy.'

'Sure, she lives right there, Miss Livy and her sister.' I pointed at the house across the way.

Simon had a good look at it. He's a scrawny boy, for all his digging. His face is pinched round the eyes and his wrists are all red and knobbly, busting out of a jacket too small for him.

'Wait here a minute,' I said. I went into the kitchen, where Mrs Baker was cutting up a chicken.

'Who's that boy?' she said right away. She don't miss nothing round here. Can't keep a thing from her. I seen how she looks at me sideways these days, though she don't say nothing.

I ignored her, cut a slice of bread and spread it with butter. Then I took it out to Simon, who looked glad to see it. He ate it fast. I shook my head and went in to get some more. As I was spreading the butter, thicker this time, Mrs Baker said, 'If you give a stray scraps, it'll never leave you alone.'

'Mind your business,' I snapped.

'That bread is my business. I baked it this morning and I'm not baking more today.'

'Then I'll go without.'

'No you won't,' she said. 'If I let you, you'd eat the entire kitchen these days. You watch yourself, Jenny Whitby.'

'Leave me alone,' I said, and ran out before she could say more.

While Simon ate the bread I started to beat the rugs again.

'Look,' he said after a bit, 'there's Livy in the window. What's she doing?'

I looked up. 'They do that all the time, them two. Stand in the windows of their nurseries and make signs at each other. Got their own language no one understands but them.'

'Bet I'd understand it.'

I snorted. 'What's she saying, then?' Miss Livy was pointing up and bowing her head. Then she pulled a finger across her throat and pouted.

'She's talking about the cemetery,' Simon said.

'How'd you know that?'

'That's what the angel on her grave looks like.' Simon bowed his head and pointed. 'Or did, anyway. The head come off — that's why she did that with her throat.'

Then he told me about what happened to the angel and how his Pa saved the guv's life. It were thrilling stuff.

'Look,' Simon said then. 'Livy's seen me.'

Miss Livy was pointing at Simon.

I heard a window open above us and when I looked up Miss Maude was poking her head out to look down.

'I should go,' Simon said. 'I got to help our Pa with the grave.'

'Nah, stay. Miss Maude'll be down to see you.'

'Thanks for the bread,' Simon said, getting up anyway.

'If ever you come there's always bread for you here,' I

said, looking out over the garden and not at him. 'And you don't need to climb the fence to get back here. If the gate's locked the key's hid under the loose stone by the coal chute.'

Simon nodded and went out of the gate.

I should've given him something to take with him. I hate to see a boy go hungry like that. Made me hungry just thinking of it. I went inside to get some of that bread for me. To hell with Mrs Baker.

# LAVINIA WATERHOUSE

I went star-gazing on the Heath with Maude and her father tonight. I wasn't sure I ought to do such a thing on the night of the very day of dear Auntie's funeral, but Mama and Papa said I should go. They both seemed very weary – Mama even snapped at me. I looked up in *Cassell's* and *The Queen* under star-gazing, but neither mentioned it, which I took as a sign that I could go, as long as I didn't enjoy it too much.

And I didn't, at first. We went at twilight because Maude's father wanted to see the moon just as it appeared above the horizon. He was looking for something called Copernicus. I thought that was a person, but Maude said it was a crater that used to be a volcano. I am never certain what she and her father mean when they talk about the moon and stars. They let me look through the telescope and asked me if I could see any craters – whatever they are. Really I couldn't see anything but to please them I said I could.

I much preferred looking at the moon without the tele-scope – I could see it so much better. It was lovely to look at, a half-moon hanging all pale orange just above the horizon.

Then I lay down on a blanket they had brought with them and looked up at the stars, which were just appearing in the sky. I must have fallen asleep because when I woke it was dark and there were many more stars. And then I saw a falling angel, and then another! I pointed them out to Maude, though of course they were gone by the time she looked.

Maude said they are called shooting stars but are actually little pieces of an old comet burning up, and are called meteors. But I know what they really are – they are angels stumbling as they take messages from God to us. Their wings make streaks across the sky until they are able to find their footing again.

When I tried to explain this, Maude and her father looked at me as if I were mad. I lay back down to look for more, and kept it to myself when I saw one.

# RICHARD COLEMAN

The moon was magnificent tonight, with Copernicus clearly visible. I was reminded of a night years ago when I took Kitty and her brother out to look at the moon. We were able to see Copernicus then almost as clearly. Kitty looked so lovely in the moonlight and I was happy, even with Harry babbling on in the background about Copernicus the man, trying to impress me. I decided that night I would ask her to marry me.

Tonight, for the first time in a long while, I wished Kitty were with us instead of sitting at home with a book. She never comes star-gazing now. At least Maude is interested. Sometimes I think my daughter is the saving grace of this family.

# KITTY COLEMAN

When it came to it at last, he did not hesitate at all. He laid me back on a bank of fading primroses, my body crushing them so that their almond scent filled the air around us. An angel hovered overhead, but he did not want to move. He was daring it to frighten him as the other angel had yesterday. I did not mind it being there, its head bowed so that it looked straight into my eyes – I had cause to thank an angel for driving him into my arms.

I lifted up the skirt of my grey dress and bared my legs. They looked like mushroom stems in the dim light, or the stamens of some exotic flower, an orchid or a lily. He put his hands on me, parted my lips down there, and pushed himself into me. That much was familiar. What was new were his hands remaining there, kneading me insistently. I pulled his head down to my breasts and he bit me through my dress.

At last the heaviness that has resided inside me since I married – perhaps even since I was born – lifted, boiling up slowly in a growing bubble. The angel watched, its gaze blank, and for once I was glad its eyes could not judge me, not even when I cried out as the bubble burst.

As I lay there afterwards with him holding me, I gazed up through the branches of the cypress arching over us. The half-moon was still low in the sky, but above me stars had appeared, and I saw one fall, as if to remind me of the consequences in store. I had seen and felt the signs inside me that day, and I had ignored them. I had had my joy at last, and I knew I would pay for it. I would not tell him, but it would be the end of us.

*May 1906*

# ALBERT WATERHOUSE

Why I have received two invoices from the mason's yard at the cemetery is a mystery. 'For repairs to grave furniture,' one read. This was separate from the invoice for chiselling my sister's name into the plinth. At her funeral I didn't notice anything wrong with the grave. Trudy said she knows nothing of it, but Livy became quite upset when I mentioned it, and ran from the room. Later she said it was because she was having a coughing fit, but I didn't hear any coughing. And Ivy May just looked at me as if she knew the answer but wasn't about to tell me.

My daughters are an even greater mystery to me than the rogue invoice – which I have sent on to the superintendent with a query. Let him sort it out – he seems a capable fellow.

*July 1906*

# EDITH COLEMAN

It has often been the case that I am the one forced to take in hand an unfortunate situation. This age has gone soft. I see it everywhere: in the foolish fashions that pass for women's dress, in the shockingly permissive theatre, in this ludicrous woman's suffrage movement we hear of. Even, dare I say it, in the conduct of our own King. I only hope his mother never got wind of his shenanigans with Mrs Keppel.

The young lack the moral fibre of their elders, and time and again my generation is required at the last to step into the breach. I do not complain of doing so – if I can be of assistance, of course I will do whatever is required, out of Christian charity. When it happens in my own son's house, however, I feel it as a more personal attack – an ill reflection on him and on the Coleman name.

It seems that Kitty is simply blind. It was I who shone the light into the dark corners and illuminated them for her.

I had come to lunch, served on that horrid black and yellow checked service – another example of the frivolities of the day. Far worse, however, was the state of their maid.

After she had banged every dish onto the table and waddled out again, I sat stunned. Kitty did not meet my eye, but pushed the poached fish and new potatoes around her plate. I disapprove of lack of appetite – it is selfish behaviour when there is so much hardship in the world. I would have said so but I was more concerned to address the problem of Jenny.

I tried at first to be gentle. 'My dear,' I said, 'Jenny is not looking her best. Have you spoken to her about it?'

Kitty gave me a puzzled look. 'Jenny?' she repeated vaguely.

'Your maid,' I said more firmly, 'is not well. Surely you can see that.'

'What is wrong with her?'

'Come now, my dear, open your eyes. It is clear as day what the trouble is.'

'Is it?'

I couldn't help but grow a little impatient with Kitty. In truth, I should like to have given her a good shake, as if she were a young girl like Maude. In some ways Maude is more mature than her mother. I had been disappointed that she did not join us for lunch – at times it is easier to speak to her than to Kitty. But I was told she was at her friend's. At least I was able to be more frank with Kitty than I could have if Maude had been with us.

'She has got herself into trouble. With a man,' I added so that there could be no doubt.

Kitty clattered her cutlery most unbecomingly and stared at me with her dark brown eyes that had made my son into a fool years before. She was very pale.

'She is six months gone at least,' I continued, as Kitty seemed incapable of speaking. 'Probably more. I always knew that girl would come to no good. I never liked her – far too insolent. You could see just by looking at her. And she sings as she works – I can't abide that in a servant. I expect the man will not marry her, and even if he does she can't possibly remain here. You don't want a married woman and mother in that position. You need a girl with no attachments.'

My daughter-in-law was still staring at me with a bewildered look. It was very clear that she could not manage – I would have to take charge.

'I shall speak to her after lunch,' I said. 'Leave it with me.'

Kitty didn't say anything for a moment. Finally she nodded.

'Now, eat your fish,' I said.

She pushed it around her plate a bit more, then said she had a headache. I don't like to see such waste, but in this instance I said nothing, as she had clearly had a shock and did look rather ill. Luckily my own constitution is more robust and I finished my fish, which was very good except that the sauce was rather rich. Thank goodness for Mrs Baker – she shall have to hold the house together for the moment until we find a replacement. I'd had my doubts about her when Kitty first hired her, but she is a good plain cook as well as a solid Christian. It does help to hire a widow – like myself she does not have great expectations of life.

Jenny came in to clear and I couldn't help but shake my head at her brazenness. How she thought she could wander about the house with such a thick waist and think no one would notice is quite astonishing. Mind you, I suppose she knows her mistress. If I had not alerted Kitty she might never have noticed until the girl held the babe crying in her arms! I saw Kitty inspect Jenny as she leaned over to gather our plates, and a look like fear crossed her face. She was most certainly not up to dismissing Jenny. I myself felt no fear, but righteous determination.

Kitty said not a word except, 'No coffee for me, Jenny.'

'Nor hot water for me,' I added. There was no point in delaying the proceedings.

The girl grunted, and as she left I thought what a blessing in disguise this was — a chance to get rid of a bad apple.

I told Kitty to go and rest, then waited a short interval before going down to the kitchen, where Mrs Baker was wiping the table clean of flour. I do not go there often, so I suppose she had reason to look surprised. But there was more to her look than that. Mrs Baker is no fool — she knew why I had come.

'The fish was quite good, Mrs Baker,' I said pleasantly. 'Perhaps a little less butter in the sauce next time.'

'Thank you, ma'am,' she replied quite correctly, but managing to sound put out as well.

'Where is Jenny? I want to have a word with her.'

Mrs Baker stopped brushing the table. 'She's in the scullery, ma'am.'

'So you know, then.'

Mrs Baker shrugged and began brushing the table again. 'Anyone with eyes to see would know.'

As I turned towards the scullery, she surprised me by adding, 'Let her be, ma'am. Just let her be.'

'Are you telling me how this house should be run?' I asked.

She did not answer.

'There is no use in being sentimental about it, Mrs Baker. This is for her own good.'

Mrs Baker shrugged again. I was surprised — she is normally a sensible woman. She is from a very different background than myself, of course, but at times I have thought she and I are not so different.

It did not take long. Jenny cried and ran from the room, of course, but it could have been worse. In a way the girl must have been relieved that it was out at last. She knew very well that someone would finally find her out. The waiting must have been excruciating, and I like to think I put the girl out of her misery.

My one regret is that Maude was there. I had thought she was at the Waterhouses', but as I came out of the scullery she was standing in the doorway of the larder. I had spoken to Jenny in a low voice, and I don't think Maude heard what I said, but she heard Jenny's shout, and I would have preferred it if she had not been there.

'Is Jenny ill?' she asked.

'Yes,' I answered, thinking that was the best way to explain it. 'She will have to leave us.'

Maude looked alarmed. 'Is she dying?'

'Don't be silly.' It was exactly the kind of dramatic question her friend Lavinia would ask — Maude was simply parroting her. I knew that girl was a bad influence.

'But what —'

'We missed you at lunch,' I interrupted. 'I thought you were at your friend's.'

Maude turned red. 'I — I was,' she stammered, 'but Lavinia has a — a cough, and so I came back. I've been helping Mrs Baker make soda bread.'

She has never been a good liar. I could have exposed the lie, but I was weary from the business with Jenny, and so I left it. And if I am honest, I didn't want to know. It gave me a pang to think that my own granddaughter would rather bake bread with the cook than have lunch with me.

# MAUDE COLEMAN

I had never thought Grandmother would come down to the kitchen. It was the one place where I thought I was safe, and could remain until she was gone – then I would not have to have lunch with her. Even Mummy thought I was at Lavinia's. I would have been, only Lavinia was out visiting her cousins.

As it was I almost managed to hide from Grandmother. I was putting the oats and flour and bicarb in the larder for Mrs Baker when I heard Grandmother come into the kitchen and speak to her. I shrank back into the larder but didn't dare close the door in case she saw it move.

She passed by without looking in and went into the scullery, where she began talking to Jenny in a low voice that sent shivers down my spine. It was the voice she uses when she has something awful to say – that she has discovered you have broken a vase, or not gone to church, or done poorly in school. Jenny began to cry, and though I had a chance to close the larder door then, I didn't – I wanted to hear what they were saying. I crept closer to the open door and heard Grandmother say, '. . . wages until the end of the week, but you must pack your things now.'

Then Jenny cried out and ran from the scullery up the stairs. Grandmother came out of the scullery, and there I was standing in the doorway, my pinafore covered in flour.

I was surprised when Grandmother then told me Jenny was ill, but indeed she had grown slow and fat these days, as if she had a blockage in her stomach. Perhaps she should be taking cod liver oil. Then Grandmother said she would have to leave because of it. I thought she must be terribly ill indeed but Grandmother wouldn't say more about it.

Luckily Grandmother decided to go then, or I might have had a tedious afternoon with her all alone, as she said Mummy had gone to bed with a headache. I saw her to the door, and as she left she said I was to tell Mummy later that everything was sorted out satisfactorily. I knew better than to ask what she meant.

After she had gone I went downstairs again and asked Mrs Baker instead. 'Is Jenny going to leave us?'

There was a pause, then Mrs Baker said, 'I expect she will.'

'Is she very ill, then?'

'Ill? Is that what she's calling it?'

There was a knock on the outside kitchen door. 'Perhaps that's Lavinia,' I said hopefully and ran to the door.

'Don't tell her any of this,' Mrs Baker warned.

'Why not?'

Mrs Baker sighed and shook her head. 'Never mind. Tell her what you like. She'll find out soon enough.'

It was Simon. He did not say hello; he never says hello. He stepped inside and looked around. 'Where's our Jenny? She upstairs?'

I glanced at Mrs Baker, who was gathering up the bowl

and sieve we had used for the bread. She frowned but did not answer.

'She's ill,' I said. 'She may have to go away.'

'She's not ill,' Simon said. 'She's banged up.'

'Banged up – is that like knocking?' I asked uneasily. I hoped no one had hurt Jenny.

'Maude!' Mrs Baker barked, and I jumped. She never shouted at me – only at the butcher's boy if the meat was off, or the baker, whom she once accused of using sawdust in his loaves. She turned to Simon. 'Is it you been teaching her this filthy language? Look at her – she doesn't even know what she's saying. Shame on you, boy!'

Simon gave me a funny look. 'Sorry,' he said. I nodded, though I didn't really know what he was apologising for. In many ways he knew so little – had never been to school, could barely read, and that learned from gravestones. Yet he clearly knew about things in the world that I had no notion of.

Simon turned to Mrs Baker. 'Is there any bread?'

'It's in the oven, little beggar boy,' Mrs Baker snapped. 'You'll have to wait.'

Simon just looked at her. He seemed not the least bothered that she had just called him a beggar. She sighed, then set down the bowl and sieve and went to the sideboard, where she found an end of a loaf. 'Go and put some butter on it,' she said, handing it to him. 'You know where it is.'

Simon disappeared into the larder.

'Make him a cup of tea, Maude,' she ordered, picking up her dishes again and heading for the scullery. 'Just one sugar,' she added over her shoulder.

I gave him two sugars.

Simon had spread the bread with great hunks of butter, as if it were cheese. I watched him eat it at the table, his teeth carving rectangular grooves in the butter.

'Simon,' I whispered. 'What does banged up mean?' It felt wicked saying the words, now that I knew they were shocking.

Simon shook his head. 'Not for me to say. Best to ask your ma.'

I knew I never would.

# SIMON FIELD

The sody bread smells good, baking in the oven. I want to wait for it, but I know I was lucky to get anything at all from Mrs Baker. She ain't so generous with the bread as our Jenny is.

I want to see our Jenny. Maude thinks she's in her room upstairs. So when I've finished the bread I pretend to leave, but don't pull the back door closed. I wait and peek through the window till I see Maude and Mrs B. go into the scullery together. Then I sneak back in real quiet and run up the stairs before anyone sees me.

I never been in the rest of the house. It's big, with lots of stairs that I keep stopping on 'cause there's so much to see. On the walls there's paintings and drawings of all sorts of things, buildings and people but mostly birds and flowers. Some of the birds I know from the cemetery, and some of the flowers too. They're proper drawings, with all the bits of the plant as well as the flower. I seen a book of Mr Jackson's at the lodge with pictures like that.

The rugs on the stairs and in the hallways are mostly green, with some yellow and blue and red bits in a pattern.

Each landing has a plant on it, them ones with long thin leaves what wave up and down as I go past. Our Jenny hates 'em 'cause she has to clean all the little leaves and it takes so long. 'No one asked me what plants they should have,' she said once. 'Why don't she get one of them aspidistras with a few big leaves that are easy to wash?'

I go on up until I'm on the top landing. There are two doors up there, both closed. I have to choose, so I open one and go in. It's Maude's room. I stand and look a long time. There's so many toys and books, more than I ever seen in a room. There's a whole shelf of dolls, all different sizes, and another shelf of games – boxes full of things, puzzles and such. There's lots of shelves of books. There's a brown and white hobby horse with a black leather saddle that moves back and forth on rollers. There's a wood dolls' house with fancy furniture in all the rooms, miniature rugs and chairs and tables. There's pictures on the walls of Maude's room, children and dogs and cats, and something that looks like a map of the sky, with all the stars connected up with lines to make pictures like what I saw in the stars that cold night in the grave.

It's toasty warm in the room – there's a fireplace just had a fire burning, and a fender in front of it with clothes hanging on it to air. I want to stay here, but I can't – I has to find our Jenny.

I go out of the room and up to the other door and knock.

'Go away,' she says.

'It's me, our Jenny.'

'Go away.'

I kneel down and look through the keyhole. Our Jenny's lying on her bed, her hands tucked under her cheek. Her eyes are red but she's not crying. Next to her is her corset. I can see the shape of her big belly under her skirt.

I go in anyway. She don't shout at me, so I sit on a chair. There ain't much in the room, just the chair and bed, a chamber pot and a bucket of coal, a green rug on the floor and a row of pegs with her clothes hanging on 'em. On the window ledge are a couple of coloured bottles, blue and green. The room is dark 'cause there's only a little window what faces north over the street.

'Jenny, our Jenny,' I says, 'what're you going to do?'

'I dunno,' she says. 'Go back to me mum, I suppose. I have to leave by the end of the day.'

'You should go to our Ma — that's what she does, delivers babies. Nellie off Leytonstone High Street, next to the Rose and Crown. Everybody knows her. Mind you, you should've gone to her earlier and she'd have got rid of it for you.'

'I couldn't do that!' Our Jenny sounds shocked.

'Why not? You don't want it, do you?'

'It's a sin. It's murder!'

'But you sinned already, ain't you? What difference does it make?'

She don't answer, but shakes her head back and forth and brings her legs up so they're curled round her belly. 'Anyway, it's too late,' she says. 'The baby's coming soon, and that's that.' She starts to cry, big ugly sobs. I look round and see a brown knitted shawl on the chair. I put it over her.

'Oh God, what am I to do?' our Jenny cries. 'Mum'll kill me. I send her most of my pay — how's she to get by without it?'

'You'll have to get another job, and your ma can look after the baby.'

'But no one'll hire me when they find out what's happened. She'll never give me a reference. This is the only job I've had. I need her reference.'

I think for a minute. 'Mrs C. will if you make her,' I say finally. I feel bad saying it, 'cause I like Maude's ma. I still remember how she smiled at me that day she wore the green dress.

Our Jenny looks up at me, curious now. 'How do you mean?'

'You know something about her,' I say. 'About her and Mr Jackson meeting in the cemetery. You could say something about that.'

Our Jenny pushes herself up so that she's sitting. 'That's wicked. Besides, there's no sin in talk. All they did was talk. Didn't they?'

I shrug.

She wipes her hair back from her face where it's stuck to her cheeks. 'What would I say?'

'Tell her you'll tell her husband about her and Mr Jackson meeting if she don't give you a good reference.'

'Ooo, that is wicked.' Our Jenny thinks for a minute. Then she gets a funny look on her face, like a thief who's just spotted an open window in a rich man's house. 'Maybe I could even keep my job. She'll have to keep me on if I'm not to tell her husband.'

I feel sick when she says that. I like our Jenny but she's greedy. 'I dunno,' I say. 'Our Pa always says never ask for too much. Ask for just what you need or you mightn't get any at all.'

'And look where your Pa's got to – a gravedigger all his life,' our Jenny says.

'Don't see as being a gravedigger's any worse'n being a maid.'

'Anyway, get out with you. If I'm to talk to her I'd best try to get my corset back on.'

From the look on her face I know there's nothing I can say will stop her. So I go out and down the stairs. I get to the next landing and there are four closed doors there. I listen for a minute but don't hear no one. I never been in a house like this. Our Ma and me sisters share a back-to-back, two rooms for the five of 'em. Five or six families could live in this house. I look at the doors. They're all oak, with brass handles shining – our Jenny's been at 'em with the polish. I choose one and open it.

I heard about rooms like this but ain't ever seen one. There's tiles everywhere, white tiles on the floor and up the sides of the walls to just over my head. One row of the tiles at the top has flowers on 'em, like tulips, red and green. There's a big white bathtub, and a white sink, with the silver pipes and taps all scrubbed shiny by our Jenny. There's big white towels hanging on a rack, and I touch one. Where I've touched it I leave a black mark and I feel bad 'cause it's so clean in here otherwise.

In a little room off this one is a WC, white too, with a seat made of mahogany, like some of the rich people's coffins I see at the cemetery. I think of the privy and bucket me and our Pa use, and it's so different from this they don't even seem like they're meant for the same thing.

I go out and choose another door, to the room at the front of the house. The walls are yellow, and though it's facing north too like our Jenny's room, there's two big windows, with balconies you can walk out on, and the light that comes in turns gold when it hits the walls. There's two sofas pushed together to make an L, and shawls decorated with butterflies and flowers spread over 'em. There's a piano and little tables with books and magazines on them, and a sideboard with photographs on it, of her and Maude and Maude's Pa and some other people.

Then I hear our Jenny talking out on the landing. There ain't time to get out of the room, and somehow I know she and Mrs C. will come in here. I crouch down quick behind one of the sofas. If I was playing hidey-seek with my sisters that's the first place they would look. But Jenny and Mrs C. ain't looking for me.

# JENNY WHITBY

For all my brave face to Simon, I was dreading talking
to the missus. She ain't been bad to me over the years,
and I do know I've sinned. Nor did I like resorting to
blackmail. But I need my place here – I need my wages. It
felt like I'd been mopping a room and not been paying
attention, and before you know it I was stuck in the corner
with a wet floor all round me. I'd have to jump far to get
free.

When I'd straightened my clothes and put on my cap
and splashed water on my face, I went downstairs. As I got
to the landing she came out of her bedroom, and I knew I
had to do it then. I opened my mouth but before I could
say a word she said, 'Jenny, I would like to speak with you,
please. Let's go into the morning room'.

I followed her in. 'Have a seat,' she said. I sat down on a
sofa. I clean in here every day but I'd never sat down before.
It's a pretty room.'

She went over to one of the windows and looked through
the blinds. She was wearing a dress the colour of bone, with
a cameo pinned at her throat. The colour don't suit her –
she looked tired and pale.

I swallowed 'cause my throat was dry and I couldn't speak yet. I hadn't really thought what I was going to say.

But then it didn't turn out like I thought it would. Not at all. Never in a million years would I have guessed what she was going to say.

She turned from the window. 'I'm sorry to hear of your troubles, Jenny,' she said first. 'And I'm sorry about the way Mrs Coleman must have treated you. She can be very harsh.'

'She's a bitch,' I said before I could stop myself. Saying that made it easier to go on. 'Now I got something to say to you, ma'am.'

'Please listen to me first. We might be able to help each other.'

'Me help you? I don't think so, ma'am. There's nothing –'

'Jenny, I need your help.'

'You need me? After you toss me out in the street like a wore-out broom, after all I done for you and Miss Maude and Mr Coleman, just because I – because I . . .' I couldn't help it. I started to cry.

She let me cry a while. Then she said something real quiet. I couldn't hear it, and she had to say it again. 'I share your predicament.'

I didn't know what that meant, but the fancy word sounded serious enough that I stopped crying.

'It's not so – advanced,' she said. 'And because of that I can still do something about it. But I don't know where to go. I don't know who to ask. I couldn't possibly ask my friends. And so I'm asking you to help me by telling me where to go to – do this. Do you understand what I'm saying to you?'

I looked at her, and I thought of the meals she'd missed,

and the headaches she'd had, and the naps in the afternoon, and the private washing I hadn't had to do for her for a couple months, and the penny dropped. I just hadn't noticed 'cause I'd had my own worries on my mind.

'Yes,' I said, quiet now. 'I understand.'

'I don't want to go anywhere where I'll be known. It must be a place far away, but not too far that I couldn't get there easily. Do you know where I can go?'

Now another penny dropped and I knew what she wanted from me. 'It's a sin,' I said.

She looked out of the window again. 'That will be on my head, not yours.'

I let her wait. She was handing the blackmail to me on a silver plate, just like I bring in the post to her in this room each morning. I wouldn't even have to say nothing about her and Mr Jackson. Just as well, 'cause I hadn't really known what they got up to – till now.

I knew why she was asking me now, too. She thought she was getting rid of me anyway, so I'd never tell nobody. But there was a price to pay for keeping me quiet. That's where the blackmail was.

'It'll cost you,' I said.

'How much do you want?' She said it like she'd been expecting me to name a price. But I surprised her.

'My position here.'

She stared at me. 'What if I gave you some money? For you and the baby, to keep you until you've found another position?'

'No.'

'I'd give you a good reference, of course. We wouldn't have to mention the baby. We could come up with another

169

reason for your leaving – that your mother was ill and you had to look after her.'

'Leave my mum out of this.'

'I'm not suggesting –'

'I want to stay here.'

'But – what will I say to Mrs Coleman? It was she who dismissed you. I can't go back on her decision.' She sounded desperate.

'You're the lady of the house, ma'am. I expect you can do what you like. You done already anyway.'

She didn't say nothing for a bit. The baby moved inside me – I could feel its little foot kicking.

'All right,' she said finally. 'You can come back to your job once you've had the baby. But you must leave today, and you can't bring the baby with you or have anyone bring it here to see you. You can see it Sundays.'

'And Saturday afternoons. I want Saturday afternoons free too.' I was surprised at myself – the success of the blackmail made me bold.

'All right, Saturday afternoons too. But you're not to tell anyone about any of this or I will make sure your baby's taken away from you. Are we clear about that?'

'Yes, ma'am.' It was strange to hear her try to sound hard – she wasn't much good at it.

'All right. Where am I to go, then?'

'Leytonstone,' I said. 'To Nellie off the High Street, next to the Rose and Crown.'

I heard a noise behind my sofa then, and I knew someone was back there. She didn't seem to notice, though – she was looking out of the window again. I glanced behind me and saw Simon crouched there. It didn't surprise me that he was eavesdropping — just like the little rascal. He was staring at me all angry for mentioning his mum. I shrugged — what else could I say?

'Go now,' she said then without looking at me. 'Go and pack your things. I'll order a cab for you.'

'Yes, ma'am.' I got up. Now we were done with the business I wanted to say something to her but I didn't know what exactly. So I just said, 'Goodbye, ma'am,' and she said, 'Goodbye, Jenny.' I went to the door and opened it. Just before I went out I looked back at her. She was still standing by the window, her eyes closed, clasping her hands in a fist against her stomach.

'Oh,' she said in a little sigh all to herself.

Simon was still hiding behind the sofa.

I hope his mum is gentle with her.

*September 1906*

# ALBERT WATERHOUSE

Don't know that I'll tell anyone, not even Trudy, but I escorted Kitty Coleman home the other night. I was coming back from nets on the Heath with Richard Coleman when I remembered that Trudy wanted me to leave a message with the vicar at St Anne's – a trifle about altar flowers or some such thing. I try not to attend to that sort of detail – best left to Trudy. But I told Richard I'd catch him up at the Bull and Last, and ran off like a good errand boy.

Afterwards I was heading towards the pub when I looked up Swain's Lane and saw Kitty Coleman, walking along slowly with her head bowed, kicking at her skirts. I thought her a peculiar sight, given it was twilight and she was alone and didn't seem to be walking anywhere in particular.

'Evening, Mrs Coleman,' I said, raising my cap. 'Nice night for a stroll, isn't it? Last spurt of summer, looks like we're having.' My choice of words made me blush. I don't know what it is about Kitty Coleman – she inspires me to say things I shouldn't.

She didn't seem to notice, though – she just stared at me like I was a ghost. I was taken aback by her appearance. Richard had mentioned she'd been ill and was not looking her finest. But it was more than that. Her looks were plainly gone, I am sorry to say.

'Are you on your way somewhere?'

Kitty Coleman hesitated. 'I have been – I wanted to climb the hill but couldn't.'

'It is steep, that hill up to the cemetery. And if you haven't been well it must seem like a mountain. Would you like me to take you to your husband? I was just going to meet him at the pub.'

'I don't want to see Richard,' Kitty Coleman said quickly.

I didn't know what to make of that, but I couldn't leave her there on her own – she seemed so ill and child-like. 'Shall I see you home, then?'

I held out my arm, feeling a little silly and wondering what Trudy would say if she could see us. I know she doesn't think much of Kitty Coleman. Luckily Trudy was safely tucked away at home with our girls. Maude was there too, staying the night.

After a moment Kitty Coleman took my arm. The quickest way to her house was straight past the Bull and Last, but I didn't go that way. It would have felt strange to parade past the pub and have Richard Coleman look out and see me with his wife on my arm when I was meant to be at the vicar's. I could have explained it, but it still didn't look right. So I took the back way, which she didn't remark upon. I tried to make conversation en route, but she didn't say much, just 'Yes' and 'Thank you' when thanks weren't even called for.

Never mind. I saw her home, feeling a little foolish but a little proud too – her face may not be so pretty now but she still carries herself well and wore a nice grey dress, even if it was a bit rumpled. A couple of passers-by stared at us and I couldn't help but hold myself a little straighter.

'Will you be all right, then, Mrs Coleman?' I asked when we got to her door.

'Of course. Thank you.'

'You look after yourself, now. Tuck yourself up with a Horlicks and get an early night.'

She nodded and slipped inside. It was only when I was heading back to the pub that I realised she hadn't said my name at all. I began to wonder if she'd even recognised me.

At the Bull and Last Richard teased me for spending so long at the vicar's. I just nodded and ordered another pint.

*October 1906*

*October 1990*

# LAVINIA WATERHOUSE

I was truly shocked when I saw Maude's mother.

We almost didn't see her. We had stopped at Maude's house on our way home from school only because I wanted Maude to lend me a book about plants so that I can copy passages from it for a school essay. Maude was reluctant to get it, and I thought it was because she disapproved of my copying, as our essays are meant to be original. (It is so tedious to think up things to write, especially about 'the life cycle of leaves'!) But now I think it was because she did not want me to see her mother. Indeed, when I think back on it, Maude has been coming to my house almost every day for months – even more than before.

She hurried me up to her room for the book and hurried me down again. Just then Mrs Coleman came out of the morning room. She looked at us so vaguely that I was not even sure she really saw us until Maude said, 'Hello, Mummy,' very softly, and she nodded slightly.

I was so surprised by her appearance that I did not even say anything about it to Maude – which made me rather sad, as I thought we shared all our thoughts. But I could not bring myself to ask her why her mother is so thin, and her hair suddenly has grey in it, and her skin looks like ditch-water. Worse than that – for one can always dye or pull out grey hair (as Mama does) and apply a tonic to dull skin – Mrs Coleman does not sparkle as she used to. Admittedly her sparkle felt a little wicked at times – which is why Mama does not care for her – but without it she is very flat indeed.

Clearly something is wrong at the Colemans'. Not only is Maude's mother not herself, but a few months ago their maid Jenny was suddenly taken ill and had to go away. Perhaps they have the same illness. Maude says Jenny is returning soon. I shall have to look to see if she has grey hairs as well. It is just as well she's coming back, for the temporary chars have been dreadful. Maude hasn't liked any of them, and the house looked none too clean, the little I saw of it. The plants on the landings were terribly dusty.

I said nothing of this to Maude, poor dear. She was very subdued as we went on to my house. I tried to be especially nice to her, even suggesting that we attend the official opening of our local public library. They have been building it on Chester Road all summer, and there is to be a ceremony on Thursday afternoon. I am not keen on going – it will be all tedious speeches – but it may cheer Maude as she is so fond of libraries. And it would mean we could leave early and miss the last class at school, which is maths. I can't abide maths – all those dull numbers. In fact I don't like any of my classes, except for domestic arts and composition, though Miss Johnson says my imagination needs reining in – a compliment, I should think!

Mama will have to get permission for us both to leave school early, as Maude's mother is clearly incapable of making such arrangements. And I expect Mama and Ivy May will have to come with us, although it is only a few minutes away. Maude and I are eleven years old, yet we are still not allowed to go anywhere alone except to walk to school together. Mama says you never know what might happen, and reads all sorts of terrible things out from the newspapers – babies left to freeze on the Heath, or people drowning in the ponds, or rough men looking for girls to prey upon.

When we arrived home I asked Mama if we could all go to the library ceremony. She said yes, the dear. She always says yes to me.

Then Maude asked a funny thing. 'Please, Mrs Waterhouse,' she said, 'could you ask my mother to come with us? She hasn't been well these past months, and she could do with getting a bit of air.'

Well, Mama was nonplussed by this request – surely Maude could ask her own mother! – but she said she would. I was a bit put out, as I am not at all sure I wish to be seen with someone who has clearly let herself go. None the less, I must stand by my friend. Besides, Mama may not be able to convince Mrs Coleman to come with us – it is not as if they are close friends. If she does, though, perhaps I will steal over to their house one night and leave a bottle of hair dye on the doorstep.

# GERTRUDE WATERHOUSE

I did not have the heart to say no to Maude. It is horrifying to think a girl cannot even ask her mother to escort her somewhere. I wanted to enquire why she felt she could not, but she looked so meek and sad that I simply said I would do my best and left it at that. I did not think I could do much good, though, even for something as insignificant as arranging an outing. I have never had any influence with Kitty Coleman, and if Maude cannot convince her to come to a little local event, I do not see how I will be able to.

None the less, I called on Kitty the next morning when the girls were at school. The moment I saw her I felt terribly guilty for not having gone there sooner. She did look awful – thin and pinched – and her lovely hair no longer glossy. It is such a surprise to see the lifeblood sapped from someone once so vital. If I were a more spiteful person, it might have made me feel better to see such loveliness brought down. Instead my heart went out to her. I even squeezed her hand, which surprised her, though she did not jerk it away. Her hand was chilly.

'Oh, you're so cold, my dear!' I exclaimed.

'Am I?' she asked absently.

I pulled the yellow silk shawl from the back of the sofa and wrapped it around her. 'I'm so sorry that you have been ill.'

'Did someone say I was?'

'Oh, I . . .' I grew flustered. 'Maude — she said you'd had pneumonia some time ago.' That much at least was true, or so I thought, though from Kitty Coleman's reaction I began to wonder.

'Is that what Maude said?' she asked. I wondered if Kitty would actually answer a question rather than ask one. But then she shrugged. 'I suppose that may as well do,' she muttered, which made no sense, but I did not try to question her.

She rang a bell, but when the girl appeared — it was not their usual maid — Kitty looked at her blankly, as if she had forgotten why she summoned her. The girl stared back just as blankly.

'Perhaps some tea for your mistress,' I suggested.

'Yes,' Kitty murmured. 'That would be good.'

When the girl had left I said, 'Have you seen a doctor recently?'

'Why?'

'Well, for your convalescence. Perhaps there's something you could take — a tonic. Or go to a spa.' I was trying in vain to name remedies for whatever afflicted her. All I could think of were novels I'd read in which the heroine went to spas in Germany, or to the south of France for the climate.

'The doctor said I must build up my strength with plenty of food and fresh air,' Kitty repeated mechanically. She looked as if she ate little more than a mouthful of food a day, and I doubt she went out at all.

'That is just what I was coming to speak to you about. I am proposing to take the girls on a little outing to the new library that is about to open on Chester Road, and I wondered if you and Maude would join us. We could go afterwards for tea up in Waterlow Park.' I felt a little silly, making it sound as if I were suggesting an expedition to Antarctica rather than a trip just around the corner.

'I don't know,' she replied. 'It's a bit far.'

'The library itself is quite close,' I said quickly, 'and we don't have to go all the way up the hill for tea – we could choose some place closer. Or you could come to me.' Kitty had never been to my house. I did not want her to sit in my cramped parlour, but I felt I had to offer.

'I'm not . . .'

I waited for Kitty to finish her sentence, but she did not. Something had happened to her – she was like a little lamb that has lost its way and is wandering aimlessly in a field. I did not relish playing her shepherd, but I also knew that God did not intend for a shepherd to judge His flock. I grasped her hand again. 'What is wrong, my dear? What has distressed you so?'

Kitty gazed at me. Her eyes were so dark it was like looking into a well. 'I have spent my life waiting for something to happen,' she said. 'And I have come to understand that nothing will. Or it already has, and I blinked during that moment and it's gone. I don't know which is worse – to have missed it or to know there is nothing to miss.'

I did not know what to say, for I did not understand her at all. Still, I had to try to answer. 'I think that you are very lucky indeed,' I said, making my voice as stern as I dared. 'You have a fine husband and a good daughter, and a lovely house and garden. You have food on the table and a cook to cook it. To many you have an enviable life.' Though not to me, I added silently.

'Yes, but . . .' Kitty stopped again, scanning my face for something. It appeared she did not find it, for she let her eyes drop.

I let go of her hand. 'I am going to send around a tonic that my mother used to prepare for me when I felt low, with brandy and egg yolk and a little sugar. I'm sure it will be an effective pick-me-up. And do you have any brilliantine? A bit on your brush will do wonders to your hair. And my dear, do come with us to the library ceremony on Thursday.' Kitty opened her mouth to speak, but I bravely talked over her. 'I insist upon it. Maude will be so pleased, as she so wants to go with you. You wouldn't want to disappoint her. She's such a good girl — top of her class.'

'She is?'

Surely Kitty must know how well her daughter was doing in her studies! 'We shall come to collect you at two thirty on Thursday. The fresh air will do you good.' Before she could object I stood up and pulled on my gloves, not even waiting for the tea to arrive (their girl is very slow) before taking my leave.

For the first time since I have known Kitty Coleman, I was in the position to dictate the tone of our relations. Rather than relishing the power, I simply felt miserable.

No one ever said Christian duty would be easy.

# MAUDE COLEMAN

I don't know why Lavinia was so keen on going to the library opening. She seemed to think I would be thrilled to go as well, but she has confused celebration with function. While I am, of course, glad we are to have a local public library, I was more interested in borrowing books than in the ceremony. Lavinia is just the opposite – she has always liked parties more than me, but she cannot sit still in a library for five minutes. She does not even like books much – though she is fond of Dickens, of course, and she and her mother like to read aloud Sir Walter Scott. And she can recite some poems – Tennyson's 'Lady of Shalott' and Keats' 'La Belle Dame sans Merci'.

But to please her I said I would go, and Mrs Waterhouse somehow persuaded Mummy to come out with us – the first time she has been out at all since she was ill. I do wish she had worn something a little gayer – she has so many beautiful dresses and hats, but she chose a brown dress and a black felt hat trimmed with three black rosettes. She looked like a mourner among partygoers. Still, at least she came – I was pleased just to walk with her.

I do not think she understood very well where the new

library is. Daddy and I had often gone on a summer evening to inspect the progress of the building, but Mummy had never come with us. Now as we turned into Chester Road from Swain's Lane she grew very agitated at the sight of the southern wall of the cemetery, which is bounded by Chester Road. She even clutched my arm, and without quite knowing why, I said, 'It's all right, Mummy, we aren't going in.' She relaxed a little, though she held on to me until we had passed by the southern gate and reached the crowd outside the library.

The library is a handsome brick building, with tan stone trimmings, a front porch with four Corinthian columns, and side sections with high arched windows. For the opening the front was decked out with white bunting, and a small platform placed on the front steps. Lots of people were milling about on the pavement and spilling into the street. It was a windy day, making the bunting shake and men's bowlers and women's feathers and flowers fly off.

We had not been there long before the speeches began. A man stepped onto the platform and called out, 'Good afternoon, ladies and gentlemen. It is my great pleasure, as Chairman of the Education and Libraries Committee of the St Pancras Borough Council, to welcome you to this most auspicious occasion, the opening of the first free library in the borough as the first step in adopting the Public Libraries' Acts in St Pancras.

'We are indebted to Alderman T. H. W. Idris, MP, and late mayor, for his successful endeavour in getting Mr Andrew Carnegie, of Pittsburgh of the United States, to give £40,000 for the purpose of the adoption of the Acts –'

Just then I felt an elbow in my ribs. 'Look!' Lavinia hissed, pointing. A funeral procession was coming along Chester Road. The Chairman on the platform stopped speaking when he saw the carriages, and the men in the crowd removed their hats while the women bowed their heads. I bowed mine as well but looked up through my lashes, counting five carriages behind the one carrying the coffin.

Then a great gust of wind made all the women grab at their hats. Lavinia and Ivy May and I were wearing our green school berets, which usually stay snug on our heads, but Lavinia pulled hers off as if the wind had loosened it, and tossed her hair and shrugged. I'm sure she did it just to show off her curls.

The undertaker's men walking alongside the front carriage clamped their hands on their top hats; one blew off anyway and the man had to run after it in his long black coat. The horses' black plumes were swaying and one horse whinnied and bucked as the wind got up its nose, so that the driver had to crack his whip, making some ladies scream, and halting the procession. Mummy trembled and clutched my arm.

The wind had loosened the bunting on the library so much that the next gust caught a length of it and blew it up in the air. The long white cloth sailed over our heads and did a kind of dance over the funeral procession, until suddenly the wind dropped and the bunting fell, landing across the carriage that carried the coffin. The crowd gasped – Lavinia of course screamed – and the nervous horse bucked again.

It was all terribly confusing. But above the shouts, the wind and the whinnying horse, I heard a woman laugh. I looked around and saw her standing on the edge of the crowd, dressed entirely in white, with a great deal of lace trim which fluttered so that she looked like a bird. Her laugh was not loud exactly, but it penetrated through everything, like the rag-and-bone man's voice as he walked along our street calling out 'Any old iron!'

Mr Jackson came out from the cemetery gate and ran up to pull the cloth off the carriage. 'Drive on!' he called. 'Quickly, before the horses bolt!' He ran back to the gate and swung it open, beckoning to the lead carriage. After the last carriage had passed inside the cemetery, he swung the gate shut, then picked up the bunting. As he began folding it he gazed at the crowd in front of the library, saw Mummy, and stopped folding the cloth. Mummy jerked as if someone had tapped her on the shoulder, and dropped my arm.

Then the Chairman stepped down from the platform and crossed the road to retrieve the bunting. Mr Jackson was forced to turn to him, and Mummy suddenly drooped. Another gust of wind blew through the crowd and she looked as if she might topple. In a moment the laughing woman was at her side, casually taking my mother's arm and holding her steady.

'Quite a show here, isn't it?' she said with another laugh. 'And the speeches have barely begun!'

She was a small woman, shorter than Mummy but with her shoulders thrown back in a way that made her look as confident as a taller woman. She had big brown eyes that seemed to sit right on the surface of her face so that you could not avoid their stare. When she smiled a tooth showed at the side of her mouth, reminding me of a horse baring its teeth.

I knew immediately that I would not like her.

'I am Caroline Black,' she said, holding out her hand.

Mummy stared at it. After a moment she took it. 'Kitty Coleman,' she said.

I was horrified to recognise the name, though Mummy clearly didn't. Caroline Black was a suffragette who conducted a long-running battle with various sceptical gentlemen about the subject of votes for women on the letters page of the local paper.

Daddy has been very scathing of the suffragettes. He says the word sounds like the term for a sort of bandaging technique developed in the Crimean War. The suffragettes have been chalking signs for their meetings on the pavements near us, and Daddy has occasionally threatened them – possibly even Caroline Black herself – with buckets of water.

The Chairman had begun speaking again. '. . . the Council has provided an open door through which every inhabitant of St Pancras can enter without fee or without challenge to enjoy the treasures of literature enshrined and stored in this building.'

The crowd began to applaud. Caroline Black did not clap, though, and neither did Mummy. I looked round for Lavinia, but couldn't see her. Mrs Waterhouse and Ivy May were still close by, and I followed Ivy May's gaze across the road. Lavinia was standing by the cemetery gate. She saw me and beckoned, pulling at the gate to show me that it was not locked. I hesitated – I did not want to leave Mummy alone with Caroline Black. On the other hand, the speeches were dull, as I had known they would be, and the cemetery would be much more interesting. I took a step towards Lavinia.

'That is all well and good, Mr Ashby,' Caroline Black

called out suddenly. I froze. 'I do applaud the idea of free access to literature and education. But can we honestly celebrate such an occasion when half the population cannot apply its newly available knowledge to that part of life so important to us all? If women do not have the vote, why bother to read the treasures of literature?'

As she spoke, people around her took a few steps back so that she was alone in a circle of spectators apart from Mummy and me standing awkwardly beside her.

Mr Ashby tried to interject, but Caroline Black continued in a smooth voice that carried a long way and would not be interrupted. 'I'm sure if our MP, Mr Dickinson, were here, he would agree with me that the subject of votes for women goes hand in hand with issues like public libraries and education for all. He is even now hoping to present a bill to Parliament about woman's suffrage. I appeal to you –' she gestured at the circle around her – 'as concerned, educated members of the public: each time you enter this building, consider the fact that you yourselves – or, if you are a man, your wives or sisters or daughters – are being denied the chance to be responsible citizens by casting your vote for those who would represent you. But you can do something about this. Come to the meetings of the local WSPU, every Tuesday afternoon at four o'clock, at Birch Cottage, West Hill in Highgate. Votes for women!' She bowed slightly, as if acknowledging applause only she could hear, and took a step back, leaving Mummy and me alone in the circle.

The faces surrounding us stared curiously, probably wondering if we were suffragettes too. Mrs Waterhouse at least gave me a look of horrified sympathy. Next to her Ivy May was staring at my mother. Mummy herself was gazing at Caroline Black, and for the first time in months she was smiling.

I looked across to the cemetery gate, but Lavinia was no longer there. Then I caught a glimpse of her inside the cemetery just before she disappeared between two graves.

# KITTY COLEMAN

Her laughter rang out like a clarion call, sending a jolt up my spine that made me open my eyes wide. I had thought it was another foggy, muffled day, but when I looked around for the source of the laughter, I discovered it was one of those crisp, windy autumn days I love, when as a girl I wanted to eat apples and kick at dead leaves.

Then I saw John Jackson across by the gate, and I had to stand very still so that he wouldn't see me. He did none the less. I had tried to walk up the hill a number of times to see him, and to explain. But I had never managed it. I suspected he understood — he understands most things.

I heard the laugh again, right at my side. Caroline took my arm, and I knew nothing would ever be the same.

# SIMON FIELD

I'm down the grave standing on the coffin when she comes along. The procession's just left, and I'm shifting dirt so it fills the cracks round the coffin. Then I've to knock out the lowest shoring wood with a hammer and our Pa and Joe'll pull 'em out with a rope. It's twelve feet deep, this one.

Our Pa and Joe are singing:

> 'She's my lady love
> She's my dove, my baby love
> She's no gal for sitting down to dream
> She's the only queen Laguna knows.'

They stop but I keeps on:

> 'I know she likes me
> I know she likes me
> Because she says so
> She is the Lily of Laguna
> She is my Lily, and my Rose.'

Then I look up and see Livy standing at the edge of the grave, laughing down at me.

'Damn, Livy,' I say. 'Wha're you doing there?'

She shakes her hair and shrugs. 'Looking at you, naughty boy,' she says. 'You mustn't say "damn".'

'Sorry.'

'Now, I'm going to get down there with you.'

'You can't do that.'

'Yes, I can.' She turns to our Pa. 'Will you help me down?'

'Oh, no, missie, you don't want to go down there. 'Tain't no place for you. 'Sides, you'll get your nice dress and shoes all dirty.'

'Doesn't matter – I can have them cleaned afterwards. How do you climb down – with a ladder?'

'No, no, no ladder,' our Pa says. 'With a deep un like this we got all this wood stuck in, see, every foot or two, to keep the sides from caving in. We climbs up and down it. But don't you go doing that,' he adds, but too late, 'cause Livy's climbing down already. All I can see of her is her two legs sticking out from a dress and petticoats.

'Don't come down, Livy,' I say, but I don't mean it. She's climbing down the wood frame like she's done it all her life. Then she's down on the coffin with me. 'There,' she says. 'Are you pleased to see me?'

'Course.'

Livy looks round and shivers. 'It's cold down here. And so muddy!'

'What'd you expect? It's a grave, after all.'

Livy scrapes her toe in the clay on the coffin. 'Who's in there?'

I shrug. 'Dunno. Who's in the coffin, our Pa?' I call up.

'No, let me guess,' Livy says. 'It's a little girl who caught pneumonia. Or a man who drowned in one of the Heath ponds trying to save his dog. Or –'

'It's an old man,' our Pa calls down. 'Nat'ral causes.' Our Pa likes to find out something about who we bury, usually from listening to the mourners at the graveside.

Livy looks disappointed. 'I think I shall lie down,' she says.

'You don't want to do that,' I say. 'It's muddy, like you said.'

She don't listen to me. She sits down on the coffin lid and then she stretches out, her hair getting mud in it and all. 'There,' she says, crossing her hands over her chest like she's dead. She looks up at the sky.

I can't believe she don't mind the mud. Maybe she's gone doolally. 'Don't do that, Livy,' I say. 'Get up.'

She still lies there, her eyes closed, and I stare at her face. It's strange seeing something so pretty lying there in the mud. She's got a mouth makes me think of some chocolate-covered cherries Maude gave me once. I wonder if her lips taste like that.

'Where's Maude?' I say to stop thinking of it.

Livy makes a face but keeps her eyes shut. 'Over at the library with her mother.'

'Mrs C.'s out and about?'

I shouldn't have said nothing, nor sounded surprised. Livy opens her eyes, like a dead un suddenly come to life. 'What do you know about Maude's mother?'

'Nothing,' I say quickly. 'Just that she was ill. That's all.'

I've said it too quickly. Livy notices. It's funny – she's not like Ivy May, who sees everything. But when she wants to she notices things.

'Mrs Coleman was ill, but that was over two months ago,' she says. 'She does look dreadful but there's something else wrong. I just know it.' Livy sits up. 'And you know it.'

I shift from one foot to the other. 'I don't know nothing.'

'You do.' Livy smiles. 'You're hopeless at lying, Simon. Now, what do you know about Maude's mother?'

'Nothing I'm going to tell you.'

Livy looks pleased and I wish I hadn't said even that. 'I knew there was something,' she says. 'And I know that you're going to tell me.'

'Why should I tell you anything?'

'Because I'm going to let you kiss me if you do.'

I stare at her mouth. She's just licked her lips and they're all glistening like rain on leaves. She's trapped me. I move towards her, but she pulls her face back.

'Tell me first.'

I shake my head. I hate to say it but I don't trust Livy. I have to have my kiss before I'll say a word. 'I'll only tell you after.'

'No, kiss after.'

I shake my head again, and Livy sees I'm serious. She lies back down on the mud. 'All right, then. But I must pretend I'm Sleeping Beauty and you're the prince who wakes me.' She closes her eyes and crosses her hands over her chest again like she's dead. I look up. Our Pa ain't hanging over the grave – he must've sat down to wait with the bottle. I don't know how long I'll be lucky, so I lean over quick and press my mouth against Livy's. She stays still. Her lips are soft. I touch them with my tongue – they don't taste like chocolate cherries, but like salt. I move back onto my heels and Livy opens her eyes. We look at each other but don't say nothing. She smiles a little.

'Simon, get yourself going, lad. We've another to dig after this,' our Pa calls down. He's standing up top leaning over like he's going to fall in. I don't know if he saw us kissing – he don't say. 'You need help up, missie?' he says.

I don't want him coming down here when Livy's with me. Three people is too much in a grave. 'Leave her 'lone,' I call up. 'I'll bring her out.'

'I'll come up myself as soon as Simon answers my question,' Livy says.

Our Pa looks like he's going to climb down, so I has to say it quick. 'Mrs C. visited our Ma,' I whisper.

'What, on a charity visit?'

'Who says we need charity?'

Livy don't answer.

'Anyhow, it were business, not charity.'

'Your mother is a midwife, isn't she?'

'Yes, but –'

'Do you mean she's had another child?' Livy's eyes get big. 'Maude has a secret brother or sister somewhere? How exciting! I do hope it's a brother.'

'It weren't that,' I say quickly. 'She don't have a brother nor suchlike. It were the other. Getting rid of the brother or sister before it's born. Else it would've been a bastard, see.'

'Oh!' Livy sits up straight and stares at me, her eyes still big. I wish I'd never said a thing. Some people's meant to be innocent of life, and Livy's one of 'em. 'Oh!' she says again, and starts to cry. She lays back down on the mud.

'It's all right, Livy. Our Ma was gentle. But it took her a time to recover.'

'What will I tell Maude?' she sobs.

'Don't tell her nothing,' I say quickly, not wanting it to get worse. 'She don't need to know.'

'But she can't possibly live with her mother in those circumstances.'

'Why not?'

'She can come and live with us. I'll ask Mama. I'm sure she'll say yes, especially when she's heard why.' Livy's stopped crying now.

'Don't tell her nothing, Livy,' I say.

Then I hear a scream overhead and look up. Livy's mother is looking down at us with Maude peeking over her shoulder. Ivy May's standing by herself on the other side of the grave.

'Lavinia, what on earth are you doing lying down there?' her mother cries. 'Get out at once!'

'Hello, Mama,' Livy says calmly, like she ain't just been crying. She sits up. 'Were you looking for me?'

Livy's mum sinks to her feet and starts to cry, not quiet like Livy did, but noisy with lots of gasping.

'It's all right, Mrs Waterhouse,' Maude says, patting her shoulder. 'Lavinia's fine. She's coming right up, aren't you, Lavinia?' She glares at us.

Livy smiles a funny smile, and I know she's thinking about Maude's ma.

'Don't you dare tell her, Livy,' I whisper.

Livy don't say nothing, nor look at me. She just climbs up the wood fast and is gone before I can say more.

Ivy May drops a clod of clay into the grave. It falls at my feet.

It's quiet when they're all gone. I start scraping mud into the cracks round the coffin.

Our Pa comes and sits down at the side of the grave, dangling his legs over the edge. I can smell the bottle.

'You going to help me or what, our Pa?' I say. 'You can bring the Lamb's box over now.'

Our Pa shakes his head. 'It's no use kissing girls like her,' he says.

So he did see. 'Why not?' I say.

Our Pa shakes his head again. 'Them girls is not for you, boy. You know that. They like you 'cause you're different from them, is all. They'll even let you kiss 'em, once. But you won't get nowhere with 'em.'

'I'm not trying to get nowhere with 'em.'

Our Pa starts to chuckle. 'Sure you're not, boy. Sure you're not.'

'Hush, our Pa. You just hush.' I go back to my mud – it's easier than talking to him.

# LAVINIA WATERHOUSE

At last I have reached a decision.

I have felt sick ever since Simon told me. Mama thinks I caught a chill down in the grave, but it is not that. I am suffering from Moral Repulsion. Even Simon's kiss — which I shall never tell a soul about — could not make up for the horror of the news about Kitty Coleman.

When they came to get me at the cemetery, I could hardly look at Maude. I knew that she was annoyed with me, but I genuinely felt ill and could not speak. Then we returned to the library and I felt even worse when I saw Maude's mother. Luckily she paid no attention to me — she was in the clutches of a frightening woman who Maude told me is a local suffragette. (I don't understand what all the fuss is about with voting. Politics are so dull — what woman would want to vote anyway?) They walked home arm in arm, talking intimately as if they had known each other for years, and ignored me, which is just as well. It is truly astonishing how brazen Maude's mother is, given what she has done.

I have not been comfortable with Maude since that day,

and, indeed, for a time felt too ill to see her or go to school. I know she thought I was simply pretending, but I felt so burdened. Then, thank goodness, it was half term, and Maude went off to see her aunt in Lincolnshire, and so I could avoid her for a time. Now she is back, though, and the burden of my knowledge is greater than ever. I hate to keep such a secret from her, and indeed, from everyone, and that has made me sick.

I have not told Mama, for I cannot bring myself to shock her. I am feeling quite fond of dear Mama and Papa, and even of Ivy May. They are simple people, unlike myself, who am rather more complicated, but at least I know that they are honest. This is not a House of Secrets.

I must do something. I cannot sit by and watch the contamination at the heart of the Coleman house spread to dear Maude. So, after three weeks of soul-searching, I sat down this afternoon in my room and wrote, in a disguised hand, the following letter:

> Dear Mr Coleman,
> It is my Christian duty to inform you of Unbecoming Conduct that has taken place in your household concerning your wife. Sir, you are encouraged to ask your wife about the true nature of her illness earlier this year. I think you will be profoundly shocked.
>
> I am writing this as behoves someone concerned with the moral welfare of your daughter, Miss Maude Coleman. I have only her best interests at heart.
>
> With respectful concern,

I wish to remain,
Yours most sincerely,
Anonymous

I shall creep round this evening and slide it under their door. Then I am sure I will begin to feel better.

*November 1906*

*November 1990*

# JENNY WHITBY

First thing was, the house were filthy. I had to clean it top to bottom, then clean it again. The only good thing about it was I didn't have time to think about Jack. That and Mrs Baker was actually pleased to see me again. I guess she'd had her fill of the replacements. Them chars was a useless lot.

Then there were my bubbies. Every few hours they'd swell and milk would pour out for Jack, right down my front. I had to wear cotton pads and change 'em all the time, and even then I'd get caught out. Luckily the missus never saw – not that she'd notice anyway. But it happened once when I were cleaning out the coal fire in Miss Maude's room. She come in and I had to quick hug a pile of linens to me, coal dust all over me and all, and make an excuse to get away. She did give me a funny look but didn't say nothing. She's so glad I'm back she's not about to complain.

I dunno how much she knows – Mrs Baker thinks not a lot, that she's still an innocent lamb. But I don't know – sometimes I catch her staring at me or her mother and I think: She's no fool.

Her mother – now there's a strange thing. I come back

209

on my tippy-toes, dreading to see her after how we parted. I thought she'd be awkward with me, but when I arrived she squeezed my hand and said, 'So lovely to see you again, Jenny. Come in, come in!' She brought me into the morning room, where a fluttery little woman, a Miss Black, jumped up and shook my hand too.

'Jenny is our treasure,' the missus said to Miss Black. Well, I blushed at that, thinking she was teasing me. But she seemed genuine enough, as if she'd forgot all about the blackmail.

'I'll just settle my things in my room and get started,' I said.

'Miss Black and I are plotting great things, aren't we, Caroline?' the missus said like she didn't hear me. 'I'm sure you could be of great help to us.'

'Oh, I don't know, ma'am. Perhaps I'll just fetch you some tea.'

'Tell me, Jenny,' Miss Black said, 'what do you think about woman's suffrage?'

'Well, we all suffer, don't we?' I said carefully, not sure what there was to say.

Miss Black and the missus laughed, though I'd not made a joke.

'No, I mean votes for women,' Miss Black explained.

'But women don't vote,' I said.

'Women *aren't allowed* to vote, but they should have every right to, the same as men. That is what we are fighting for, you see. Don't you feel you have as much right as your father, your brother, your husband to elect who is to govern this country?'

'Haven't got none of them.' She hadn't mentioned sons.

'Jenny, we are fighting for your equality,' the missus said.

'That's very kind of you, ma'am. Now, will you be wanting coffee or tea?'

'Oh, coffee, I think, don't you, Caroline?'

Them two are together all the time now, plotting against the government or some such thing. I should be pleased for the missus, that she seems happier than before. But I ain't. There's something about her don't seem right, like a top that's been wound too tight – it's spinning like it should, but it might just break.

Not that it matters so much to me now – I got others to think of. The first Saturday I went back to Mum's I cried when I saw Jack. Only five days away and he looked like someone else's baby. I'd still a little milk left in me then, but he wouldn't take it – he wanted the girl across the way who's nursing him after losing her own. I cried again to see him at her bubbies.

How I'm to pay her all these months I don't know. Wish I'd thought of that when I were securing my job here with the missus. Four months ago she'd have given me anything, but now if I asked for better wages she'd probably just lecture me about women suffering. One thing I've learned – you've to be scared of blackmail for it to work. I don't think she cares about nothing now except votes for women.

Here's another funny thing – the missus is busy acting like nothing happened to her this summer, but someone ain't forgot. I were putting the shoes out in the hallway, all polished and ready for the next day, when a letter gets slid under the front door, addressed to Mr Coleman. I picked it up and looked at it. It were in a funny hand, like a schoolgirl writing it on a wobbly chair. I opened the front door and looked out. It were a foggy night and I could just make out Miss Lavinia running up the street before she disappeared.

I didn't put the letter on a tray for the master, but kept it with me. Next morning I sat down for a cuppa in the kitchen and showed it to Mrs Baker. Funny how she and I are friendlier since Jack. She don't know about the blackmail, but she must suspect as much. She never asked how I got my job back.

'What would she be writing to the master for except to make trouble?' I said.

Mrs Baker studied the letter, then took it over to the kettle and in a minute had steamed it open. That's what I like about her — she can be horrible mean sometimes, but she's definite.

I read over her shoulder. When we'd finished we looked at each other. 'How does she know about all that?' I wondered aloud, before I realised Mrs Baker mightn't have known about the missus' predicament.

But she did. Mrs Baker's no fool. She must've worked it out for herself.

'That silly girl,' she said now. 'Trying to stir things up.' She opened the door of the range and threw the letter into the flames.

As I said, she's definite.

# EDITH COLEMAN

When she opened the door I thought for a moment that I was dreaming. But I knew very well that I was wide awake – I am not the dreaming type. Of course there was a smirk on her face to tell me she knew I was surprised.

'What on earth are you doing here?' I asked. 'Where is the char I hired?' I had taken on the running of the house while Kitty was ill and had been hiring chars until we could find a proper maid.

'I work here again, ma'am,' the impertinent girl replied.

'According to whom?'

'Best ask my mistress, ma'am. May I take your coat, ma'am?'

'Don't you touch my coat. Go and wait in the kitchen. I'll see myself up.'

The girl shrugged and I thought I heard her say, 'Suit yourself.'

I wanted to say something but didn't bother – it was not she I must speak to. Clearly Jenny would not be here if Kitty had not let her come back – behind my back and against my orders.

I walked into the morning room unannounced. Kitty was

213

sitting with Miss Black, whom I had met briefly on another occasion. I had not thought much of her at the time. She had gone on and on about woman's suffrage, a subject I find intolerable.

They both stood now and Kitty came and kissed me. 'Let me take your coat, Mother Coleman,' she said. 'Why didn't Jenny take it at the door?'

'That is what I should like to discuss with you,' I replied, keeping my coat on for the moment – I was no longer sure that I would be staying. It was unfortunate that Kitty was not alone, as I was reluctant to talk about Jenny in front of others.

'Mother Coleman, you have met Caroline Black before,' Kitty said. 'Caroline, you do remember my mother-in-law, Mrs Coleman.'

'Of course,' Miss Black said. 'It's a pleasure to see you again, Mrs Coleman.'

'Will you sit with us?' Kitty asked, gesturing towards the sofas. 'Jenny's just brought up the tea and Mrs Baker has made some lardy cakes.'

I sat down, feeling very awkward in my coat. Neither woman seemed to notice.

'Caroline and I have been discussing the Women's Social and Political Union,' Kitty said. 'Did you know that they have opened an office in London just off the Aldwych? It's very handy for the newspaper offices, and they can lobby Parliament about woman's suffrage much more effectively from a base here rather than from Manchester.'

'I don't approve of women voting,' I interrupted. 'They don't need to – their husbands are perfectly capable of doing so on their behalf.'

'There are plenty of unmarried women – myself included – deserving of representation,' Miss Black said. 'Besides, a woman doesn't always have the same views as her husband.'

'In any sound marriage the woman is in perfect agreement with her husband. Otherwise they shouldn't have married in the first place.'

'Really? Would you always vote the same way as your husband, Kitty?' Miss Black asked.

'I would most likely vote Conservative,' Kitty said.

'You see?' I said to Miss Black. 'Colemans always vote Conservative.'

'But that is only because a Conservative candidate now seems more likely to agree actively to support woman's suffrage,' Kitty added. 'If a Liberal or even a Labour candidate were openly supportive, I would vote for them.'

I was horrified by such an announcement. 'Don't be silly. Of course you wouldn't.'

'I'm not concerned with the political parties. I'm concerned with a moral issue.'

'You should be concerned with moral issues much closer to home,' I said.

'Whatever do you mean?' I noticed Kitty spoke without looking at me.

'Why is Jenny here? I dismissed her in July.'

Kitty shrugged and smiled at Miss Black as if to apologise for me. 'And I hired her again in October.'

'Kitty, I dismissed your maid four months ago because her conduct was immoral. Such behaviour is irreversible, and she is not fit to work in this house.'

At last my daughter-in-law met my eye. She looked almost bored. 'I asked Jenny to come back because she is a very good maid, she is available, and we need a good maid. The chars you hired were unacceptable.'

Something in her face told me that she was lying, but I did not know what the lie could be.

'Have you forgot what she has gone and done?' I asked.

Kitty sighed. 'No, I have not forgot. I just do not happen to think it is very important. My mind is on other matters, and I simply wanted to hire someone I knew would work well in the house.'

I drew myself up. 'That is ridiculous,' I said. 'You can't have a girl here who has –' I stopped and glanced at Miss Black, who was gazing at me calmly. I did not wish to mince my words but it would be unseemly to be so frank in front of a stranger. I did not complete my sentence, knowing that Kitty could. Instead I said, 'What kind of example does that set for Maude or my son?'

'They don't know of it. They think Jenny was ill.'

'The moral foundation of this house will be undermined by her presence, whether they know of the circumstances or not.'

Kitty smiled, which seemed to me to be a most inappropriate response. 'Mother Coleman,' she said, 'you know that I am so very grateful to you for looking after this house while I was ill. You have been generous with your time and efforts. Now, however, it is time that I took charge of my own house once more. I have decided that Jenny may work for us again, and there is really nothing more to be said about it.'

'What does my son say to this?'

'Richard is blissfully ignorant of household matters. That, I believe, is what you taught me about running a house: never worry your husband.'

I ignored her remark, but I did not forget it. 'I shall have to have a word with him.'

'Do you think he would welcome that?'

'I think any man would want to know if his house is morally threatened.'

'Will you stay for tea?' Kitty said it pleasantly enough, but her words implied that she thought I might wish to go.

I did wish to go. 'I will not stay to tea,' I said, standing up. 'I will not set foot in this house while she is here. Goodbye, Kitty.' I turned and walked out. Kitty did not follow me, and it was just as well that the impertinent maid was not in the hallway to see me out, or I don't know what I might have said to her.

One of the unfortunate consequences of being of what I would call a definite disposition is that occasionally I am caught in a dilemma. I had no qualms about cutting off contact with Kitty if necessary, but I could not say the same for my son and granddaughter. After all, it is not their fault that Kitty is morally lax. However, I was reluctant to involve Richard in what, as Kitty herself reminded me, are women's affairs.

None the less, I did feel he should know something of his wife's impropriety – if not about her decision to take Jenny back, then at least about her friendship with a dubious woman. I invited him over one evening on his own, under the guise of discussing something about his late father's property. The moment I saw him, however, I knew I would not say a word to him either about Jenny or about Caroline Black. He was glowing, even after a day at work, and I was reminded of how he looked when he and Kitty had returned from their honeymoon.

So that is how it is, I thought frankly. She has taken him into her bed again so that she can do what she likes outside of it.

She is no fool, my daughter-in-law. She has come a long way since the day Richard first introduced her to me, a slight, gawky girl from the provinces wearing dresses two years out of fashion. I do not like to play games, and as I looked at my son now, I knew that she had outplayed me.

# RICHARD COLEMAN

This year we will be staying at home for New Year's.

*February 1907*

# GERTRUDE WATERHOUSE

Oh dear – I have just returned from one of Kitty Coleman's
At Homes with such a headache.

In January something happened that I had always dreaded
might one day. Kitty Coleman changed her At Homes to
Wednesday afternoons so that she could attend some sort
of meeting in Highgate on Tuesdays. (At least that means
she will not be coming to my At Homes!) Now I have felt
obliged to go – not every week, I should hope, but at least
once or twice a month. I managed to get out of the first
few, saying I had a chill, or that the girls were unwell, but
I couldn't use that excuse every time.

So today I went along, taking Lavinia and Ivy May with
me for support. When we arrived the room was already full
of women. Kitty Coleman welcomed us and then flitted
across the room without making introductions. I must say
it was the loudest At Home I have ever attended. Everyone
was talking at once, and I am not sure anyone was actually
listening. But I listened, and as I did my eyes grew big and
my mouth small. I didn't dare say a word. The room was
full of suffragettes.

Two were discussing a meeting they were to attend in

Whitechapel. Another was passing around a design for a poster of a woman waving a sign from a train window that read 'Votes for Women'. When I saw it I turned to my daughters. 'Lavinia,' I said, 'go and help Maude.' Maude was serving tea across the room, and looked as miserable as I felt. 'And don't listen to what anyone around you is saying,' I added.

Lavinia was staring hard at Kitty Coleman. 'Did you hear me, Lavinia?' I asked. She shook her head and shrugged, as if to shake away my words, then made a face and crossed the room to Maude.

'Ivy May,' I said, 'would you like to go downstairs and ask the cook if she needs help, please.'

Ivy May nodded and disappeared. She is a good girl.

A woman next to me was saying she had just been speaking at a rally in Manchester and had rotten tomatoes thrown at her.

'At least it wasn't rotten eggs!' another woman cried, and everyone laughed.

Well, almost everyone laughed. A few women like myself were very quiet, and looked just as shocked as I felt. They must have been Kitty's old friends who came to the At Home expecting pleasant conversation and Mrs Baker's excellent scones.

One of them, less timid than me, finally spoke. 'What is it that you speak about at these rallies in Manchester?'

The tomato woman gave her an incredulous look. 'Why, for women to have the vote, of course!'

The poor woman turned bright red, as if she herself had been hit by a tomato, and I was mortified for her.

To her credit, Caroline Black came to her rescue. 'The

Women's Social and Political Union is campaigning to have a bill brought before Parliament that would allow women the right to vote in government elections, just as men do,' she explained. 'We are rallying the support of women and men all over the country by speaking publicly, writing to newspapers, lobbying MPs, and signing petitions. Have you seen the WSPU's pamphlet? Do take one and read it – it is so informative. You can place a donation for it on the table by the door when you go. And don't forget to pass on the pamphlet when you are done – it is really surprising how much life there is in a little pamphlet when you hand it on to others.'

She was in her element, speaking so smoothly and gently and yet also forcefully that several women indeed took away pamphlets and left coins by the door – myself included, I am ashamed to admit. When the pile of pamphlets reached me, Caroline Black was watching me with such a sweet smile on her face that I had to take one. I could not bring myself to hide it down the back of the sofa as I might have liked. I did that later, at home.

Kitty Coleman did not take the floor in quite the same way as Caroline Black, but she was still in an excited state, her eyes glittering, her cheeks flushed as if she were at a ball and had not stopped dancing once. She did not look entirely healthy.

I know I should not say this, but I wish she and Caroline Black had never met. Kitty's transformation has been dramatic, and undoubtedly it has pulled her out of the bad way she was in, but she has not gone back to her old self – she has changed into something altogether more radical. Not that I was greatly enamoured of her old self, but I prefer

that to her present state. Even when she is not at her At
Homes with suffragettes everywhere, she still talks incess-
antly about politics and women this and women that till I
want to cover my ears. She has bought herself a bicycle and
goes around even in the wind and rain, getting grease marks
all down her skirts – if they are not already covered in chalk
from all the signs she has been drawing on pavements about
meetings and rallies and such. Whenever I find her crouched
somewhere with a bit of chalk, I cross the road and pretend
not to see her.

She is never at home now in the afternoons, but always
at a meeting, and neglects poor Maude shamelessly. Sometimes I think of Maude as my third daughter, she is at our
house so often. Not that I am complaining – Maude is
very thoughtful, helping me with tea or Ivy May with her
schoolwork. She sets a good example for Lavinia, who I am
sorry to say never seems to take it up. It is very peculiar
that one daughter can have a mother who pays her no
attention and yet turns out well, while the other gets all
the attention in the world and yet is so difficult and selfish.

It was a relief to leave Kitty's At Home. Lavinia seemed
eager to come away as well. Back at home she was very
kind to me, sending me off to bed to nurse my head while
she insisted on making supper. I don't even mind that she
burned the soup.

# JENNY WHITBY

Lord, I hope these At Homes don't last. Since the missus switched 'em to Wednesdays I'm run off my feet. At least I've got Maude to help — though I don't know that she'll stick it. The whole afternoon she looked like she wanted to bolt, even when Lavinia came to keep her company.

That one makes me laugh. When she's here she watches the missus with an outraged look on her face. And when the master's home, she looks at him all puzzled and sorrowful. She hasn't said nothing, though, nor tried to send another letter — I've kept an eye out. I've no intention of letting her wreck this house — I need my wages. As it is I'm not managing to pay for Jack. Or I am, but I've had to do something I never thought I'd stoop to — taking spoons to sell from an old silver set in the sideboard what the missus' mum left her. They don't use it, and no one but me ever polishes it. It ain't right, I know, but I don't have no choice.

I finally listened to them suffragettes today as I passed round the scones. What I heard made me want to spit. They talk about helping women but it turns out they're choosy about who exactly gets the help. They ain't fighting for my vote — only for women who own property or went to university. But that Caroline Black had the nerve to ask me to donate some of my wages 'for the cause'. I told her I wouldn't give a penny until the cause had anything to do with me!

I were so mad I had to tell Mrs Baker about it when we were washing up afterwards.

'What did she say to that?' Mrs Baker asked.

'Oh, that men would never agree to give the vote to everyone all at once, that they had to start with some women and once they'd secured that they would fight for everyone. But ain't it always the way that they put themselves first? Why can't they fight for us first, I say. Let working women decide what's what.'

Mrs Baker chuckled. 'You wouldn't know who to vote for if they bit you on your arse, and you know it.'

'I would!' I cried. 'I ain't that stupid. Labour, of course. Labour for a labouring woman. But these ladies upstairs won't vote Labour, or even Liberal. They're all Tories like their husbands, and them Tories'll never give the vote to women, no matter what they say.'

Mrs Baker didn't say nothing. Maybe she was surprised I was talking politics. To be honest, I were surprised at myself. I've been round too many suffragettes – they're starting to make me talk a load of rubbish.

*July 1907*

# MAUDE COLEMAN

Daddy and I were on the Heath when I felt it. It was our Friday night together, and we had set up the telescope on Parliament Hill. We had looked at a few stars and were waiting for Mars to appear. I didn't mind the wait. Sometimes we talked, but mostly we simply sat and observed.

As I was sipping a cup of tea from our flask I began to feel a dull ache in my stomach, as if I had eaten too much. Yet I had hardly touched Mrs Baker's welsh rarebit at supper – I am never hungry in hot weather. I shifted on my folding stool and tried to concentrate on what Daddy was saying.

'At the Society meeting recently someone said the opposition of Mars is likely to be very good this month,' he said. 'I don't know if this telescope is powerful enough. We should have borrowed the Society's, though someone else may have it tonight. All this will be a damn sight easier when the observatory is built.'

'*If* it is built,' I reminded him. The Hampstead Scientific Society had been trying to find a site on the Heath where it could build an observatory, but there had been objections to each spot, with a debate raging about it on the letters page of the local paper.

The place between my legs itched: it was damp there, as if I had spilled tea in my lap. Suddenly I understood what was happening. 'Oh,' I said before I could stop myself.

Daddy raised his eyebrows.

'It's nothing. It's –' I stopped, wincing with pain.

'Are you all right, Maude?'

The pain was suddenly so strong I could barely breathe. It ceased for a moment and then began again, like a hand clamped over my stomach, squeezing then letting go.

'Daddy,' I gasped, 'I'm not feeling well, I'm afraid. I'm so sorry, but I have to go back.'

Daddy frowned. 'What is it? What's wrong?'

I was so embarrassed I hardly knew what to say. 'It's – something I need to see Mummy about.' Immediately I wished I had simply said I had a stomach ache. I am not much good at lying.

'Why –' Daddy stopped. I think he understood. At least he did not ask more questions. 'I'll see you back,' he said, reaching for the wing nut that held the telescope to its stand.

'I can go on my own. It's not far, and you don't want to have to set up everything all over again.'

'Of course I'll see you back. I won't have my daughter wandering about alone on the Heath at night.'

I wanted to tell him that since Mummy became so busy with the suffragettes, I'd begun going all over on my own – to the cemetery, up to the Village, even across the Heath to Hampstead. Sometimes Lavinia came with me, but often she was too nervous to go far. But now was not the time to say such things to Daddy. Besides, he did not know how deeply involved Mummy had become – she talked about woman's suffrage with everyone but him, and for the most part confined her WSPU activities to the daytime, and nights when she knew Daddy was busy. For all he knew, she sat at home every day reading and gardening, as she used to.

We packed up in silence. I was glad it was too dark for Daddy to see my face, for I had gone bright red. I trailed down the hill after him, forced to slow down when the pain got too strong. Daddy didn't seem to notice, but continued down the path as if nothing were wrong. When I could I hurried to catch up with him.

We reached the edge of the Heath, where the Bull and Last spilled men with their pints into the street. 'I can walk home from here, Daddy,' I said. 'It's not far and there are plenty of people in the street. I'll be fine.'

'Nonsense.' Daddy kept walking.

When we got home he unlocked the door. A lamp was burning on the hall table. Daddy cleared his throat. 'Your mother is out visiting a friend who's taken ill, but Jenny can see to you.'

'Yes.' I kept my back to the wall in case there was a stain on the back of my dress. I would have died of shame if Daddy had seen.

'Well, then.' Daddy turned to go, pausing at the door. 'Will you be all right now?'

'Yes.'

When the door closed behind him I groaned. My thighs were sticky and chafed and I wanted to lie down. First, though, I needed help. I lit a candle and went upstairs, hesitating outside Mummy's morning room. Perhaps she was there after all, sitting on the sofa reading a book. She would look up and say, 'Hello there, what heavenly sights have you seen?' in the way she used to.

I opened the door. Of course Mummy wasn't there. Sometimes I felt as if the room was no longer Mummy's, but a cause's. The old traces of Mummy – the yellow silk shawl on the sofa, the piano with a vase of dried flowers on it, the prints of plants – were still there. But what I noticed instead was the half-finished banner draped across the sofa that read DEEDS NOT WORDS; the stack of WSPU pamphlets on the piano; the scrapbook on the table, newspaper cuttings, letters, photographs piled next to it along with scissors and a gluepot; the box of chalk, the handbills, the sheets of paper scribbled with lists. Daddy never came in here. If he did he would be very surprised.

I closed the door, climbed the stairs to Jenny's room and tapped on it. 'Jenny?' I called. There was no answer at first, but when I tapped again I heard a grunt, and Jenny opened the door, squinting, a red crease across her cheek where it had pressed against the pillow. She wore a long white nightgown and her feet were bare. 'What's wrong, Miss Maude?' she murmured, rubbing her face.

I stared at Jenny's thick yellow toenails. 'I need your help, please,' I whispered.

'Can it not wait till morning? I was asleep, you know. I have to get up earlier than you lot.'

'I'm sorry. It's – my courses have begun and I don't know what to do.'

'What?'

I repeated myself and turned red again.

Oh, Lord, the curse,' Jenny muttered. She looked me up

and down. 'Blimey, Miss Maude, twelve's young to start — you've not got even a trace of bubbies yet!'

'I'm not so young. I'll be thirteen in — in eight months.' I knew how silly I sounded and began to cry.

Jenny opened her door wide. 'There, now, no need for that.' She put her arm round me. 'You'd best come in — it won't get sorted out with you standing there bawling.'

Jenny's room had been Nanny's room when I was small. Although I had been in it only once or twice since Jenny moved into it, it still felt familiar. It smelled of warm skin and wool blankets and camphorated oil, like the presses Nanny used to heat for my chest when I had a cold. Jenny's dress, apron and cap were hung on pegs. Her hairbrush sat on the small mantel over the fire, and also a photograph of Jenny with a baby in her lap. They were sitting in front of a backdrop of palm fronds, and Jenny wore her best dress. Both looked serious and surprised, as if they had not expected the camera to flash.

'Who's that?' I asked. I had never seen the photograph.

Jenny was wrapping a robe around herself and barely looked up. 'My nephew.'

'I've not heard you mention him. What's his name?'

'Jack.' Jenny crossed her arms. 'Now, has your mum told you anything, or sorted out anything for you?'

I shook my head.

'Of course not. I might've known. Your mother's so busy saving women she don't even look after her own.'

'I know what's happening. I've read about it in books.'

'But you don't know what to do, do you? That's what's important, what you *do* about it. Who cares what it is? "Deeds not words," ain't that what your mum's always saying?'

I frowned.

Jenny pursed her lips. 'Sorry, Miss Maude,' she said. 'All right – I'll lend you some of mine till we've got you what you need.' She kneeled by a small chest where she kept her things and took out a few long thick pieces of cloth and a curious belt I had never seen. She showed me how to fold the cloth in three and fasten it to the belt. She explained about the bucket and salt water to soak the cloths in, to be left under the bed by the chamber pot. Then she went downstairs for a bucket and a hot-water bottle for the pain, while I washed myself and tried on the towel and belt in my room. It felt like my petticoats and bloomers had become all wadded up and caught between my legs, making me waddle like a duck. I was sure everyone would be able to tell.

As awful as it had been having such a thing happen when I was with Daddy, I was glad at least that Lavinia was not there too. She would never forgive me for starting first. She has always been the pretty one, the womanly one – even when we were younger she reminded me of the women in Pre-Raphaelite paintings, with her curly hair and plump figure. Jenny was right – I am flat and, as Grandmother once said, my clothes hang from me like washing from a line. Lavinia and I always assumed that she would get her courses first, would wear a corset first, would marry first, would have children first. Sometimes I've been bothered by this, but often I've been secretly relieved. I have never told her, but I am not so sure that I want to be married and have children.

Now I would have to hide my belts and towels and pain from her. I didn't like keeping secrets from my best friend.

But then, she was keeping one from me. Ever since Mummy took up with Caroline Black, Lavinia has been peculiar about her, but won't say why. When I ask her she simply says that suffragettes are wicked, but I'm sure there's more to it than that. It was something to do with Simon and being down that grave. But she won't say, and neither will Simon. I went to the cemetery on my own and asked him, but he just shrugged and kept on digging.

When Jenny came back with the bucket she gave me a hug. 'You're a woman now, you know. Before you know it you'll be wearing a corset. That's something to tell your mum tomorrow.'

I nodded. But I knew that tomorrow I would say nothing to Mummy. She wasn't here now when she was needed most. Tomorrow did not matter.

*February 1908*

# KITTY COLEMAN

To my surprise, it was harder facing Maude than Richard.

Richard's response was predictable – a rage he contained in front of the police but unleashed in the cab home. He shouted about the family name, about the disgrace to his mother, about the uselessness of the cause. All of this I had known to expect, from hearing of the reactions of other women's husbands. Indeed, I have been lucky to go this long without Richard complaining. He has thought my activities with the WSPU a harmless hobby, to be dabbled in between tea parties. It is only now he truly understands that I too am a suffragette.

One thing he said in the cab did surprise me. 'What about your daughter?' he shouted. 'Now that she's firmly on the road to womanhood, she needs a better example than you are setting.'

I frowned – the phrase he used was so awkward it must be masking something. 'What do you mean?'

Richard stared at me, both incredulous and embarrassed. 'She hasn't told you?'

'Told me what?'

'That she's begun her ... her ...' He waved his hand vaguely at my skirt.

'She has?' I cried. 'When?'

'Months ago.'

'How can you know when I don't?'

'I was with her at the time, that's why! And a humiliating moment it was, for both of us. She had to go to Jenny in the end — you weren't home. I should have guessed then how deeply you were into this ridiculous nonsense.'

Richard could have said more, but must have sensed he didn't need to. I was remembering when my own courses began — how I had run to my mother, crying, and how she had comforted me.

We were silent the rest of the way back. When we got home I took a candle from the hall table and went directly up to Maude's room. I sat on her bed and looked at her in the dim light, wondering what other secrets she was keeping from me, and how to tell her what I must tell her.

She opened her eyes and sat up before I had said anything. 'What is it, Mummy?' she asked so clearly that I am not sure she had been asleep.

It was best to be honest and direct. 'Do you know where I was today while you were at school?'

'At the WSPU headquarters?'

'I was at Caxton Hall for the Women's Parliament. But then I went to Parliament Square with some others to try to get in to the House of Commons.'

'And — did you?'

'No. I was arrested. I've just come back from Cannon Row Police Station with your father. Who is furious, of course.'

'But why were you arrested? What did you do?'

'I didn't do anything. We were simply pushing through the crowd when policemen grabbed us and threw us to the ground. When we got up, they threw us down again and again. The bruises on my shoulders and ribs are quite spectacular. We've all got them.'

I did not add that many of those bruises came from the ride in the Black Maria — how the driver took corners so sharply I was thrown about, or how the cubicles in the van were so small that I felt I had been shut in a coffin standing up, or how it smelled of urine, which I was sure the police had done themselves to punish us further.

'Was Caroline Black arrested too?' Maude asked.

'No. She had fallen back to speak to someone she knew, and by the time she caught up the police had already got us. She was terribly upset not to be taken. She even came down to Cannon Row on her own and sat with us.'

Maude was silent. I wanted to ask her about what Richard had told me in the cab ride home, but found I couldn't. It was easier to talk about what had happened to me.

'I'll be in court early tomorrow,' I continued. 'They may send me straight to Holloway. I wanted to say goodbye now.'

'But — how long would you be in — in prison?'

'I don't know. Possibly up to three months.'

'Three months! What will we do?'

'You? You'll be fine. There is something I want you to do for me, though.'

Maude gazed at me eagerly.

Even before I pulled out the collecting card and began to tell her about self-denial week — a campaign drive the WSPU was initiating to raise money — I knew I was doing the wrong thing. As her mother I should be comforting and reassuring her. Yet even as her face fell I continued to explain that she should ask all our neighbours as well as any visitors to place donations in the card, and that she should send it to the WSPU office at the end of the week.

I don't know why I was so cruel.

# DOROTHY BAKER

As a rule I don't involve myself in this family's comings and goings. I arrive at half-seven in the morning, I cook for them, I leave at seven at night – six if the supper's a cold one. I stay out of the way, I don't have opinions. Or if I do I keep them to myself. I have my own little house, my grown children with their dramas – I don't need more. Not like Jenny, who given half a chance pokes her nose into every story going. It's a miracle she's not had it cut right off.

But I do feel sorry for Miss Maude. I was going home the other evening through a thick fog when I saw her walking just ahead of me. I'd never seen her in Tufnell Park before. She's got no reason to come over here – her life goes in other directions, north and west towards Highgate and Hampstead, not east towards Tufnell Park and Holloway. That's to be expected of a family of that class.

The streets here are not so rough, but all the same I didn't like to see her on her own, especially in that peasoup. A person could disappear for good in one. I felt I ought to follow to make sure she came to no harm. It was clear enough where she was headed. Can't say I blame her – I'd have done the same in her shoes, though living near it as I do, I don't feel much draw to see it. But then, I don't have family inside. My children act out their dramas within the bounds of the law.

Miss Maude found her way there easy enough – even with the fog and the strange streets she's got a level head on her. When she got there she stopped and stared. The look of the place when it loomed out of the fog must have thrown her. The Castle, they call it round here. True enough it resembles one, with a big arched entrance and stone towers with ramparts. Most peculiar for a prison. My children used to play knights and maidens in front of it, when they dared. There are also rows of little windows set in a brick wall far back from the road, where the prisoners must be.

Then we both got a surprise – blow me if that Black woman wasn't marching up and down in front of the entrance. She's a little thing, but she wore a long grey coat that flapped round her ankles and made her look taller. She was singing this:

'Sing a song of Christabel's clever little plan
Four and twenty Suffragettes packed in a van
When the van was opened they to the Commons ran
Wasn't that a dainty dish for Campbell-Bannerman?
Asquith was in the treasury, counting out the money
Lloyd George among the Liberal women speaking
    words of honey
And then there came a bright idea to all those little
    men
"Let's give the women votes," they cried, "and all be
    friends again."'

Then she turned to the little windows and shouted, 'Chin

up, my dear — you're halfway through now. Only three weeks to go! And we have so much to do when you come out!' Her voice hardly carried in the fog, though — don't know how she thought anyone inside would hear her.

Miss Maude had seen enough — she turned and ran. I followed but my running days are long over and I lost sight of her. It was dusk now, and I began to worry. The shops were closed, and soon there wouldn't be any decent people out on the street for her to ask directions of.

Then I turned a corner and she was rushing out of the fog towards me, looking very frightened.

'Miss Maude, what on earth are you doing out here?' I said, pretending not to know.

'Mrs Baker!' She was so relieved to see me that she clutched my arm.

'You should be at home,' I scolded, 'not wandering the streets.'

'I've been — for a walk and got lost.'

I looked at her. There was no point in being coy. 'Wanted to see where she is?'

'Yes.' Miss Maude hung her head.

I shuddered. 'Grim place. I've never liked having it on my doorstep. Here, you!' I called to a passing figure.

'Hallo, Mrs Baker.'

'Miss Maude, this is Jimmy, my neighbour's son. See her to the Boston Arms, will you, Jimmy? She'll know her way from there.'

'Thank you, Mrs Baker,' Miss Maude whispered.

I shrugged. 'It's not my business,' I said. 'Not a word of this to anyone. Take care how you go in the fog.'

I keep my word.

March 1908

# SIMON FIELD

It's chucking down, so our Jenny lets me in from the rain.
Mrs Baker don't say nothing when she sees me — just grunts.
Makes me a soft egg, though.

'Lord,' our Jenny says, looking out of the window while
I sit at the table eating. 'What a day to be visiting prison.'

'Who's going to prison?' I ask.

Mrs B. bangs a pot of water onto the range and gives our
Jenny a look. Jenny ignores her — she says whatever she
likes.

'The master and Miss Maude. They ain't been able to visit
till now — them suffragettes can't have visitors the first four
weeks. First it were to be just the master, but I heard 'em
arguing and Miss Maude got her way, bless her. She misses
her mum. Though heaven knows why, the woman were
hardly round before anyway.'

'That's enough, Jenny,' Mrs B. says.

'It don't matter — it's just Simon.'

'What doesn't matter?' Maude has come down the stairs,
and is standing with her arms clutched over her stomach.
She looks peaky to me.

Our Jenny and Mrs B. both turn quick to look at her.

'Nothing, Miss Maude,' our Jenny says. 'You had enough to eat?'

'I'm not much hungry, thanks.'

'Terrible luck, getting the curse on top of the rain on your visiting day.'

Maude looks at me then glares at our Jenny.

'For pity's sake, Jenny, leave the girl alone!' Mrs B. don't often shout. 'Get upstairs and clear away the dishes.'

Our Jenny runs off. I've enough sense not to say nothing 'bout the curse. 'Hallo,' is all I says.

'Hello.'

Hard to imagine Maude's ma in prison. Whoever thought she'd end up there? When I first found out from our Jenny, I let it slip real casual one day to Mr Jackson that Mrs C. were in Holloway. He jumped like someone'd pinched him.

'Good Lord. Why is she there?'

I didn't really know why, to be truthful. 'Women's things, sir.'

He stared at me so hard I had to say something more. 'You know, them women what goes round on bicycles, chalking signs on the pavement and shouting at rallies and that.'

'You mean suffragettes?'

'I suppose so, sir.'

'Good Lord,' he said again. 'Prison is a terrible place for a woman. I hope she is not being mistreated.'

'Probably no more'n anyone else in prison, sir. My cousin got out after six months with nothing worse'n flea bites.'

'That is not much comfort, Simon.'

'Sorry, sir.'

I want to say something to Maude now, but can't think of nothing that would help. Then there's a knock at the back door, and Livy comes in dripping wet, and there ain't much chance for me to get a word in. Maude don't look too happy to see her. Livy rushes over and gives her a big hug. She sees me over Maude's shoulder but don't say nothing. She's been funny with me ever since I kissed her. That were over a year ago and she ain't been the same since. Our Pa were right, I guess.

Fact is, this is the first time all three of us has been together in a long while. Not like when the girls was younger and used to visit the cemetery all the time.

'Oh, my dear, you look so pale!' Livy says now. 'You must be terribly upset about your visit.'

The thing about Livy is that she says things like that but she means something else. She don't think it's terribly upsetting Mrs C. is in Holloway – to her it's great fun, though she would never admit it. She looks so excited now, that I know what's to come next.

She sits Maude down at the table. 'Now,' she says, 'I want to suggest something to you.' She's acting like no one else is there – like I'm not sitting at the table too, and Mrs B. ain't peeling potatoes at the sideboard, and our Jenny ain't taking a tray with the breakfast things through to the scullery. But she knows we're there and listening. 'I know you'll say no, so I want you to promise to be quiet until I've finished what I have to say. Do you promise?'

'All right,' Maude says.

'I want to come with you this morning to visit your mother.'

'You can't –'

253

'I haven't finished yet.'

Maude frowns but stays quiet.

'You know it will be horrid and it will upset you. Don't you want your friend to be there with you, holding your hand and helping you to be as brave as you can in front of your mother?'

We all wait to hear what Maude will say – our Jenny standing in the scullery door, Mrs B. frowning at a potato skin like she's not listening. 'But what about your mother?' Maude says. 'And Daddy? I'm sure he won't let you.'

Livy smiles. 'Mama needn't know, and don't you worry about your father. He'll say yes – I'll make sure of it.'

She will, too. Livy can make a man do anything she likes. I've seen her at the cemetery, rolling her eyes and swirling her skirt, and men do what she says. Even Mr Jackson fetches her a watering can if she wants one – though that may be 'cause he still feels bad about her angel getting broke. Unless you look real hard you can't see the join in the neck where the mason fitted the head back on, but they made a mess of the nose. Probably should've left it chipped. Once I took Livy round the angels and showed her all the chips and scratches on them. I did it to make her feel better but it just seemed to upset her.

'Maude, are you ready?'

Everybody turns to stare at Maude's Pa come down the stairs. The way our Jenny and Mrs B. act – Jenny's eyes get big, and Mrs B. lets her knife slip so she cuts her thumb and has to suck it – it's clear he don't ever come down here. He must be feeling nervous about going to Holloway, or he don't like the whole house above us all empty, and has come looking for people.

Even Maude jumps to see him here. 'Yes, Daddy, I just need to – to get one thing in my room. I'll be right back.' She looks at Livy, then squeezes past her Pa and runs upstairs. He still stands at the bottom of the stairs, looking like he's surprised himself that he's down here.

Livy's getting ready to work her charm. 'Mr Coleman –'

But Mr C. has spotted me. 'Mrs Baker, who is this boy eating our bread?'

Mrs B. don't even flinch. 'Gardener's boy, sir.' She chose well – the garden is Mrs C.'s territory. Mr C. probably don't even set foot in it except to smoke a cig. He won't know which is the gardener's boy.

Mr C. looks out at the rain. 'Well, he certainly picks his days, doesn't he?'

'Yes, he does, sir. Do you hear, Simon? There'll be no gardening for you. Off you go, now.'

I gulp down the rest of my tea, put on my cap and step out into the rain. I don't get to say nothing to Maude, nor hear Livy's sweet talk. Never mind – at least my tum's full.

# LAVINIA WATERHOUSE

Really it was not at all difficult. I simply appealed to his softer nature. And he does have a soft nature. He clearly is a broken man with his wife in prison — anyone can see that if they only look. But I am not sure anyone is looking except me. I do feel too that he and I have a special connection, because of the letter. Although he does not know that I wrote it, he must know someone is looking out for him.

For a long time I could not understand why he did not throw his wife out once he had read the letter, but now that I am older and beginning to understand men better, I see that he has quite gallantly set aside his own feelings in order to protect the family name from scandal.

He said yes when I asked to accompany them to Holloway. I repeated more or less what I had said to Maude — that I would be a comfort to her in difficult circumstances — but also suggested he was being an exemplary father and gentleman to consider his daughter's needs in that way.

I cannot help but think that he said yes in part because he prefers my company to Maude's. Certainly I was the livelier one in the cab over. But how could I not be – we were to see the inside of a prison! I couldn't think of anything more deliciously exciting.

The only dampening element (apart from the rain, ha ha!) was that as the cab drove past our house I saw Ivy May had pulled aside the net curtain and was looking out of the window. She seemed to look right at me, and I had to pray that she would not tattle on me – Mama thinks Maude and I were at the library.

I had never seen Holloway prison before. As we walked up to the arched wooden doors of the main entrance, I squeezed Maude's arm. 'It looks like a castle!' I whispered.

To my amazement Maude wrenched her arm away. 'This isn't a fairy tale!' she hissed.

Well. I was a little put out, but soon recovered when I saw the woman who opened the side door to let us in. She was short and fat and wore a grey uniform, with a big bunch of keys hanging at her waist. Best of all, she had a huge mole on her upper lip. She was just like a character out of Dickens, though I didn't say so to Maude. I had to clap my hand over my mouth so the woman wouldn't see me laughing. She did, though, the troll.

We went into a reception room, and Maude and I sat on a narrow bench while Troll opened a ledger book and took down Mr Coleman's details. I was amazed she could read and write.

Troll looked up at us. 'Only one of youse can come in,' she said. 'Only three visitors allowed at one time, an' one's already there. One of youse'll have to wait here.' She fixed a yellow eye on me.

'Another visitor?' Mr Coleman looked puzzled. 'Who?'

257

Troll put her finger on a page in the ledger. 'Miss C. Black.'

'Damn her! What the devil's she doing here?'

'She arranged a visit, same as you.'

'She's no relation to my wife. Tell her she has to go.'

Troll smiled slyly. 'She's a right to see 'er, same as anyone else. It's your wife decides who she sees an' don't sees.'

Poor Mr Coleman was furious but there was nothing he could do. 'You two wait here for me,' he said to us.

'But I've come to see Mummy!' Maude cried.

'It's best if you stay here with Lavinia. We can't leave her alone.'

He turned to the woman. 'Can the girls wait here for me?'

Troll just grunted.

I smiled, relieved by his chivalry.

'But Lavinia will be fine here on her own,' Maude insisted. 'Won't you, Lavinia?'

I opened my mouth to protest, but that nasty woman jumped in. 'I don't want two of youse cluttering up my bench.' She pointed at Maude. 'You go with your Da, and you –' pointing at me – 'wait where you are.' She went to the door and called out something into the corridor.

I was so shocked I couldn't speak. Being left alone in a prison with a horrid troll? And for such a silly reason as the space needed on a hard bench? Clearly Troll was saying this simply to get at me. I turned to Mr Coleman for help. Unfortunately he then revealed that he is not so gallant as I thought – he simply nodded at Troll.

Another woman came in, tall this time, also wearing the

grey uniform, and jangling her keys in a most irritating manner.

'H15, second division,' Troll said to her. 'Another un's already there.'

The wardress nodded and gestured for Mr Coleman and Maude to follow — which they did, neither of them giving me even a backward glance.

Well. When they were gone, Troll grinned at me from behind her table. I was surprised to see she had a full set of teeth — I would have expected them to be black and falling out. I ignored her and sat very quietly, like a little mouse. For I was rather terrified.

The thing about a little mouse, though, is that it can't help looking around for some crumbs to munch on. There was not much to see in the room — just the table and a few benches, all empty — and I found myself studying Troll. She was sitting behind the table, writing something in the ledger. She really was quite repulsive, even worse than something Dickens would have thought up. Her mole positively gleamed on her lip. I wondered if there were hairs growing out of it. The thought made me giggle. I didn't think she could see me spying on her — I was looking at her through my lashes while pretending to study my fingernails — but she growled, 'What you laughing at, gal?'

'My own little joke,' I said bravely. 'It's nothing to do with you. And really, you had better call me Miss Waterhouse.'

She had the impudence to laugh, so I felt obliged to explain that I was almost certain we were related to the painter J. W. Waterhouse, even though Papa thinks not, and that I had written to him to discover the connection. (I didn't tell her that Mr Waterhouse never responded to my letter.) Of course I was assuming far too much of a prison gatekeeper with a mole on her lip, even if she can write — she clearly had never heard of JWW, not even when I described his painting of the Lady of Shalott that hangs in the Tate. She hadn't even heard of her! Next she would be asking who was Tennyson.

Fortunately this fruitless conversation was interrupted by the arrival back of yet another wardress. Troll said she was glad the other had come because I could 'talk the ear off an elephant, an' all of it rubbish, too.'

I was very tempted to stick out my tongue at her — the longer I sat there the less terrified I was. But then a bell rang, and she went off to answer the door. The other wardress just stood there and stared at me as if I were a piece in a museum exhibition. I glared at her but it didn't seem to put her off. I expect they don't often see girls like me sitting on the bench — no wonder that she stared.

Troll came back with a man in tow, dressed in a dark suit and bowler hat. He stood at the table while Troll looked in her ledger and said, 'She's already got her visitors for today. Popular lady. Did you write ahead to arrange it?'

'No,' the man said.

'You have to write ahead for permission,' Troll said gleefully. She did delight in other's misfortunes. 'And then it's up to her to say she'll see you.'

'I see.' The man turned to leave.

Well. I was rather beyond surprise by that time. So when he glanced over at me and started like a skittish horse, I simply smiled my sweetest smile and said, 'Hello, Mr Jackson'.

Luckily he left before Maude and her father returned or

there would have been an awkward scene. For once Troll held her tongue rather than make everyone's misery worse, and I kept quiet as well. It was very odd indeed that Mr Jackson should want to visit Maude's mother.

It was such a trying day that when I got home I had to have a long nap and a bowl of bread-and-butter pudding to comfort me, as if I were ill. All the while there were thoughts racing around my head that kept trying to fit themselves together. They were to do with Maude's mother and Mr Jackson. I tried very hard not to let them fit together, however, and I think I succeeded.

# MAUDE COLEMAN

Daddy and I followed the wardress down a corridor and into a large internal courtyard. From the ground we could see all the way up to the roof. The walls were lined with tier after tier of doors. Outside the rows of doors were gangways of black ironwork, along which other wardresses dressed in grey were walking.

Our wardress led us up two flights of stairs and out along one of the gangways. From the iron railing at my side to the other across the courtyard a wire net had been stretched over the empty space. There were strange things caught in it — a wooden spoon, a white cap, a cracked leather shoe.

In the centre of each cell door hung a leather flap. As I passed one I had an overwhelming urge to lift it. I slowed down so that Daddy and the wardress were several paces ahead, then quickly lifted the flap and put my eye up to the peephole.

The cell was very small — perhaps five feet by seven, not much larger than our scullery. I could see very little — a plank of wood leaning against a wall, a towel hanging from a nail, and a woman sitting on a stool in the corner. She had dark brown hair piled on her head, olive skin, and a strong jaw and mouth set in the manner of a soldier as he marches in a parade. She held herself very straight, as Grandmother is always nagging me to do. She wore a dark green dress with white arrows sewn on it — the badge of a prisoner — a checked apron, and a white cap like the one caught in the net outside the cells. A ball of wool and knitting needles sat in her lap.

I wanted her to look at me. When at last she met my eye, I knew exactly who she was. I had never seen Mrs Pankhurst before — the remarkable Emmeline Pankhurst, leader of the suffragettes. Mummy always hoped she would come to an At Home, but she never did. I heard Caroline Black once describe her leader's eyes as 'deep blue and so penetrating that you would do anything for them — take a spade to Mount Snowdon if she said it ruined her view.'

Mrs Pankhurst smiled at me.

'Maude!'

I jumped back from the peephole. Daddy was staring at me in horror. The wardress was still rushing forward but stopped when she heard Daddy's shout.

I ran to him.

'What in hell's name were you doing?' he whispered, grabbing my arm.

'Sorry,' I whispered.

The wardress grunted. 'Look sharp, keep up with me or you won't see 'er at all.'

Farther along the gangway two women were standing at a cell door — one a wardress, the other Caroline Black. Under her grey coat she was wearing a brilliant white dress with several rows of lace trim across her chest, and a hat trimmed with wilting primroses. She looked as if she should be strolling in Hyde Park. My own plain blue coat and old straw hat were very drab in comparison.

As we approached she was saying into the cell, 'The colours are to be purple for dignity, white for purity, and green for hope. Isn't it a splendid idea? I would've worn them myself today except I wanted to wear primroses for you. Think how striking it will look in public gatherings to see everyone dressed in the same colours!' She glanced at us, smiled, and announced, 'More visitors!'

'Who has come?' I heard from inside the cell.

'Mummy!' I cried. I darted forward, but then stopped — although the door was open, there were still bars across the doorway. I wanted to cry.

Mummy's cell was identical to Mrs Pankhurst's, down to the ball of grey wool sitting on the stool, a grey sock with red stripes at the top almost finished between the knitting needles. Mummy stood against the back wall. 'Hello, Maude,' she said. 'Come to see your old mother locked away, then?' Like Mrs Pankhurst, she too was dressed in dark green serge dotted with white arrows. The dress was too big for her — it covered her feet and hid her waist. Big as it was, I could see from her pinched face that she had lost weight. She had dark circles under her eyes and her skin was blotchy and yellow. Her eyes were bright, as if she had a fever.

'Hello, Richard,' she said to Daddy, who hovered behind me and Caroline Black.

We were all three standing awkwardly in the doorway, stepping from side to side and peeking around each other, as if trying to look at an animal at the zoo. The two ward-resses stood on either side of the doorway like sentinels.

'For God's sake, Kitty, haven't you been eating?' Daddy said.

I flinched, and Caroline Black shook her head slightly, the primroses fluttering on her hat. I wished he had said something else instead of blurting out the first thing that popped into his head, but I felt sorry for him, too – he looked so strained and uncomfortable.

Mummy didn't seem bothered, though, but smiled as if he had told a joke. 'If you saw what we get as rations, you wouldn't eat either. I cracked my tooth on a bit of gravel in my bread the other day. It's rather put me off.'

'Mummy, I wrote to you,' I said quickly, 'but the letter was returned.'

'We're not allowed letters for the first four weeks,' Mummy said. 'Caroline could have told you that. And how much did you raise during self-denial week? A good amount, I hope.'

'I – I don't remember,' I whispered.

'You don't remember? Of course you do. It was only four weeks ago, and you've a good memory for figures. Or are you embarrassed that it wasn't much? I don't mind – I didn't expect you to raise what I would have. How much did you get – ten pounds?'

I bowed my head. I had raised barely a tenth of that. I had been meant to ask neighbours and visitors for donations, but couldn't bring myself to do it. Instead I had given up all my pocket money for a month, and Mrs Baker and Mrs Waterhouse had given me a few shillings. I had come to hate that collecting card.

'Did you know,' Caroline Black said, 'that some women ate only brown bread and gruel for the whole week, in tribute to you lot in here? They donated the money they saved from eating a "prison diet" to the WSPU!'

She and Mummy laughed, Caroline Black showing her side tooth.

'How is Mrs Pankhurst?' she asked. 'Have you seen her?'

'We're a bit worried,' Mummy said. 'She didn't come to exercise yesterday, nor to chapel this morning. I do hope she isn't ill.'

'I saw her,' I declared, pleased to be able to say something useful.

'Saw her? When did you see her?' Mummy demanded.

'Just now. A few cells down.'

Mummy and Caroline Black gazed at me with delight. Our wardress, however, frowned.

'How did she look?' Mummy asked eagerly. 'What was she doing?'

'She was knitting.'

'Did she say anything?'

'No, but she smiled at me.'

'Stop this at once!' our wardress cried. 'You're not to talk about such things. I should march you right out of here.'

'That's good news,' Mummy declared, ignoring the wardress. 'Knitting, was she? Just like me.' She glanced at the wool on her stool and laughed. 'The thing I'm worst at they're forcing me to do. By the time I leave I'll be an expert, at knitting socks, anyway.'

'Are those for you?' I had a hard time imagining Mummy wearing grey socks with red stripes.

'No, no! They're for male prisoners. Something to keep us busy. Otherwise it really is agonizingly dull in here. I thought at first I might go mad. But I haven't. Oh, and I've got my Bible to read.' She pointed at a shelf that held two books as well as a tin plate and cup, a wooden salt cellar, a piece of yellow soap, and a small brush and comb. 'And look what they've given us!' She held up the other book. I squinted at the title: *A Healthy Home and How to Keep It*. 'I've read it cover to cover. And d'you know what it tells us — sleep with your window open at night!' Mummy looked up at the small, barred window high above her head and began to laugh again. Caroline Black joined her.

'Kitty,' Daddy said quietly.

To my relief, Mummy stopped laughing.

'Have you learned your lesson in here?' Daddy asked.

Mummy frowned. 'What do you mean by "lesson"?'

'Enough is enough, now. When you get out we can get back to normal.'

'That rather depends on what you mean by "normal"'.

Daddy did not reply.

'Are you suggesting that I give up the fight when I've got out?'

'Surely you're not going to continue?'

'On the contrary, Richard, I think prison has been the making of me. Oddly enough, dullness has made me into a rod of iron. "That which does not defeat me makes me stronger." That's Nietzsche, you know.'

'You read entirely too much,' Daddy said.

Mummy smiled. 'You didn't think that when you first met me. Anyway, when I get out I will have far too much to do to read.'

'We'll discuss this when you are back home,' Daddy said, glancing at Caroline Black. 'You can't be expected to think properly in here.'

'There's nothing to discuss. It's a decision I have made. It has nothing to do with you.'

'It has everything to do with me – I'm your husband!'

'Pardon me, Richard, but nothing I've done in my little life has had any significance whatsoever until I joined the WSPU.'

'How can you say that in front of Maude?'

Mummy looked at me. She seemed genuinely puzzled. 'What about Maude?'

'Are you saying having a child has not been significant?'

'Of course it has. Maude is the reason I'm sitting in this prison cell. I'm doing this so that she will be able to vote.'

'No, you're doing it so that you can swan about town, feeling self-important, making silly speeches and neglecting your home and family.'

'I do feel important,' Mummy replied. 'For perhaps the first time in my life I have something to do, Richard. I'm working! I may not be optimistic like Caroline and the Pankhursts that we'll see suffrage voted in in my lifetime. But our work will one day lead to it. Maude will see those results, even if I don't.'

'Oh, climb down from your soapbox!' Daddy cried. 'You claim to be doing this for your daughter. Have you ever asked Maude what she thinks of you leaving her all alone like this? Have you?'

Five sets of eyes turned on me. Daddy's were furious, Mummy's curious. The two wardresses inspected me without interest. Only Caroline Black's dog-like brown eyes showed any sympathy. I turned red. My stomach was aching.

I took a step backwards and then another, and before I knew it I had turned and started to run.

'Hey! Stop!' I heard a wardress shout.

I continued to run along the gangway, back along the route we had taken — down the stairs, through the court-yard, and along a corridor, accompanied the whole way by shouts from women in grey uniforms, who never managed to catch up with me. I reached a door, opened it, ran to the bench and fell into Lavinia's arms.

'Oh, my poor dear,' Lavinia said, patting me on the back as I sobbed. 'There, now. There, now. It's just as well I came. I suppose.'

# RICHARD COLEMAN

When we got back from Holloway I went straight to Kitty's morning room, where she keeps her books. There I saw just how far she has fallen into the black pit that is this cause.

I had been planning to find and burn the Nietzsche, but instead I burned every handbill, every newspaper, every banner I could lay my hands on.

*May 1908*

# ALBERT WATERHOUSE

Poor Richard. I didn't think I would ever be embarrassed for the chap, but I am. I always said his wife would be a handful.

He and I were on the roster to roll the cricket pitch tonight, and were just walking over to the Heath when we saw her. I must say I'm glad Trudy has never asked for a bicycle. Kitty Coleman was riding along merrily, her dress rising to her knees as she pedalled. I caught a good glimpse of an ankle – and a fine one it was, too – before I managed to look away.

Richard made as if he didn't see her, so I pretended not to as well, but then she rang a little bell and we had to raise our hats at her. She waved, then went on her way with a flash of the other ankle.

I thought she was looking remarkably well for having been six weeks in Holloway, but I did not say so to Richard. In fact it seemed best not to say anything at all.

But Richard did, which surprised me, as we're not ones for confidences. 'Tell me, Albert, how do you handle your wife?'

I stumbled over a paving stone. 'How do I handle my wife?'

With firm affection, I thought, as I regained my balance. I did not say so aloud — there are things men do not say aloud.

'Kitty has blackmailed me,' Richard continued.

'How so?'

'She says that if I try to forbid her to work for the suffragettes she will begin giving speeches at rallies. Can you imagine the Coleman name all over those infernal handbills they pass out? Or plastered on posters, or chalked on the pavement? Holloway almost killed my mother from the shame of it — this would finish her off. What would you do in my situation?'

I was trying to picture Trudy making such a threat, but it was impossible to imagine. If anything she is more concerned about the Waterhouse name than I am. And she would rather eat a plate of coal than speak in public. The kinds of threats she makes to me are to do with the colour of the front parlour curtains or which seaside town we are to go to for a holiday.

Richard was looking at me as if he expected a response. 'Perhaps it's just a phase your wife is going through,' I suggested. 'Perhaps the suffragette movement will die out. They're planning a demonstration in Hyde Park in June, aren't they? Even Trudy knows of it, and she's no suffragette. Perhaps that will satisfy them, and afterwards your wife will settle down.'

'Perhaps,' Richard repeated, but I am afraid he did not sound convinced.

# KITTY COLEMAN

Maude has been avoiding me for weeks now, ever since I came out of Holloway. At first I didn't notice, as there was so much to do, what with the march to organise for June. It is to be the largest public gathering of people anywhere, ever in the world. We are run off our feet with tasks — booking trains from all over the country, getting permission for the march routes and use of Hyde Park, conferring with the police, finding speakers and marching bands, making banners. It is like planning a battle. No, not just a battle — an entire war.

On that theme, Caroline has had a wonderful idea of what she and I can dress as for the procession. It is to be very dramatic, and I plan to celebrate my liberation from both Holloway and my despair with a liberating costume. It will be a great day.

In the midst of all the activity, though, I did notice that Maude left rooms as soon as I entered them, and was eating more meals at the Waterhouses' than at home.

Richard simply shrugged when I mentioned this to him. 'What did you expect?' he said. It is hard to talk to him now — since I got out of Holloway he has been avoiding me too. Just as well that I have grown a thick skin!

I was not really surprised to see what he had done to my morning room. Other suffragettes' husbands have done worse. To put an end to such behaviour I had to resort to blackmail, which I am not proud of but which was necessary. It worked, too — he may hate what I am doing but he fears his mother more.

On Saturday morning I caught Maude moping in the drawing room and had an idea. 'Come with me into town,' I suggested. 'There's a motor to take us. See?' I pointed out of the window at the Jenkinses' motor-car sitting in front of the house. Mrs Jenkins, a wealthy WSPU member in Highgate, has kindly donated it for WSPU business around town. Her husband doesn't know — we only use it when he's at work or away — and we have had to bribe Fred, the driver, to keep him quiet. It has been worth every penny.

Maude gaped at the car, which was gleaming in the sun. I could see that she wanted to say yes but she felt she shouldn't.

'Do come,' I said. 'It's a lovely day — we can ride with the top down.'

'Where are you going?'

'To Clements Inn. But not for long,' I added quickly, knowing that she did not like the WSPU. 'Then on to Bond Street. Afterwards we could stop at the soda fountain at Fortnum and Mason's — we haven't had an ice-cream there in such a long time.'

I don't know why I was trying so hard. I have never been an attentive mother, but now I feel as if I am fighting for something on Maude's behalf, and want to include her, even if it means bribing her with an ice-cream.

'All right,' she said at last.

I had her and Jenny help bring out the stacks of banners I'd been sewing – or rather, that I'd begun and found I hadn't the time for, and so paid Jenny and Mrs Baker extra to sew. I am still far behind the number I've promised to make. I am going to have to enlist Maude, though her sewing is worse than mine.

It was thrilling to be driven through London. I have done it many times now, but I still love it. Fred wears goggles when he drives, but I refuse to – I feel I never see anything if I have them on. We had tied our hats down with scarves – mine a purple, green and white one that reads 'Votes for Women' (I offered one to Maude but she refused) – but everything flapped like mad in the wind anyway, and dust from the street flew into our clothes and hair. It was terribly exciting. The speed was so exhilarating – we zoomed past milk carts, horse-drawn omnibuses, men on bicycles, and raced alongside motorised cabs and other private cars. Pubs, wash houses, tea shops, all passed by in a blur.

Even Maude enjoyed herself, though she did not say much – not that one can talk over the noise of the engine. For the first time in months she seemed to relax, snug in the back seat between me and the banners. As we drove through an avenue of plane trees, their leaves forming a canopy overhead, she leaned her head back and looked up at the sky.

She helped me unload the banners at Clements Inn – Fred never lifts a finger to help, as he disapproves of suffragettes – but would not stay in the office, preferring to wait outside with Fred. I tried to be quick about it, but there were so many comrades to greet, questions to answer, and points to be raised, that by the time I got back to the car Maude and Fred were both sulking.

'Sorry!' I cried gaily. 'Never mind, let's go on. Colling-wood's on Bond Street, if you please, Fred.' This stop wasn't strictly WSPU business, but it was certainly to do with woman's suffrage.

Maude looked surprised. 'Has Daddy bought you something new?' Collingwood's was where Richard went for jewellery for me.

I laughed. 'In a manner of speaking. You'll see.'

But when she saw the necklace in the black velvet box which the jeweller proudly presented to me, she didn't have quite the response I'd expected. She said nothing.

The necklace was made up of emeralds and amethysts and pearls, clustered together to form purple and white flowers with green leaves. The stones came entirely from necklaces I already owned: pearls I had received for my confirmation, amethysts inherited from my mother, and emeralds from a necklace Mrs Coleman gave me when I got married.

'You've done a marvellous job,' I said to the jeweller. 'It's exquisite!'

Maude was still staring at the necklace.

'Don't you like it?' I asked. 'It's the colours, don't you see? The WSPU colours. Lots of women are having pieces made up in them.'

'I thought . . .' Maude stopped.

'What is it?'

'Well — was I to inherit the necklaces that it is made from?'

'Gracious, is that what the matter is? So now you'll inherit this one instead.'

'Daddy will be furious,' Maude said quietly. 'And Grandmother. Those were her emeralds.'

'She gave me that necklace to do with what I liked. It's mine now — it's not for her to say.'

Maude was silent, a silence worse than the sulk earlier.

'Shall we go to Fortnum and Mason's for ice-cream?' I suggested.

'No, thank you, Mummy. I think I'd like to go home now, please,' Maude said in a small voice.

I thought she would love the necklace. It seems that I can never please her.

# RICHARD COLEMAN

I noticed them immediately. Kitty was in the hallway, preening herself in the mirror before we left for Mother's party. Jenny stood holding her wrap while Maude watched from the steps. Kitty's dress was cut low, and as I glanced at her décolletage I recognised the emeralds. I had seen my mother wear them many times when she and my father went to parties and functions, and once to meet the Queen. They looked hideous now, made up in a new necklace with other stones.

I said nothing – Kitty's blackmail has effectively cut out my tongue. Instead I grew furious with myself for being so powerless with my wife. Surely this was not how a husband should be, so helpless and without authority. Kitty knew exactly what she was doing.

Later, when I saw the look on my mother's face as she gazed at Kitty's necklace, I could have throttled my wife's lovely white throat.

# EDITH COLEMAN

I think she enjoys tormenting me.

It has been bad enough this past year the few times when, for form's sake, I have had to visit my son at their house. Worse still when she was sent to Holloway and the Coleman name appeared in the papers. I was mortified, but it blew over more quickly than I had expected. My friends – my good friends – did not mention it, sparing me further embarrassment. I was just glad that James is not alive to see his name brought so low.

But the worst has been the emeralds. James's mother gave them to me the night before our wedding, with the understanding that I would cherish and preserve them, to pass on to my own son's wife. In those days such an understanding was unspoken. It would never have occurred to me to do anything other than wear the emeralds proudly and pass them on willingly when the time came. It could never have occurred to any of us Coleman women to desecrate them as Kitty has done.

She wore them to my annual May party, with a dark green silk dress cut far too low. I knew immediately what they were, even if the necklace itself was not familiar to me.

I would have known my emeralds anywhere. She saw me recognise them as well. Poor Richard standing next to her had no idea. Emeralds are in a woman's realm, not a man's. I shall never tell him.

I did not make a scene — I could not in front of everyone, and I would not do so to please her either. Instead I waited until the last guest had gone. Then I sat in the dark and wept.

*June 1908*

June 1905

# LAVINIA WATERHOUSE

At first I refused to help Maude. I wanted nothing to do with any suffragettes' banners. But Maude is no seamstress, and when I saw her poor fingers at school one day, all pricked and torn from the needle (someone must teach her how to use a thimble properly!), I took pity on her and began going over in the afternoons to help.

It is a good thing I have! She is so slow, the dear, and her awful mother has left her with the most impossible pile of banners to sew. It was odd at first sitting in that morning room sewing – I was worried that at any minute Maude's mother would come in, and I have not felt comfortable around her ever since I Found Out. As it happened, though, she is rarely at home, and when she is she is talking on the telephone she had installed, and doesn't even notice us. That telephone makes me nervous – I always jump when it rings, and I would hate to answer it. Maude has to all the time when her mother is out, and takes endless messages about meetings and petitions and other nonsense.

Luckily my sewing is very good – I get through three banners to Maude's one, and you can see her stitches. And it is rather fun sitting there together – we talk and sing, and sometimes Maude gives up sewing altogether when her fingers are bleeding too much, and reads a book aloud while I work. Jenny brings us endless cups of tea, and even coffee once or twice when we beg her.

All we have to do is to sew, thank goodness. We receive the cloth and letters already cut, and the slogan written on a piece of paper pinned to the cloth. The letters are usually white, the cloth green or black. I don't think I could make up a slogan if you paid me. Some of them are so complicated I can make neither head nor tail of them. What on earth does TAXATION WITHOUT REPRESENTATION IS TYRANNY mean? Or worse, WOMEN'S 'WILL' BEATS ASQUITH'S 'WON'T'? What does the Prime Minister have to do with it?

The best part has been the mistakes. It first happened when I was sewing on letters for one of the endless banners that read DEEDS NOT WORDS. (I am sick to death of those words!) As I was folding the finished banner I happened to glance at it and discovered I had sewn on WORDS NOT DEEDS. I was all ready to unpick the letters, but I peeked at Maude and saw that she hadn't noticed – she was frowning over her banner, sucking on another pricked finger. So I quietly folded the banner, put it on the pile, and smiled to myself. Apparently there are to be thousands and thousands of banners – women all over the country are sewing them. Every few days Maude's mother rushes in, grabs the pile of finished banners, and rushes out again without so much as a thank you. I doubt anyone will trace the mistake back to me.

After that I began to make more 'mistakes' – a few more WORDS NOT DEEDS, and then I sewed WEEDS NOT RODS, and stuffed the extra D in my pinafore pocket. It was great

fun creating errors: WORKING WOMEN DEMAND THE VOTE
became VOTING WOMEN DEMAND WORK; HOPE IS STRONG
became ROPE IS THONG.

I had done half a dozen or so when Maude caught me
out. She was helping me fold one when she suddenly said,
'Stop a moment,' and spread out the banner. It read WHO
WOULD FLEE THEMSELVES MUST STRIKE THE BROW.

'Lavinia! That's meant to read "Who would be free themselves must strike the blow"? You know, from Byron!'

'Oh dear,' I said, and giggled.

'Haven't you even been reading what you're sewing? And
where are the B and E for "BE"?'

I smiled sheepishly and pulled the letters out from my
pocket. 'I thought they were left over, or a mistake,' I said.

'You know very well what it was supposed to say,' Maude
muttered. 'What shall we do with it? It's too late to change
it, and we can't hide it – Mummy's sure to count them and
will want to know why one is missing.'

I struck my own brow. 'Oh dear, I'd best flee.' It was silly
but it made Maude laugh. Soon we were laughing so hard
we were crying. It was good to see her laugh. She has been
so serious these days. In the end we simply folded up the
banner and added it to the pile.

I had not thought I would go to the Hyde Park march
– the thought of being among thousands of suffragettes
made me shiver. But after so many days of sewing and
overhearing things about it, I couldn't help but wonder if
it wouldn't be rather fun. There are to be women from all
over the country, not all of them suffragettes per se, and
there will be bands and speakers, and spectacles all over.
And then Maude told me everyone is to wear white and

287

green and purple, and I thought up the perfect outfits for us. We would wear our white dresses, and trim our straw hats with flowers from the Colemans' garden. Maude's mother may be sinful, but she has cultivated the most wonderful flowers.

'Delphiniums, cornflowers, star jasmine and Persian jewels, all wound round with green leaves,' I decided. 'It will look ever so beautiful.'

'But you said you didn't want to go,' Maude said. 'And what will your mother say?'

'Mama shall come with us,' I said. 'And we won't necessarily march, but we can be spectators.'

Maude thinks Mama will never agree, but she always says yes to me.

# GERTRUDE WATERHOUSE

I felt very silly doing it, but I couldn't see any other way to stop her. When Livy and Ivy May came home from school my ankle was wrapped in a bandage and propped on a footstool. 'I tripped over the threshold,' I said when Livy exclaimed over it. 'It's only a sprain, thankfully, no broken bones.'

'Oh, Mama, you are so clumsy,' she said.

'Yes, I know.'

'How long did the doctor say you must stay off it?'

'A week at least.'

'But that means you can't take us to the march Sunday!'

'Yes, I know. I'm sorry, dear — I know how much you were looking forward to it.' I myself had been dreading it.

Livy cried out. 'But we must go! We can't miss it, can we, Ivy May?'

Ivy May was inspecting the bandage. I should have wound it more tightly.

'Perhaps Papa can take us,' Livy suggested.

'No,' I said quickly. I would not have Albert involved. 'You will be at church with him in the morning, and he is playing cricket in the afternoon. No, I think it best if you stay home.'

'Well, then, we could go with Maude and her mother.'

'No,' I said again, even more quickly.

'We'll be perfectly safe.'

'No.'

Livy glared at me so hard I almost couldn't bear it. 'Really, Livy, dear,' I said as lightly as I could, 'I don't understand why you want to go so badly anyway. It's not something that is of interest to you; nor should it be. I'm sure whoever you marry will be quite capable of deciding for you whom to vote for.'

'On the contrary,' Livy announced, 'I do support woman's suffrage.'

Ivy May tittered. 'Livy doesn't want to be left out,' she said.

'Shush, Ivy May, I'm sure you want to go to Hyde Park too,' Livy said.

'Do you really support woman's suffrage?' I asked, surprised at my daughter.

'I do! I think the colours are splendid — the scarves and jewellery in violet, green and white. And the women whizzing about in motor-cars, so lively and passionate —' Livy stopped when she saw my face.

'I do not approve of the suffragettes, nor of the march,' I said sternly, hoping that would be the end of the matter.

Of course it was not. Livy cried for two days and would not speak to me, until at last, the night before the march, I gave in. Nothing stops her getting what she wants, not even her silly mother's schemes. I did not want Livy to discover I had tried to deceive her, so in the end I could not even go with them, but had to hand them over to Kitty Coleman.

Ivy May caught me walking on my 'sprained' ankle. Bless her, she said not a word.

# MAUDE COLEMAN

We got off the omnibus at Euston Station and began to wade through the crowds of people already gathered on the pavement. Women were pouring out of the station, having ridden down on special trains from the north. Lavinia and I each grabbed one of Ivy May's hands and held tight as we were pushed and shoved among a sea of accents from Birmingham and Manchester and Lancashire.

Mummy moved quickly through the crowds – the crush did not seem to bother her, which surprised me given how much she hates being confined. When we got to the road in front of St Pancras Station, she began scanning the faces of women in white dresses who had gathered in the road with their banners. 'Ah, there they are!' she cried, and pushed through the crowd on the pavement to get onto the road itself.

There I breathed more freely, for there was more room. It was strange to stand in the middle of such a big road and have no coaches or carts or cabs to dodge – just a long line of women in white dresses stretched ahead and behind, with men and women on the pavement watching us.

Mummy led us over to a group of women, many of

whom I recognised from her At Homes. 'Here they are, Eunice,' Mummy said, laying her hand on the arm of a tall woman with a face full of freckles who wore a sash that read BANNER CAPTAIN. 'And there's Caroline!' Mummy cried, waving. 'Caroline!'

Caroline Black hurried over, flushed, her hair coming down from under her hat. Over her shoulder she carried a large bundle tied to a pole. Mummy kissed her. 'Have you got everything?'

'Yes, I think so,' panted Caroline Black, 'though thank heavens I gave the boy the armour yesterday to bring down. I'd never have made it otherwise.'

I did not know what they were talking about, but before I could ask, Mummy turned to me. 'Now, Maude, I'm going to leave you with Eunice, who will look after you.'

'But you're marching too, aren't you?' I asked, trying to keep the panic out of my voice. 'You're marching with us.'

'I will be in the procession, yes, but I've got something to do in another part of it. You'll be fine here – you know most of these women.'

'Where are you going? What are you doing?'

'It's a surprise.'

'But we thought we were going to be with you. We told Mrs Waterhouse you were looking after us.'

Mummy shook her head impatiently. 'What I have to do is far more important than looking after you. And frankly, Eunice is probably better at sorting you out than I would be. She's Banner Captain for this section of the procession and is very capable. You're in good hands with her. I'll meet you at the end of the day, after the Great Shout at five o'clock. Come to Platform 5, where Mrs Pankhurst is speaking. I'll see you there. Now, we really must be off. Have fun, girls! Remember, Maude, Platform 5 after the Great Shout.' She took Caroline Black's arm and rushed away into the crowd. I tried to keep my eyes on them but couldn't — it was like following the progress of a twig through a fast-flowing stream.

Lavinia had turned pale. 'What shall we do without her?' she moaned, which was rather hypocritical given how much she dislikes Mummy.

'Well, girls, we'll have a grand day, eh?' Eunice cried as she helped two women next to us secure their banner that read HOPE IS STRONG. 'I've got to check the other banners along my section. You stay here by this banner until I return.' She strode away before we could say anything.

'Bloody hell,' I said quietly. We had been abandoned.

Lavinia looked at me, shocked as much by my swearing as by our predicament, I expect. 'Perhaps Mama was right,' she said. 'Perhaps I should have stayed home. I'm feeling rather faint.'

'Stop it,' I said sharply. 'We'll manage.' It was going to be a grim afternoon, and worse if she fainted as well. I looked around for something to distract her. 'Look at the band — the Hackney Borough Brass Band,' I read from their banner. 'Aren't their uniforms lovely?' I knew Lavinia preferred men in uniforms. She was already saying she planned to marry a soldier. The musicians were smirking at the surrounding women. A euphonium player winked at me before I could look away.

Lavinia was staring up at the banner we were meant to stay with. 'Rope is thong,' she announced suddenly, and giggled.

'What did you say?'

'Nothing, nothing.'

After a bit we began to feel better. The women around us were all talking and laughing, clearly excited to be there. The overall effect was of a great buzz of female sound, at times high-pitched, loud but not frightening as it might be if it were all men. It was hard not to be infected by the high spirits. And they did not all appear to be suffragettes. Many of them were just like us, there for the afternoon out of curiosity, not necessarily waving a banner and shouting. There were lots of women with their daughters, some of them quite young. There were even three little girls, all dressed in white with green and purple ribbons in their hair, sitting in a pony-cart near us.

Lavinia squeezed my arm and said, 'It is terribly exciting, isn't it? Everyone is here!'

Except Mummy, I thought. I wondered what she and Caroline Black were doing.

Then the band, led by a man with a handlebar moustache, began to play a march from *Aida* and everyone stood up straighter, as if a wire had been pulled taut all up and down the procession. An expectant hum rose from the crowd. Eunice reappeared suddenly and called out, 'Right, then, banners up!' Women around her raised their poles and fitted them into the holders at their sides; then others who saw those banners go up lifted theirs, until as far ahead and behind as I could see there were banners sailing above a sea of heads. For the first time I wished I too was carrying a banner.

The hum died down after a few minutes when we hadn't moved.

'Aren't we ever going to start?' Lavinia cried, hopping from foot to foot. 'Oh, I can't bear it if we don't go soon!'

Then, suddenly, we did. The banners ahead jerked and a space opened up in front of us.

'Onward!' Eunice cried. 'Come, now, girls!'

As we began to walk, the spectators on the pavement cheered and I felt tingles up and down my back. There were six other processions beside ours, coming from points all around London, bringing marchers towards Hyde Park. It was terribly thrilling to feel a part of a larger whole, of thousands and thousands of women all doing the same thing at the same time.

It took some time for the procession to assume a steady pace. We kept stopping and starting, making our way past St Pancras, then Euston Station. On both sides, men watched us pass, some frowning, a few jeering, but most smiling the way my uncle does when he thinks I've said something silly. The women on the sidelines were more supportive, smiling and waving. A few even stepped in to join the marchers.

At first Lavinia was very excited, humming along with the band, laughing as a banner ahead of us caught a breeze and started to flap. But once we began walking more steadily, when we had passed Euston and were heading towards Great Portland Station, she sighed and dragged her feet. 'Is this all we're going to do? Walk?' she complained.

'There will be speeches at Hyde Park. It's not so far. And we'll be going along Oxford Street and you can see the shops.' I said this with authority, but I didn't really know where the route would take us. My London geography was shaky – I had not been into town very often, and then I simply followed Mummy or Daddy. I knew the principal rivers of Africa better than the streets of London.

'There's Simon.' Ivy May pointed.

It was a relief to see a familiar face among the mass of strangers. 'Simon!' Lavinia and I called at the same time.

When he saw us his face lit up and he stepped out of the crowd to fall in beside us.

'What are you doing here, naughty boy?' Lavinia asked, squeezing his arm.

Simon turned red. 'Came to find you.'

'Are you going to march with us?' I asked.

Simon looked around. 'There ain't no men, is there?'

'The bands are all men. Stay with us.'

'Well, maybe for a little bit. But I has to go and get the horse at Hyde Park.'

'What horse?'

Simon looked surprised. 'The horse for the ladies. For your ma. Didn't she tell you?'

'Mummy doesn't have a horse. She hates horses.'

'It's a friend of Mr Jackson what has the horse. They're just borrowing it for the day.'

'Mr Jackson? What does he have to do with it?'

Simon looked like he'd rather not have said anything. 'Your ma asked Mr Jackson if he knew anyone could lend her a horse. A white horse, it had to be. And he has a friend has one, up off Baker Street. So he lent it to her, and asked me to fetch it and bring it back. Paid me and all.'

The band began to play the Pirate King song from *The Pirates of Penzance*. I was trying to take in what Simon was saying, but it was difficult to think in the middle of so many people and so much noise. 'Mummy never goes to the cemetery. How could she see Mr Jackson?'

Simon shrugged. 'He visited her at Holloway. And I heard 'em talking at the cemetery not long ago – about the suffragism and that.'

'She's not riding the horse, is she? Where exactly is she?'

Simon shrugged again. 'See for yourself. They're at the start of the procession.'

'Is it far?'

'I'll show you.' Simon immediately plunged back into the crowd on the pavement, probably relieved to leave the procession of women.

I began to follow but Lavinia grabbed my arm. 'What about me?' she cried.

'Stay here. I'll come back to you.'

'But you can't leave me alone!'

'You're not alone – you're with Ivy May. Stay with the banner,' I added, gesturing at HOPE IS STRONG. 'I'll come back to you. And Eunice is bound to return soon. Tell her I've gone to look at the banners. Don't say I've gone to see Mummy.'

'We're coming with you!' Lavinia cried, but I wrenched my arm away and pushed into the crowd before she could follow. Whatever Mummy was doing, I didn't want Lavinia to see it.

# SIMON FIELD

All I can say is, Mrs C. weren't wearing that when I handed over the horse to her earlier. Must've had it on under her dress.

I'm surprised but try not to show it. Can't take my eyes from her legs. I only seen a woman's legs like that once at a panto of Dick Whittington, and even then she wore tights and the tunic came to her knees. Mrs C. ain't dressed as Dick, though, but as Robin Hood. She wears a short green tunic belted in the middle, little green boots, and a green and purple cap with a white feather in it. She's got bare legs, from her ankles up to – well, up high.

She's leading the white horse what Miss Black's riding. You'd think Miss Black'd be dressed as Maid Marian or Friar Tuck or some such, but instead she's got on a full suit of armour and a silver helmet with a white feather in it that bobs up and down in time with the horse, just like the ostrich feathers on the horses in a funeral procession. She holds the reins in one hand and a flag in the other with words on it I can't read.

Maude just stares. Who can blame her – everyone's staring at Kitty Coleman's legs. I has to say – they're fine legs. I'm bright red looking at 'em, and go hard, right among all them people. Has to cross my hands in front of me to hide it.

'Who's Miss Black meant to be?' I ask, to distract myself.

'Joan of Arc.' Maude says it like she's spitting the words.

I never heard of this Joan, but I don't tell Maude. I know she don't want to talk.

We've been standing on the pavement a bit ahead of 'em, so we can watch 'em approach. As they pass by Maude looks like she wants to say something to her ma, but she don't. Mrs C. ain't looking at her – she has a funny smile on her face and seems to be looking way ahead, like she sees something on the horizon she can't wait to get to.

Then they're past. Maude don't say nothing, and neither do I. We just watch the procession go by. Then Maude snorts.

'What?' I say.

'Caroline Black's banner has a mistake on it,' she says, but she won't tell me what it is.

# KITTY COLEMAN

For most of the march I felt as if I were walking through a dream.

I was so excited that I hardly heard a thing. The buzz of spectators, the jangling and creaking of the bridle, the clanking of Caroline's armour — they were all there, but distant. The horse's hooves sounded as if they were muffled by blankets, or as if sawdust had been strewn along the route, as it sometimes is for funerals.

Nor could I really see anything. I tried to focus on faces along the route but they were all a blur. I kept thinking I saw people I knew — Richard, John Jackson, Maude, even my dead mother — but they were just resemblances. It was easier to look ahead towards our destination, whatever that would be.

What I did feel sharply was the sun and air on my legs. After a lifetime of heavy dresses, with their swathes of cloth wrapping my legs like bandages, it was an incredible sensation.

Then I heard a bang that was not muffled. I looked into the crowd, suddenly able to see, and there was someone who looked like my late brother on the pavement opposite me. He was staring at Caroline with such a perplexed expression that I couldn't help but step across to see what he was looking at.

There was another bang. Just before the horse reared I saw Caroline's banner – it read WORDS NOT DEEDS.

Blast, I thought, who made such a silly mistake? Then the hoof came down on my chest.

# LAVINIA WATERHOUSE

At first I would not speak to Maude when she and Simon came back — not all the way down Portland Place or Upper Regent Street, nor when we were stopped for a time along Oxford Street. I could not forgive her for leaving me like that.

She did not speak either, just marched with a face like thunder, and did not seem to notice that I had sent her to Coventry. There is nothing more annoying than someone not realising you are punishing them. Indeed it rather felt as if it were me being punished — I was immensely curious about Maude's mother and the horse but since I was not speaking to her I could not ask about it. I wished Ivy May would talk to me, to make my silence with Maude all the more pointed. I straightened her hat for her, as it was tilted dangerously far back, but Ivy May simply nodded at me in thanks. She was not in the habit of saying things when one wanted her to.

Then the procession halted again. Simon ran off to collect his horse, and we moved towards the Marble Arch entrance to Hyde Park. We were pressed closer and closer together, as many of the people on the pavement squeezed into the crowd to enter as well. It was like being a grain of sand in an hourglass, waiting our turn to funnel through the tiny hole. It grew so crowded that I grabbed Maude and Ivy May's hands.

Then we were through, and suddenly there was open space, sunny and green and full of fresh air. I gulped at it as if it were water.

A great sea of people had gathered in the distance around various carts where handfuls of suffragettes perched. In their white dresses and all piled up above the crowd they reminded me of puffy clouds on the horizon.

'Move along, move along,' called a woman behind us who wore a sash reading CHIEF MARSHALL. 'There's thousands more behind you, waiting to get in. Move along to the platforms, please, keeping in formation.'

The procession was meant to continue all the way to the platforms, but once inside the park everyone began rushing to and fro, and we lost all order. Men who had been spectators along the route were now mingling with all the ladies who had marched, and as we moved willy-nilly towards the platforms it became more crowded again, with them pushing in on us. Mama would be horrified if she could see us, unchaperoned, caught among all these men. I saw that silly Eunice for a moment, shouting at someone to bring her banner around. She was hopeless at looking after us.

There were banners everywhere. I kept looking for one I had sewn but there were so many that my mistakes were lost among them. I had not imagined that so many people could gather in one place at one time. It was frightening but thrilling as well, like when a tiger at the zoo stares straight at you with its yellow eyes.

'Do you see Platform 5?' Maude asked.

I couldn't see numbers anywhere, but Ivy May pointed to a platform, and we began to make our way over. Maude kept pulling me into walls of people, and I had to grip Ivy May's hand harder, as it was growing sweaty.

'Let's not go any further,' I called to Maude. 'It's so crowded.'

'Just a little bit – I'm looking for Mummy.' Maude kept pulling my hand.

Suddenly there were too many people. The little spaces we had managed to push into became a solid wall of legs and backs. People pressed up behind us, and I could feel strangers pushing at my arms and shoulders.

Then I felt a hand on my bottom, the fingers brushing me gently. I was so surprised that I did nothing for a moment. The hand pulled up my dress and began fumbling with my bloomers, right there in the middle of all those people. I couldn't believe no one noticed.

When I tried to shift away, the hand followed. I looked back – the man standing behind me was about Papa's age, tall, grey-haired, with a thin moustache and spectacles. His eyes were fixed on the platform. I could not believe it was his hand – he looked so respectable. I raised my heel and brought it down hard on the foot behind me. The man winced and the hand disappeared. After a moment he pushed away and was gone, someone else stepping into his place.

I shuddered and whispered to Maude, 'Let's get away from here,' but I was drowned out by a bugle call. The crowd surged forward and Maude was pushed into the back of the woman ahead of her, dropping my hand. Then I was shoved violently to the left. I looked around but couldn't see Maude.

'If I may have your attention, I would like to open this

meeting on this most momentous occasion in Hyde Park,'
I heard a voice ring out. A woman had climbed onto a box
higher than the rest of the women on the platform. In her
mauve dress she looked like lavender sprinkled on a bowl
of vanilla ice cream. She stood very straight and still.

'There's Mrs Pankhurst,' women around me murmured.

'I am delighted to see before me a great multitude of
people, of supporters – both women *and* men – of the simple
right of women to take their places alongside men and cast
their ballots. Prime Minister Asquith has said that he needs
to be assured that the will of the people is behind the call
for votes for women. Well, Mr Asquith, I say to you that if
you were standing where I am now and saw the great sea
of humanity before you as I do, you would need no more
convincing!'

The crowd roared. I put my hands on the shoulders of
the woman beside me and jumped up to try and see over
the crowd. 'Maude!' I called, but it was so noisy she would
never have heard me. The woman scowled and shrugged
off my hands.

Mrs Pankhurst was waiting for the sound to die down.
'We have a full afternoon of speakers,' she began as it grew
quiet, 'and without further ado –'

'Maude! Maude!' I cried.

Mrs Pankhurst paused, and jerked her head slightly. 'I
would like to introduce –'

'Maude!'

'Lavinia!' I heard, and saw a hand fluttering above the
crowd far to my right. I waved back and kept waving as I
began to push towards the hand.

Mrs Pankhurst had stopped again. 'Shh! Shh!' women on

the platform began to hiss. I continued to push, forcing spaces to open in front of me, ignoring whatever was happening on the platform. Then ahead of me I saw the garland of delphiniums and star jasmine I had woven that morning for Maude's straw hat, and with one last shove I had found her.

We held onto each other tightly. Maude's heart was beating hard, and I was trembling.

'Let's get away from all these people,' Maude whispered. I nodded and, still holding tight to Maude, let her push away from the platform and out of the jam of people listening to Mrs Pankhurst.

At last there was space again. When we reached the trees on the far edge of the crowd I stopped. 'I'm going to be sick,' I said.

Maude led me to a tree, where I could kneel away from everyone. Afterwards we found a shady spot to sit a little away from the base of the tree. We didn't say anything for a few minutes, but watched people stroll or hurry past, detaching themselves from one wheel of spectators around a platform, joining another. We could see four platforms from where we sat. In the distance the women speaking on them were tiny figures whose arms moved about like windmills.

I was very thirsty.

Maude would speak eventually, I knew, and ask the question that must be asked. I dreaded it.

'Lavinia,' she said at last, 'where is Ivy May?'

For the first time all day I began to cry. 'I don't know.'

# MAUDE COLEMAN

Mummy was sitting just two trees away. We didn't discover that until after the meeting had ended.

There was no point in searching for anyone while the speeches were being made and the crowd so tightly packed in. Lavinia was in despair, but I knew that Ivy May was a sensible girl – she might say little, but she heard everything, and she would know that we were to meet Mummy at Platform 5 after the Great Shout, whatever that was.

That is what I kept telling myself, and repeating to Lavinia, whenever she would listen. Eventually she laid her head in my lap and fell asleep, which is just like her in a dramatic moment. It is melodrama that she loves – to her true drama is dull. I fidgeted, waiting for the speeches to finish and for Lavinia to wake.

At last a bugle sounded. When it sounded a second time, Lavinia sat up, her face red and crumpled. 'What time is it?' she said, yawning.

'I'm not sure. Close to five o'clock, I expect.'

The distant crowds were waving their arms and cheering. The bugle sounded once more. A chant rose up like an orchestra swelling to a crescendo in a symphony. It sounded as if everyone were saying, 'Folks are swimming'. Only the third time did I realise they were calling, 'Votes for women!' The last one was loud like a thunderclap, and the cheers and laughter that followed like rain released from clouds.

Then, suddenly, the crowd broke up and a surge of people moved towards us. I scanned the passing faces for someone familiar. I did spy Eunice, who rushed past with a stray banner and pole. She did not see us and we did not try to stop her.

'We should go to Platform 5,' I said. 'Someone is bound to be there.'

We linked arms and began to wade through the crowd, but it was very difficult as everyone was moving away from the platform rather than towards it. Everywhere there were exhausted faces – thirsty children, impatient women, concerned men wondering how they would get home through such crowds. Now that people were not marching in organised processions, the streets outside Hyde Park would be in chaos, jammed with people and cabs and overfull omnibuses. It would take hours to get home.

Finally we drew close to what I remembered as Platform 5, but the banner with the Number 5 on it had been taken down. Mrs Pankhurst and the other women had climbed down from the cart, and a man was hitching a horse up to it.

'They're taking away the platform!' I cried. 'How will we ever find Mummy without it?'

'There's Caroline Black,' Lavinia said, pulling at my sleeve. 'What on earth is she wearing?'

Caroline Black was hopping from foot to foot, still in her Joan of Arc armour. The white plume in her helmet bobbed up and down as she moved. She looked very grim, and my stomach turned over to see her alone.

'There you are!' she cried, not smiling sweetly at me as she usually did. 'Where have you been? I've been looking for you for ages!'

'Where's Mummy?' I demanded.

Caroline Black looked as if she might cry. 'Your mother – she's had a little mishap.'

'What happened?'

'It all went so well, that's the shame of it.' Caroline Black shook her head. 'We had a marvellous time, with such support from our comrades and the spectators. And the horse was lovely, so gentle and a dream to ride. If only –'

'What happened? Where is she?' It was all I could do not to shriek the words.

'Someone let off firecrackers in the crowd along Oxford Street. The horse shied, and at that moment Kitty stepped in front of it to look at my banner – I don't know why. The horse reared – I just barely kept my own seat. When it came down it kicked her in the chest.'

'Where is she now?'

'The daft thing insisted on finishing the march, leading the horse and all, as if nothing had happened. She said she was fine, just a bit breathless. And I stupidly allowed her. Then she wouldn't leave during the speeches – she said she had to be here to find you afterwards.'

'Where in God's name is she?' I cried. Lavinia jumped at my tone and people around us stared. But Caroline Black didn't even flinch.

'She's sitting over in the trees.' She pointed back the way we had come.

Lavinia grabbed my arm as I began to walk towards the trees. 'What about Ivy May?' she cried. 'We must find her!'

'Let's get to Mummy and then we'll look for her.' I knew Lavinia was angry at me but I ignored her and kept going.

Mummy was propped up against the trunk of the tree, one leg folded under her, a bare leg stretched out in front.

'Oh my Lord,' Lavinia murmured. I had forgot that she hadn't seen Mummy in her costume.

Mummy smiled as we came up, but her face was tense, as if she were struggling to hide something. Her breathing was laboured. 'Hello, Maude,' she said. 'Did you enjoy the procession?'

'How do you feel, Mummy?'

Mummy patted her chest. 'Hurts.'

'We must get you home, my dear,' Caroline Black said. 'Can you walk?'

'She mustn't walk,' I interrupted, remembering my first aid lessons from school. 'That may make it worse.'

'Going to be a doctor, are you?' Mummy said. 'That's good. I thought you might become an astronomer, but I've been known to be wrong. As long as you become something, I don't mind what it is. Except perhaps a wife. But don't tell Daddy that.' She winced as she took a breath. 'Go to university.'

'Hush, Mummy. Don't talk.'

I looked around. Caroline Black and Lavinia were watching me as if I were in charge.

Then I saw a familiar figure striding towards us.

'Thank heaven you're here, Mr Jackson!' Lavinia cried, grabbing his arm. 'Can you find Ivy May for us?'

'No,' I interrupted. 'You must get Mummy to a cab. She needs a doctor quickly.'

Mr Jackson looked at Mummy. 'What has happened, Kitty?'

'She's been kicked by a horse and can't breathe,' I said.

'Hello, John,' Mummy murmured. 'This is what happens, you see – I dress up as Robin Hood and get kicked by the pantomime horse.'

'Ivy May is lost, Mr Jackson!' Lavinia shouted. 'My little sister has been lost in that horrid crowd!'

Mr Jackson looked from Mummy to Lavinia. I knew he could not make the decision himself – I would have to do it. 'Mr Jackson, go and find a cab,' I ordered. 'You're more likely to get one than me or Lavinia, and you can carry Mummy to it. Caroline, you wait here with Mummy, and Lavinia and I will look for Ivy May.'

'No!' Lavinia cried, but Mr Jackson had already run off.

Mummy nodded. 'That's right, Maude. You're perfectly capable of taking charge.' She remained against the tree, with Caroline Black kneeling awkwardly beside her in her armour.

I took Lavinia's hand. 'We'll find her,' I said. 'I promise.'

# LAVINIA WATERHOUSE

We did not find her. We searched everywhere, but we did not find her.

We walked back and forth across the park where the crowds had stood, the grass all trampled as if a herd of cattle had passed through. There were many fewer people now, so it should have been easy to see a little girl on her own. But there were none. Instead there were groups of young men roving about. They made me very nervous, especially when they called out to us. Maude and I linked arms tightly as we walked.

It was so frustrating — we could not find any policemen, nor even any of the suffragettes who had been running about during the procession wearing sashes that read BANNER CAPTAIN or CHIEF MARSHALL. Not one responsible grown-up was about to help.

Then a group of very rough men shouted, 'Ahoy there, girls! Fancy a drink?' and came towards us. Well. Maude and I fairly ran our legs off to get out of the park. The men didn't follow, but I refused to go back in — it was far too dangerous. We stood at the Marble Arch entrance and looked out across the grass, shielding our eyes from the early evening sun.

I was looking not just for Ivy May, but for Simon as well. We had not seen him since he left the procession to go and collect the horse (led by Maude's mother in that costume! I am speechless. It was no wonder that the horse kicked her). He had said he might come back to the park after. I kept thinking as I looked that they would be together — that Simon would appear, leading Ivy May by the hand. They would be eating ice-creams and they would have them for Maude and me as well. Ivy May would give me a cheeky look, with a little smile and glittering eyes, and I would pinch her for frightening me so.

'She's not here,' Maude said. 'We would have seen her by now. Perhaps she's gone home. She may have retraced the route we took, back to Euston and got on an omnibus. She's not stupid, Ivy May.'

I held up the little purse that dangled from my wrist. 'She had no money for the bus,' I whispered. 'I made her give it to me for safekeeping, so she wouldn't lose it.'

'She may have found her way back,' Maude repeated. 'Perhaps we should walk along the procession route and look for her.'

'I'm so very tired. I don't think I could take another step. Let's stay here just a little longer.'

Then we did see him coming towards us. He looked so small in that great grass expanse, with his hands at his sides, kicking at things that had been left behind — bits of paper, flowers, a lady's glove. He seemed unsurprised to see us, and unsurprised when Maude said, 'Ivy May is missing'.

'Ivy May's gone,' I said. 'She's gone.' I began to cry.

'She's missing,' Maude repeated.

Simon gazed as us. I had never seen him look so grave.

'We think she may have gone along the route we marched,' Maude said. 'Come with us to look.'

'What were she wearing?' Simon asked. 'I didn't notice before.'

Maude sighed. 'A white dress. A white dress like everyone else. And a straw hat with flowers around the brim, like ours.'

Simon fell in beside us and we began walking back down Oxford Street. This time we could not walk down the middle of the street, for it was full of horse-drawn cabs and omnibuses and motor-cars. We stayed on the pavement, crowded with people walking back from the demonstration. Simon crossed over to search the other pavement, looking in doorways and down alleys as well as scanning the faces around him.

I could not quite believe we were going to have to walk the whole route again – I was so thirsty and footsore that I did not think I could manage it. But then, as we were going along Upper Regent Street, I saw down a mews a pump for watering horses, and went up and put my whole face under the stream of water that gushed out. I didn't care if the water was bad or my hair got wet – I was so thirsty I had to drink.

The bell in the clock tower of St Pancras Station was striking eight when at last we arrived back at our starting point.

'Mama will be frantic with worry,' I said. As tired as I was, I dreaded arriving home to face Mama and Papa.

'It's still so light out,' Maude said. 'It's the longest day of the year – did you know that? Well, second longest, perhaps, after yesterday.'

'Oh, for pity's sake shush, Maude.' I could not bear to hear her talk like a teacher in a classroom. Besides which, I had a fearsome headache.

'We'd best go home,' Maude said, ignoring me. 'Then we can tell your parents and they can contact the police. And I can find out about Mummy.'

'Your mother,' I began. Suddenly I was so angry I wanted to spit. Maude had sent Mr Jackson off with her mother rather than have him help us. He would have found Ivy May, I was sure of it. 'Your bloody mother got us into this mess.'

'Don't blame her!' Maude cried. 'It was you who wanted so badly to come on the march!'

'Your mother,' I repeated. 'You don't know the half of it about her.'

'Don't, Livy,' Simon warned. 'Don't you dare.'

Maude looked between us. 'I don't want to hear it, whatever it is,' she said to me. 'Don't you ever say a word of it to me.'

'Go home, both of you!' Simon said. I'd never heard him raise his voice before. 'There's an omnibus there.' He even pushed us towards it.

'We can't leave Ivy May,' I declared, stopping in my tracks. 'We can't just jump on a bus and leave her at the mercy of this awful city.'

'I'll go back and look for her,' Simon said.

For that I could have kissed him, but he was already off at a run, back down along the Euston Road.

# JENNY WHITBY

Never did I expect to see such a sight.

I didn't know who it could be, ringing the bell on a Sunday evening. I'd just returned from Mum's, didn't even have my cap and apron on yet. I weren't even there normally – I usually came back later, after Jack was asleep, but today he were so tired from running about that after tea he just fell into his bed.

Maybe it were the missus and Miss Maude, had their key pickpocketed in the crowd. Or a neighbour meaning to borrow a stamp or run out of lamp oil. But when I opened the door, it were the man from the cemetery, carrying the missus in his arms. Not only that – she weren't wearing a proper skirt! Her legs were bare as the day she was born. Her eyes were just open, like she'd been woke up from a nap.

Before I could say a word but stare with my eyes popping, Mr Jackson had pushed inside, with that suffragette lady Miss Black fluttering behind him. 'We must get her to her bed,' he said. 'Where is her husband?'

'At the Bull and Last,' I said. 'He always goes there after his cricket.' I led the way upstairs to her room. Miss Black was wearing some sort of metal suit what clanked as she went up the stairs. She looked so strange I began to wonder if I were dreaming it all.

Mr Jackson laid the missus on her bed and said, 'Stay with her – I'll get her husband.'

'And I'll fetch a doctor,' said Miss Black.

'There's one on the Highgate Road, just up from the pub,' I said. 'I can –'

But they were gone before I could offer to go so Miss Black could stay with her friend. It were like she didn't want to stay.

So it were just me and the missus. She lay there staring at me. I couldn't think what to do. I lit a candle and were just about to close the curtains when she whispered, 'Leave them open. And open the window.'

She looked so silly in her green outfit, her legs all naked. Mr Coleman would have a fit if he saw her like that. After I opened the window I sat on the bed and began to take off her little green boots.

'Jenny, I want to ask you something,' she said real quiet.

'Yes, ma'am.'

'Does anyone know about what happened to me?'

'About what happened to you, ma'am?' I repeated. 'You've had a little accident, is all.'

The missus' eyes flared and she shook her head. 'Jenny, there is no time for this silliness. For once let us be clear with each other – does anyone know what happened to me two years ago?'

I knew what she were talking about the first time, even though I acted like I didn't. I set the boots on the floor. 'No one knows but me. And Mrs Baker – she guessed. Oh, and Simon.'

'The cemetery boy? How could he know?'

'It were his mum you went to.'

'And that is all – no one else knows?'

I didn't look in her eyes, but tugged at the green cap in her hair. 'No.' I didn't say anything about Miss Livy's letter. There seemed no point in agitating her in her state. Simon and Mrs Baker and me, we could keep our counsel, but there was no guessing what Miss Livy might say one of these days – or said already, like as not. But the missus needn't know that.

'I don't want the men to find out.'

'No.' I reached round and began to unbutton the back of her tunic.

'Promise me they won't.'

'They won't.'

'Promise me something else.'

'Yes, ma'am.'

'Promise me you won't let my mother-in-law get her claws into Maude.'

I pulled off the tunic and gasped. Her chest was one big black bruise. 'Lord, what happened to you, ma'am?'

'Promise me.'

Now I understood why she was talking like that. 'Oh, ma'am, you're going to be just fine in a day or two. The doctor will be here soon and he'll sort you out. Miss Black's gone to fetch him. And Mr – the gentleman's gone to get your husband.' The missus tried to say something, but I wouldn't let her – I just ran on and on, saying whatever popped into my head. 'He's down the pub just now, but it won't take him a minute to get back. Let's just get this nightgown on before they come, shall we? It's ever so pretty,

319

this one, what with the lace at the cuffs and all. Let's just pop this over your head and pull it down. There. And your hair, that's it. That's better now, ain't it?'

She lay back again, like she were too weak to fight my words. Her breathing were all wet and ragged. I couldn't bear to hear it. 'I'll just run and light the lamps,' I said. 'For the master and doctor. Won't be a second.' I ran out before she could say anything.

Mr Coleman came home as I was lighting the lamps in the front hallway, and then the doctor and Miss Black. They went upstairs, and then it went all quiet up there. I couldn't help it – I had to go and listen outside the door.

The doctor had such a low voice that all I could hear was 'internal bleeding.'

Then Mr Coleman laid into Miss Black. 'Why in hell didn't you find a doctor the moment the horse kicked her?' he shouted. 'You were boasting there would be a huge crowd – surely among 200,000 people there was a doctor!'

'You don't understand,' Caroline Black said. 'It was so crowded it was difficult to move or even speak, much less find a doctor.'

'Why didn't you bring her home at once? If you had shown any sense whatsoever she might be all right now, with nothing more than a few bruises.'

'Don't you think I didn't beg her to? You clearly don't know your wife well if you think she would have done what I asked her to. She wanted to get to Hyde Park and hear the speeches on such an historic occasion, and nothing I nor anyone else – not even you, sir – said could have dissuaded her.'

'Hyperbole!' Mr Coleman shouted. 'Even at a time like

this you suffragettes resort to hyperbole. Damn your historic occasion! Did you even look at her chest after it happened? Did you even see the damage? And who on God's green earth told Kitty to lead a horse? She's a disaster around horses!'

'It was her idea. No one forced her. She never told me she didn't like horses.'

'And where's Maude?' Mr Coleman said. 'What's happened to my daughter?'

'She's – she's on her way home, I'm sure.' Caroline Black was crying now.

I didn't stay to hear more. I went down to the kitchen and put the kettle on. Then I sat at the table and began to cry myself.

# IVY MAY WATERHOUSE

Over his shoulder I saw a star fall. It was me.

# SIMON FIELD

I never seen a dead body before. That sounds strange coming
from a gravedigger. All day long I got dead bodies round
me, but they're in boxes, nailed shut tight and covered with
dirt. Sometimes I'm standing on a coffin in a grave, and
there's only an inch of wood 'tween me and the body. But
I ain't seen it. If I spent more time out of the cemetery I'd
see dead bodies all the time. Funny, that. Our Ma and sisters
has seen hundreds, all them women and babies died in birth,
or neighbours, died of hunger or the cold.

It's strange seeing someone I know like that. If I
didn't know to be looking for her I wouldn't recognise her.
It's not that she's cut or crushed or anything like that. It's
just that she ain't there. There are the legs, arms, head, all
in the right places, lying down the back of a mews behind
a stack of bricks. And the face is clean and smooth even,
the mouth shut, her eyes a little open like she's looking
through her lashes and don't want you to know she's
looking. But when I look at the face I just can't see her.
She ain't a person no more, but a thing like a sack of
spuds.

'Ivy May,' I call softly, squatting beside her. I say it even though I know she's dead. Maybe I'm hoping she'll come back if I say her name.

But she don't. She don't open her eyes and look at me with that look she has of knowing everything what's happening and never saying. She don't sit up with her legs straight out in front of her the ways she likes to sit. She don't stand solid, looking like you could never knock her down, as hard as you pushed.

The body just lays there. And I have to get it back somehow, from a mews off the Edgware Road to Dartmouth Park.

How am I going to get her all that way without someone seeing me? I wonder. Anyone sees me will think I did it.

Then I look up at the end of the mews and see a man standing there. A tall man. Can't see much of his face 'cept the glint of his specs in the streetlamp and a thin moustache. He's staring at me, and when he sees me looking at him he steps back behind the building.

Could be he thinks I've done it and he's off to tell someone. But I know he's not. It's him what done it. Our Pa says men can't leave their crimes alone — they got to come sniffing round again, like worrying a loose tooth or picking a scab.

I run out the mews to look for him, but he's gone. I know he'll come back again, though, and if I don't take her now he will.

I straighten out her dress a bit, and her hair, and I buckle on one of her shoes what'd come off. When I lift her onto my back I see her straw hat's been under her. It's all broken, and the flowers crushed, and too much trouble to pick it up with Ivy May heavy on my back, so I leave it on the ground.

If anyone asks, I'll say she's my sister and fallen asleep. But I stay away from the pubs and keep to the little streets and then the parks, Regents then Primmers Hill then the bottom of the Heath, and I don't see many folk. And none ask. That time of night the people out are too drunk to notice, or else up to their own mischief and don't want to draw attention to themselves.

All the way home I keep thinking 'bout that hat. I wish I hadn't left it. I don't like leaving any part of her there. So when it's over, when I've got her home, I go back, all the way through the parks and the streets. It takes no time, not without her weight on my back. But when I get to the mews and look behind the bricks the hat is already gone, flowers and all.

# MAUDE COLEMAN

I waited on the wrought-iron steps that led from the French doors down into the garden. The air smelled of jasmine and mint and grass sprinkled with dew. I could hear frogs croaking in the pond at the bottom of the garden and, from the window below me, Jenny sobbing in the kitchen.

I have never been good at waiting — it always seems so wasteful, and I feel guilty, as if I should be doing something else. But I could not do anything else now — there was nothing to be done. Grandmother had arrived and was sitting in the morning room, knitting furiously, but I did not want to be busy like that. Instead I looked up at the stars, picking out the constellations — the Great Bear, the Crow, the Wolf.

The church bells close by struck midnight.

Daddy came and stood in the open French doors and lit a cigarette. I did not look at him.

'It's a clear night,' he said.

'Yes.'

'Pity we can't set up the telescope in the garden — we might even see Jupiter's moons. But of course it wouldn't be right, would it?'

I did not answer, though I'd had the same thought myself.

'I'm sorry I shouted at you when you arrived home, Maude. I was upset.'

'That's all right.'

'I was afraid I'd lost you too.'

I shifted on the cold metal. 'Don't say that, Daddy.'

He coughed. 'No, you're right.'

Then we heard the scream, long and high-pitched, from the direction of the Waterhouses' house. I shivered.

'What in God's name was that?' Daddy asked.

I shook my head. I had not told him about Ivy May going missing.

A throat cleared behind us. The doctor had come downstairs to get us. Now that the waiting was over I did not want to move from the steps. I did not want to see my mother. I had been waiting for her all my life, and now I preferred to be waiting for her always, if that was the only alternative.

Daddy flicked his cigarette into the garden and turned to follow the doctor. I could hear it sizzling in the dewy grass. After it stopped I went inside too.

Mummy was lying very still, her face pale, her eyes open and unnaturally bright. I sat down next to her. She fixed her eyes on me. I knew she was waiting for me to speak.

I had no idea what to say or do. Lavinia and I had rehearsed such scenes many times when we were play-acting, but none of that seemed right now that I was actually here with Mummy. It felt silly to say something melodramatic, ridiculous to say something banal.

In the end, though, I did resort to the banal. 'The garden smells nice tonight. The jasmine especially.'

Mummy nodded. 'I've always loved jasmine on a summer's night,' she said. Then she closed her eyes.

Was that all we were going to talk about – jasmine? It seemed so. I squeezed her hand tightly and looked hard at her face, as if that would help me to remember it better. I could not bring myself to say goodbye.

The doctor touched my shoulder. 'It's best if you go now, Miss.'

I let go of Mummy's hand, and went downstairs and back out into the garden, wading through the wet grass down to the back fence. The ladder was still there, although Lavinia and I did not meet each other over the fence so much now. I climbed to the top of the wall. The Waterhouses' ladder was not up. I balanced there for a moment, then jumped, landing in the wet grass and smearing my dress. When I got my breath back I walked up the garden to the French doors that led directly into the Waterhouses' back parlour.

The family was arranged in a semicircular tableau that a painter might have set up. Ivy May lay across the chaise longue, hair spread around her face, eyes closed. Lavinia lay at her sister's feet, her head resting on the edge of the chaise longue. Mrs Waterhouse sat in an armchair near Ivy May's head, holding her hand. Mr Waterhouse leaned against the mantelpiece, a hand covering his eyes. Simon hovered near the door with his head bowed.

I knew just from looking at them, gathered together yet so separate in their grief, that Ivy May was dead.

I felt as if my heart had been hollowed out, and now my stomach was too.

When I came in they all looked at me. Lavinia jumped up and threw herself into my arms, weeping. I gazed over her shoulder at Mrs Waterhouse. It was as if I were seeing myself mirrored in her face. Her eyes were quite dry, and her expression was of someone who has been struck a blow from which she will not recover.

Because of that, I spoke the words directly to her. 'My mother is dead.'

# KITTY COLEMAN

All her life Maude was a presence at my side, whether she was actually there or not. I pushed her away, yet she remained.

Now I was holding on to her hand and I did not want to let go. It was she who had to let go of me. When she did at last, I knew I was alone, and that it was time for me to depart.

# SIMON FIELD

Next day Mr Jackson went out and shot that white horse through the head.

Later, as our Pa and Joe and me was digging, the police came to take me away for questioning. Our Pa didn't even look surprised. He just shook his head and I knew what he were thinking – I should never have got in with them girls.

The police asked me all kinds of things about what I did that day – not just about looking for Ivy May, or finding her, but about the horse and Kitty Coleman and Mr Jackson. They seemed way off the mark to me, and none too nice about it neither. It were like they wanted to make their lives easy and say I did the crime.

When it sounded like they was ready to accuse me I said, 'Who would be stupid enough to do that to a girl and then bring her home to her parents?'

'You would be surprised what criminals do,' one of the policemen said.

I thought of the tall man with the specs at the end of the mews. But when it came time to describe finding Ivy May I didn't tell 'em about him. Would've been easier on me if I had – given 'em someone else to look for.

But I knew he was long gone – them bumblers would never find him.

I would, though, some day. Find him. For Ivy May.

# JOHN JACKSON

I arranged to meet Miss Coleman at her family grave. I'd considered asking her to come to Faraday, where her mother and I used to meet. But it was a silly, sentimental thought, and risky besides – questions might be asked if we were seen alone in the Dissenters, whereas in the meadow we could be thought to be discussing burial arrangements.

She was dressed all in black, with her hair up under a black straw hat. I had never seen her before with her hair up – she looked several years older. She has no idea but she is beginning to resemble Kitty.

'Thank you for coming, Miss Coleman,' I said as we stood side by side next to the grave. 'I'm so sorry for your loss. It has been a great shock to us all. But your mother is with God now.' I blinked rapidly at the ground. I often express my condolences to mourners at the cemetery, but this time I felt the inadequacy of the words.

'My mother did not believe in heaven,' Maude said. 'You know that.'

I wondered what those last three words were meant to signal. How much did she know about my intimacy with her mother? Her expression was so guarded that it was impossible to guess.

'Simon didn't tell me what you wanted to see me about when he delivered the message,' she said. 'I assume it is to do with my mother's burial, which I thought my father went over with you.'

'He was here yesterday, yes. There was something I wished to discuss with him but did not. I thought that perhaps you and I might do so.'

Maude raised her eyebrows but said nothing.

There was no easy way to say it – no stock expressions or careful euphemisms to smooth the shock of the idea. 'Your mother told me she wished to be cremated rather than interred.'

Maude looked up at the Coleman urn, studying it as if she had never seen it before. 'I know that. She was always worried she might be buried alive.'

'Then perhaps you could tell your father what she told you.'

'Why didn't you tell him yesterday?'

I paused. 'She spoke of it only unofficially – she did not put it in writing or tell her husband. It would not be appropriate for me to tell him.'

Maude pursed her lips. 'Daddy already knows she wanted to be cremated. They used to argue about it. He feels we should do what society dictates concerning the disposal of – of bodies.'

'He won't agree to it even if he knows it was his wife's fervent wish?'

'He'll do what looks best.' Maude paused. 'He lost her, and now he has got her back he will be sure to keep her.'

'What people do with their dead is usually a reflection of themselves rather than of their loved one,' I said. 'Do you think all these urns and angels mean anything to the dead? It takes a very unselfish man to do exactly what his wife wants without his own — or society's — desires and tastes entering into it. I had rather hoped your father was that man.'

'But surely if all these monuments mean nothing to the dead, then nothing we do to them does?' Maude replied. 'If they don't care, shouldn't we then do what is important to us? It's we who are left behind, after all. I've often thought this place is really for the living, not the dead. We design the grave to remind us of the dead, and of what we remember of them.'

'Will the urn on your family grave remind you of your mother — of what she was and what she wanted?'

'No, there is nothing of my mother on it,' Maude admitted. 'If my mother were to choose her own grave it would have a statue of Mrs Pankhurst on it and under her name it would read "Votes for Women".'

I shook my head. 'If your mother were to choose her own grave there would be no monument or words at all. It would be a bed of wildflowers.'

Maude frowned. 'But Mummy is dead, isn't she? She really is dead. She's not going to design her grave.'

She was a remarkable young lady — there are few who could say what she said without flinching.

'And because she's dead,' she continued, 'surely she won't care what happens to her body. She won't be buried alive — we know that. It's we who care — my father most of all. He represents all of us, and he must decide what is best.'

I leaned over and brushed away a spider from the Waterhouse grave. I knew it was not fair of me to make demands on her — after all, she was only thirteen years old and has just lost her mother. But for Kitty's sake I must. 'All I would ask of you, Miss Coleman,' I said gently, 'is that you remind your father of what you know — of what he must already know — of your mother's wishes. It is of course for him to decide what will then be done.'

Maude nodded and turned to go.

'Maude,' I said.

'Yes?'

'There is something else.'

She closed her eyes briefly, then looked at me.

'Your mother's —' I stopped abruptly. I could not tell her — it would be a breach of my professional duties, and I could lose my position for saying anything. But I wanted somehow to warn her. 'It would be best if you spoke to your father sooner rather than later.'

'All right.'

'It is a matter of urgency. Perhaps more than you know.'

'I'll speak to him today.' Maude turned and hurried down the path that led to the entrance.

I stood there for some time, studying the Coleman grave. It was hard to imagine Kitty being buried there. That absurd urn made me want to snort with laughter.

# RICHARD COLEMAN

She came to see me in my study as I was going through papers. I stopped writing. 'What is it, Maude?'

She took a deep breath — she was clearly very nervous. 'Mummy said to me once that she wanted to be cremated and her ashes scattered.'

I looked down at my hands. There was a spot of ink on the cuff of my shirt. 'Your mother said a great many things that have not come to pass. She once said she wanted four children. Do you see any sisters or brothers about? Sometimes what we think and what we do are not meant to be the same.'

'But —'

'That's enough, Maude. There is nothing more to be said on the matter.'

Maude shuddered. I'd spoken more sharply than I'd intended. These days I find it difficult to control my tone.

'I'm sorry, Daddy,' she whispered. 'I was only thinking of Mummy. I didn't mean to upset you.'

'You haven't upset me!' I pressed my pen so hard into

the paper that the nib suddenly cracked. 'Damn!' I threw down the pen.

Maude slipped out without another word.

The sooner this week is over the better.

# LAVINIA WATERHOUSE

Purchased from Jay's in Regent Street, 22$^{nd}$ June 1908:

1. 1 black dress in paramatta silk for me – for the funeral and for Sundays; my old merino dress is for everyday. There was an even lovelier silk dress, with crape all round the neck, but it was too dear.
2. 1 black bombazine dress for Mama. It looks so cheap and shiny that I tried to convince her to buy paramatta instead, but she said we didn't have the money and she would rather I had the silk as it matters more to me. Sweet of her.
3. 1 black cotton petticoat for me, 2 pairs bloomers threaded with black ribbon.
4. 1 black felt hat with veil for me. I insisted on the veil – I look so awful when I've been crying and shall need to pull down the veil often to hide my red eyes and nose. Mama did not buy a hat for herself but said she would dye one of her bonnets. She did at least buy a few ostrich feathers to trim it with.
5. 2 pairs black cotton gloves for Mama and me. They have 4 lovely jet buttons up the cuff. Mama had chosen

plain ones without buttons, but did not notice when I switched them. Also, pair of gloves, a hatband, and black cravat for Papa.

6. 7 black-edged handkerchiefs — 2 for Mama, 5 for me. I wanted many more but Mama would not let me. She has not cried at all, but I insisted she should have a few, just in case she does cry.

7. 200 sheets stationery with medium-band black edging.

8. 100 remembrance cards on order that read as follows:

### IVY MAY WATERHOUSE
#### AGE 10

'A lovely flower, soon snatched away,
To bloom in realms divine;
Thousands will wish, at Judgement Day,
Their lives were short as mine.'

I chose the epitaph, as Mama was overcome in the shop and had to go outside for some air. The shop assistant said the epitaph was meant for a baby, not someone Ivy May's age, but I think it's lovely, especially the phrase 'To bloom in realms divine', and I insisted it remain.

I could have spent all day in Jay's — it is so comforting to be in a shop devoted entirely to what one is experiencing. But Mama refused to linger and became quite short with me. I don't know what to do about her — she is very pale, poor dear, and hardly says a word except to be contrary. Much of the time she remains in her room, lying in bed as if she is ill. She rarely emerges for visitors, and so it has been up to me to see to the entertaining — pouring out cups of tea, asking Elizabeth to bring in more cake and crumpets. So many cousins arrived today that we ran out and I had to send Elizabeth to the baker's for more. I myself cannot eat a thing, except for the odd slice of currant bread, which the King's physician recommends for keeping the strength up.

I have tried to interest Mama in the letters of condolence we have received, but she does not seem to read them. I have had to answer them myself, as I worry that if I leave them with Mama she will simply forget, and it does not do to delay a reply.

People have said the most surprising things about Ivy May – how angelic she was, how she was the perfect daughter and such a support to Mama, how tragic for us and how much she will be missed. Indeed, I sometimes want to write back and ask if they thought it was *I* who died. But instead I make sure simply to sign my name large and clear, so that there will be no doubt.

Mama said to me at breakfast that she does not want me to go back to school, that I can finish the term by studying at home. (Just as well, as I am in no mood to sit in class. I should probably interrupt everything by weeping at the wrong moments.) And that next term I am to switch schools and attend the Sainte Union on the Highgate Road. My heart did a little leap, as the girls there have such smart uniforms. I was surprised, of course, as the school is Catholic, but perhaps I shouldn't be – Mama asked for the priest from St Joseph's in Highgate to come and see her last night. Papa said not a word. If reverting to Catholicism is a comfort to her, what is one to say?

Papa has been kept very busy with the arrangements, and that is good, I think. I helped him when I could, as Mama is unable. When the undertaker came to see us it was I who chose the dress Ivy May is to wear (white cotton with puffed sleeves that used to be mine) and the flowers (lilies) and what to do with her hair (loose curls and a crown woven of white roses). Papa answered the other questions about the coffin and horses and such. He also met with the cemetery people and the vicar, and with the police.

The latter gave me rather a shock, as Papa brought a policeman home to question me! He was nice enough, but asked me so many questions about that awful afternoon in Hyde Park that I began to be confused about exactly when Ivy May went missing. I tried to be brave but I'm afraid I went through all the handkerchiefs we had just bought. Luckily Mama was upstairs and so did not have to hear the details. Papa had tears in his eyes by the time I finished.

The policeman kept asking me about the men in the crowd. He even asked about Simon, as if Simon were someone to be suspicious of! I put him straight there. And I told him about the men who chased Maude and me at the demonstration, and how frightened we were.

I did not tell him about the man who put his hand on my bottom. I knew that I should have, that it was just the thing he was looking for. But I was embarrassed to have to speak of it. And I could not bear to think that that man got hold of my sister. Telling the policeman about him would be like an admission that he had. I wanted to keep Ivy May safe from him, in my mind if nowhere else.

No one has talked about what actually happened to Ivy May. But I can guess. I am no idiot. I saw the marks on her neck.

Tonight I was standing at my window when I saw Maude

342

standing at hers. We waved to each other, but it felt very peculiar, and after a moment I stepped back from the window. We are not allowed to visit each other, as one is not meant to pay visits while in mourning. Besides which, I don't think seeing Maude would bring much comfort to me now – all I can think of is her mother abandoning us in that huge crowd, and Ivy May's sweaty hand slipping from mine.

I sat on my bed and looked at Ivy May's little white bed in the corner. We would never lie in our beds again at night and whisper and tell each other stories – or rather, I told them and she listened. I am all alone now.

It hurt so much to look at that bed that I went down right then and asked Papa to move it.

# GERTRUDE WATERHOUSE

I am so heavy with guilt that I cannot get out of bed. The priest has come, and the doctor, and neither can rouse me.

I did not tell them, nor Albert either, that I pretended to have a sprained ankle. Albert, bless him, thought it was real. If I had not pretended, if I had taken the girls to the march – or indeed if I had stood up to Livy and not allowed her to go – Ivy May would be sitting here with me now.

I have killed my daughter with my own stupidity, and if she is not here I do not want to live either.

# EDITH COLEMAN

The first thing I did was to give that impertinent maid her notice. I am sorry to admit that anything in a house of mourning could give me satisfaction, but that did. Of course she wailed and wrung her hands, but her dramatics had no effect on me – if anything they made me more determined that I had done the right thing, and none too soon.

Jenny had the nerve to mention Maude. 'What will she do?' she kept crying.

'Maude will continue as she has always done. I will look after her – I have come to stay and will remain for as long as I am needed. But that is no concern of yours.'

Jenny looked stricken.

'I let you go two years ago,' I reminded her, 'for reasons I'm sure you remember. My daughter-in-law should never have taken you back. Pack your bag and go. Your final wages will be sent to you.'

'What about my reference?'

I snorted. 'Do you think I would give a reference to a girl like you?'

'But how am I to get another position?'

'You should have thought of that when you lay with that man.'

The girl ran from the room. To my surprise Mrs Baker appeared a few minutes later, asking me to keep Jenny on.

'Why should I keep on a girl of such lax morals?' I replied. 'Believe me, she will be much better off staying home and looking after her child, the poor mite.'

'And what will she feed him — air?'

'I beg your pardon?'

'Never mind about Jenny's son, ma'am,' Mrs Baker said. 'It's for Miss Maude's sake that I'm asking you to keep Jenny. The poor girl's just lost her mother — I hate to see her losing the people round her too. Jenny's been here since Miss Maude was a baby. She's like family to her.'

'That girl is nothing like family to Maude!' I was so furious it was a struggle to keep my voice down. 'How dare you compare her to the Colemans! And Maude doesn't need her — she's got me.' By losing a mother, she has gained a grandmother, I almost said, but thought the better of it.

So Jenny went. Maude said, not a word, though she stood in the hallway and watched her go with a very pale face.

Then, for her sake and Richard's, I made another decision. Already the morning after Kitty's death the flowers had begun arriving — elaborate arrangements of lilies, irises, corn-flowers, white roses, all tied up with purple, green and white ribbons. The cards read things like 'To our Fallen Comrade' and 'Hope is Strong — In Heaven as on Earth' and 'She Gave Herself to the Cause'. And that infernal telephone rang so much that I had a man come and disconnect it. Then suffragettes began coming to the door to ask about the funeral, until I had the hired girl who replaced Jenny turn them away. It was clear that Kitty was becoming a martyr to them. I dreaded to think what would happen if the suffragettes turned up en masse to the funeral – they might take it over and turn it into a political rally. I would never forgive myself for allowing James's family name to be dragged through the mud yet again.

I would not let it happen. I spoke to Richard of my plan and he readily agreed. After that it was not so difficult to arrange things to our satisfaction – after all, discretion is paramount in the undertaking trade.

# JENNY WHITBY

She come running after me as I walked down the street
with my bag. I'd stopped crying by then – I were too scared
of what was to become of me even to cry. She didn't say
nothing, just threw her arms round me and hugged me
tight.

There ain't nothing she can do – a girl of thirteen up
against such a grandmother? I feel terrible for breaking my
promise to her mum about that witch, but I got no influence
with someone like that – the missus should've known that.
Nor can I do nothing about keeping her secret from the
men. That's in God's hands now – or Miss Livy's, more like.

None of this should be my concern now, though – I got
my own troubles, like how to keep me mum and me son
and me on no wages and no reference. I've no time for
tears. I've the rest of the missus' silverware in my bag, but
that won't last forever.

# ALBERT WATERHOUSE

I am rather ashamed of my daughter. I know these are difficult days for her, as they are for us all; indeed I've wondered if she would hold up under the strain. But I wish Livy and Maude had not said such awful things to each other in public, and right at Ivy May's grave – my poor Ivy May, whom I could not protect from evil men. I am just glad Trudy was being comforted by a sister and did not hear them – she would have been horrified to hear herself argued over.

It was at first something to do with Maude's dress. I am no judge of these things, but she was wearing a rather fine silk dress that Livy clearly envied. Livy said something about the dress being ostentatious for a girl of thirteen to wear.

Maude then replied, 'Lavinia, you can't spell the word, must less understand what it means. Mourning dresses by definition are not ostentatious.'

I was a bit surprised, as Maude is usually so soft spoken. But then, she has just lost her mother. And Livy was shocked – and livid, I am sorry to say.

'I know enough to know that you should not be wearing

a boater with that dress,' Livy said. 'Nor should you put your hair up under a boater – it just looks silly. And it's coming down at the back. Your hair isn't thick enough to put up the way mine is.'

'Perhaps you forget that I have no mother to ask advice of,' Maude said. 'Nor a sister, nor even a maid, now.'

'I don't have a sister either! Have you forgot that?'

Maude looked mortified at her slip, and if Livy had allowed her to apologise, as she seemed about to do, their argument might have blown over. But of course Livy couldn't resist pressing her point. 'All you think of is yourself. Have you spared a thought for poor Mama, who has lost a daughter? Is there anything worse than losing one's child?'

'Losing one's mother, perhaps,' Maude said in a low voice.

These comparisons were so odious that I finally had to step in – wishing I had done so earlier. (I often wish that, when it is too late.) 'Livy, would you like to walk with your mother down to the carriage?' I asked, at the same time giving what I hoped was a sympathetic look to Maude.

'Papa, how often must I remind you – it's Lavinia.' Livy turned her back on Maude and went over to her mother. I was about to say something – what, I did not know – but before I could, Maude slipped away and ran up the path farther into the cemetery.

Later that night, I could not sleep and came downstairs with my candle to get out *Cassell's* and *The Queen*. I have never looked in women's manuals before – thankfully I have little to do with household sorts of things. But at last I found what I was looking for: both manuals say that a child mourns its parent and a parent its child for the same period of time – one year.

I left both books on the table open to those pages, but
when I came down the next morning they had been put
away.

# MAUDE COLEMAN

I could not stop shaking. I have never been so furious.

What I hated most were the horrid things I said as well. Lavinia brought out the worst in me, and it is much harder to live with that than with her remarks. I have learned to expect her to say silly and stupid things, and I have usually managed not to sink to her level, until now.

I sat for a long time by the sleeping angel. I had not known where I was running to until I ended up there. And that is where he found me. I suppose I knew he would. He sat down at the end of the slab of marble but did not look at me or say anything. That is his way.

I looked up into the bright blue sky. It was an obscenely sunny day for a funeral, as if God were mocking us all.

'I hate Lavinia,' I said, swatting at some vetch that was growing at the base of the angel's plinth.

Simon grunted. 'Sounds like something Livy would say.' He was right.

'But you ain't Livy,' he added.

I shrugged.

'Listen, Maude,' he said, then stopped.

'What is it?'

Simon tapped his finger on the marble. 'We're digging your ma's grave now.'

'Oh.' I could not think what more to say.

'It's too early to be digging it. For a funeral meant for the day after tomorrow, in sandy soil? We should be digging it tomorrow afternoon. Else it could cave in, sitting there an extra day. Dangerous enough as 'tis. Shoring don't always work in sand. And Ivy May's grave so close. Don't like to dig two graves close together like that at the same time — the dirt don't hang together so well on that side. No choice about it, though, is there?'

'Who told you to dig Mummy's grave now rather than tomorrow?'

'The guvnor. Told us this morning. Our Pa tried to argue with him but he just said to get on with it once Ivy May's funeral's done. Said he'd handle the consequences.'

I waited for Simon to continue. I could see from his face that there was something he would eventually tell me, laying it out step by step in his own time.

'So I had a little look round. Couldn't see nothing from the work map in the lodge. Then I heard that the chapel here's been booked for tomorrow morning. Now I knows the other graves dug for tomorrow's all got coffins coming from outside. Don't say which the chapel is for.'

I shook my head. 'Mummy's service is at St Anne's on Friday afternoon. Daddy told me.'

'Then one of the mutes at Ivy May's funeral just now told me they're doing a funeral at the chapel here tomorrow,' Simon continued as if I had not spoken. 'Has to be your ma. Hers is the only grave ready with nothing to go in.'

I stood up – it hurt to hear him talk about Mummy like that, but I did not want him to see how much his words upset me. 'Thank you for telling me,' I said. 'I'll try to find out from Daddy if something has been changed.'

Simon nodded. 'Just thought you'd want to know,' he said awkwardly.

I wondered if Simon knew that Mr Jackson had asked me about cremation – he seemed to find out about everything else. If he did, though, he didn't say. At Ivy May's grave Mr Jackson had caught my eye, and to his unspoken question I'd simply shaken my head. He must have guessed by then anyway that Daddy had said no – otherwise he would have heard from us.

Instead I asked Simon about something else – something I was sure he knew. 'What happened to Ivy May that day?' I said, looking straight at him. 'No one will tell me.'

Simon shifted on the marble. For a long time he didn't say anything and I wondered if I would have to repeat myself. Then he cleared his throat. 'Someone strangled her.'

His answer was so stark that I could feel my own throat tightening. 'By a man?' I managed to say.

Simon nodded, and I saw from his face that I should not ask more.

We sat for a moment without speaking.

'I'm sorry 'bout your ma,' Simon said suddenly. He leaned across and quickly kissed me on the cheek, then jumped off the grave and was gone.

Back at home I ran into Grandmother in the front hall, inspecting a bouquet of flowers that had arrived – lilies tied with green, white, purple and black ribbons. 'Suffragettes!'

she was muttering. 'Just as well we –' She stopped when she saw me. 'Back already from the meal?'

'I haven't been to the Waterhouses' yet,' I confessed.

'Not been? Get you over there, then. Pay your respects. That poor child's mother is grey with grief. Such a terrible terrible death. I hope they catch the man who –' She stopped herself.

'I will go,' I lied. 'I just – need to have a word with Mrs Baker first.' I ran downstairs so that I would not have to tell her why I was not going to the funeral meal. I just could not bear to see Mrs Waterhouse's face sucked dry of life. I could not imagine what it must feel like to lose a child, and to lose her so awfully and mysteriously. I could only compare it to how I felt losing my mother: an aching emptiness, and a precariousness about life now that one of the things I had taken for granted was gone. Mummy may have been absent or remote these past few years, but she had at least been alive. It was as if Mummy had been shielding me from a fire and then was suddenly taken away so that I could feel the scorching flames on my face.

For Mrs Waterhouse, though, there must be simply a feeling of horror that I could not begin to describe.

Was one worse than the other, as Lavinia seemed to suggest? I did not know. I just knew that I couldn't see Mrs Waterhouse's dead gaze without feeling an abyss open in myself.

Instead of going to the Waterhouses' funeral meal, I went down to ask Mrs Baker about ours. Since she was preparing it, she of all people would know if there had been a change in the arrangements.

She was stirring a pot of aspic on the range. 'Hello, Miss

Maude,' she said. 'You should eat – you haven't touched your food these last few days.'

'I'm not hungry. I – I wanted to ask if everything will be ready for Friday. Grandmother wanted me to find out for her.'

Mrs Baker gave me a funny look. 'Course it will.' She turned back to the pot. 'I just spoke to your grandmother this morning. Nothing's changed in two hours. Beef jelly will set overnight, the ham's to be delivered this afternoon. It should all be ready by the day's end. Mrs Coleman wanted me to get everything ready early so I can help her with other things tomorrow – she's not happy with the temporary help. Not that I do just anything. I won't work on my knees, no matter what.' She glared at the pot. I knew that she missed Jenny, though she would never say.

She clearly thought the funeral would be on Friday. If Daddy had changed the day, no one knew but him and probably Grandmother. I could not face asking either of them, and I knew they would not tell me anyway.

When I came down to breakfast next morning both Daddy and Grandmother were sitting at the table in their best mourning clothes, untouched cups of coffee in front of them. They had peculiar looks on their faces, but they simply said, 'Good morning, Maude,' as I sat down to a bowl of congealed porridge. I tried to eat but could not swallow, so I simply pushed at the porridge with my spoon.

The doorbell rang. Daddy and Grandmother jumped. 'I'll get it,' Grandmother said to the hired char, who was lurking by the sideboard. I frowned at Daddy but he would not look at me – he kept his eyes on the newspaper, though I don't think he was really reading it.

I heard low voices in the front hall and then heavy footsteps on the stairs, as well as creaking. Soon the footsteps sounded overhead, in Mummy's room, and I knew Simon was right.

'Why have you done this, Daddy?'

He still would not look at me. 'Finish your porridge, Maude.'

'I'm not hungry. Why have you changed the day of the funeral?'

'Go and change into your new dress, Maude.' Grandmother spoke from the doorway.

I did not move from my chair. 'I want to know why you've done this. I have a right to know.'

'You have no rights!' my father roared, banging his hand on the table so that coffee slopped from both cups. 'Don't ever let me hear you say that again. You are my daughter and you will do as I say! Now go and change!'

I did not move from my chair.

Daddy glared at me. 'Do I have no authority in my own house? Does no one obey me? Has her influence extended so far that my own daughter won't do as I say?'

I did not move from my chair.

Daddy reached over and knocked my porridge bowl to the floor. It smashed at the feet of the terrified maid.

'Richard,' Grandmother warned. She turned to me, her face more lined than usual, as if she had not slept well. 'Your mother's funeral is to be this morning. We felt it best to have a private service so that it is not taken over by the wrong element. Now, go upstairs and put on your dress. Quickly, now, while I have a word with Mrs Baker. The carriage will be here soon.'

'I didn't want it to be hijacked by the suffragettes,' Daddy said suddenly. 'You saw what happened when she was released from prison – it was turned into a victory celebration. I'm damned if I'm going to let them make a martyr of her. Fallen comrade, they call her. They can go to bloody hell!' He sat back with such a pained look that I could almost forgive him his behaviour.

I knew there was nothing I could do, so I ran upstairs. As I passed Mummy's room – which I had avoided all week, leaving anything that needed doing in there to Grandmother – I could hear tapping. They were nailing the coffin shut.

In my room I dressed quickly. Then it came to me that there *was* one thing I could do. I found paper and pen and scribbled a note, pausing for a moment to recall the address I had seen printed so often on the letters page of the local paper. Then, grabbing my hat and gloves, I raced downstairs again, passing Daddy and Grandmother's surprised faces in the front hall as I continued down to the kitchen.

Mrs Baker was standing by the table, arms crossed, glaring at the spread of food laid out, a large ham glistening with jelly the centrepiece.

'Mrs Baker,' I whispered, 'if ever you loved my mother, please find someone to take this immediately. Please, for her sake. As quick as you can, else it will be too late.'

Mrs Baker glanced at the address, then without a word she strode to the back door and wrenched it open. As I was stepping into the carriage with Daddy and Grandmother I saw her stop a boy in the street and give him the note. Whatever she said to him made him run as if he were chasing his hat in the wind.

It was pouring with rain. The undertaker had spread straw

in front of our house to muffle the horses' hooves, but it was not necessary – the rain drowned out the sound anyway. A few neighbours had seen the funeral carriages and were standing in their doorways, but most were not expecting to do so until the next day.

No one spoke in the carriage. I stared out of the window at the passing houses, and then the long brick and iron fence that separated graves from the road. The glass sides of the carriage carrying the coffin were splashed with rain. All along the route people took off their hats for a moment as we passed.

At the cemetery Mr Jackson stepped up to the carriage with a large umbrella and helped down first Grandmother and then me. He nodded at me briefly, and I managed to nod back. Then he led us through the gate to the chapel entrance, where Auntie Sarah was waiting for us. She was twelve years older than Mummy and lived in Lincolnshire. They had not been close. She pecked me on the cheek and shook Daddy's hand. Then we went into the chapel for the service.

I sat in the front pew between Daddy and Auntie Sarah, with Grandmother next to Daddy. At first it was just the four of us and the vicar of St Anne's, who led the service. But when we began the first hymn, I heard voices behind me joining in to sing 'Nearer my God to Thee', and turned to see Mr Jackson and Simon standing at the back.

Just as we'd finished the second hymn, 'Abide with me' (which, of course, Mummy had detested), the door banged open. Caroline Black stood in the doorway, breathing heavily, her hat askew, her hair tumbling down. Daddy stiffened. 'Damn her,' he muttered. Caroline Black took a seat halfway up the aisle and caught my eye. I nodded at her. When I turned back to face the front I could feel Daddy's fury next to me, and I smiled a little and lifted my chin, as Mummy used to do when she was being defiant.

Damn you, I thought. Damn you yourself.

When it was all done – when the coffin had been taken into the cemetery and laid in the grave with the gigantic urn looming over it; when Simon and his father began to fill it, working steadily in the pouring rain; when I stepped away from my mother to begin the journey home – Caroline Black reached over and took my hand. It was then that I at last began to cry.

# DOROTHY BAKER

The waste of all that food was a crime. She didn't even apologise – just said there had been a change in plans and there would be just four for the funeral meal. And there was me preparing for fifty!

I nearly walked out then and there, but for Miss Maude. In a week she's lost her mum and Jenny – and her best friend, from what the Waterhouses' char says. She doesn't need me leaving too.

# SIMON FIELD

What happens today I'll never tell Maude. Probably won't tell no one.

After Kitty Coleman's funeral our Pa and Joe and me start filling the grave. The soil's sandy, makes it hard to shovel much in at once, even in the rain. It's always harder digging in the meadow, in the sand. Clay needs more cutting with the spade, but it sticks together so you can handle it easier than sand.

We been real careful with this grave, it being so close to Ivy May's. It's twelve feet deep, so Maude and her Pa and Gran can fit in when their time comes. We done extra shoring and made sure the wood were tight as we could get it against sand. Sand can be a killer if it ain't handled right.

We're shovelling in the sand a while, and the grave's half full. It's chucking down rain and we're soaked. Then our Pa's cap falls in.

'I'll get it,' I says to our Pa.

'Nah, son, I'll get it,' he says, and jumps right in like he's a boy again. Lands straight on his cap and starts to laugh. 'Bull's eye,' he says. 'You owe me a pint.'

'Where are you going to get a pint?' I laugh. 'You'll have to walk a long way for it.'

Only pub round here that'll serve gravediggers is the Duke of St Albans the bottom of Swain's Lane, and they won't let our Pa in any more 'cause he got so drunk he tried to kiss the landlady, then wrecked a chair.

Just then there's a crack and the shoring on the side by Ivy May's grave pops out. It does that when the ground round it's shifting. Before our Pa can do anything but duck the flying wood, that side of the grave collapses.

It must happen fast, but it don't seem like it. Seem like I got lots of time to watch our Pa look up like he's just heard thunder overhead and is waiting for the next flash of lightning. 'Oh,' I think I hear him say.

Then the dirt is raining down on him, piling round him up to his waist. There seems to be a little pause then but it can't be long 'cause Joe and I ain't moved at all yet, ain't said a word, ain't even breathed.

Our Pa catches my eye for a second and seems to smile at me. Then a pile of dirt comes down and knocks him over.

'Man in!' I shout as loud as I can through the rain. 'Man in!' It's words no one likes to hear in this place.

The dirt is still moving like it's alive but I can't see our Pa now. Just like that he's not there. Joe and I scramble round the grave, trying to keep from setting off more dirt. The hole's three-quarters full now. We need a big timber or ladder to lay 'cross the hole, to give us something stable to work from, but there ain't one around. We had a ladder but someone's borrowed it.

There ain't no time to wait when a man's buried like

that. He'll die in a few minutes if he ain't got no air. I jump into the hole though I'm not supposed to, landing in the mud on all fours like a cat. I look and look and then I see the thing our Pa taught me. I see his finger sticking out the dirt, just the tip of it, wiggling. He remembered to put his hand up. I start clawing round the finger with my hands. Don't dare use a shovel. I dig so hard the sand gets jammed under my nails and it hurts bad.

'Hang on, our Pa,' I say as I'm digging. 'We're getting you out. I see your fingers. We're getting you out.'

Don't know as he can hear me, but if he can it might make him feel better.

I'm digging and digging, trying to find his face, hoping he put the other hand up to it. There ain't no time, not even to look up. If I did look up, though, I know I'd see Joe standing on the edge of the grave, looking down at me, hands at his sides. He's a big man, and can dig for hours without stopping, but he's no thinker. He don't do the delicate work. He's better off up there.

'Joe, start counting,' I say as I keep clawing at the sand. 'Start from ten and keep counting.' I reckon I've dug ten seconds.

'Ten,' Joe says. ''Leven. Twelve.'

If he gets to two hundred and I ain't found our Pa's face it'll be too late.

'Thirty-two.'

'Sixty-five.'

'One-twenty-one.'

I feel something overhead and look up. There's a ladder 'cross the grave now. If more dirt comes down I can reach up and grab hold of the rungs so it don't get me. Then someone jumps into the grave beside me. It's Mr Jackson. He reaches out with his arms wide and hugs the pile of dirt I been digging. I didn't think he were that strong but he shifts the pile back so I got more room. He do just what I need him to do without me having to say it.

'One-seventy-eight.'

My fingers touch something. It's our Pa's other hand. I dig round the hand and find his head, then dig round that and lift his hand so his mouth and nose are clear. His eyes are closed and he's white. I put my ear up to his nose but don't feel a breath tickle it.

Then Mr Jackson pushes me aside and puts his mouth over our Pa's like he's kissing him. He breathes into his mouth a few times, then I see our Pa's chest go up and down.

I look up. Round the grave, all silent and still, there's a circle of men standing – other diggers, gardeners, masons, even dung boys. Word got out fast and everybody came running. They've all took their caps off, even in the pouring rain, and are watching and waiting.

Joe's still counting. 'Two-twenty-six, two-twenty-seven, two-twenty-eight.'

'You can stop counting, Joe,' I says, wiping my face. 'Our Pa's breathing.'

Joe stops. The men all move, shifting feet, coughing, talking low – everything they held back while they was waiting. Some of 'em don't like our Pa for his love of the bottle, but no one wants to see a man caught down a grave like that.

'Hand us a spade, Joe,' Mr Jackson says. 'We've got a lot of work to do yet.'

I never been down a grave with Mr Jackson. He ain't so handy with a spade as me or other diggers but he insists on staying there with me till we get our Pa out. And he don't tell the other men to get back to work. He knows they want to see this through.

I like working side by side with him.

It takes a long time to uncover our Pa. We have to dig careful so we don't hurt him. For a time he has his eyes closed like he's asleep, but then he opens 'em. I start talking to him as I'm working so he won't get scared.

'We're just digging you out, our Pa,' I say. 'The shoring come down with you in the grave. But you covered your face like you taught me, and you're all right. We'll be moving you out in a minute.'

He don't say nothing, just keeps looking up at the sky, with the rain coming down so fast and going all over his face. He don't seem to notice it. I start to have a bad feeling which I don't say nothing 'bout 'cause I don't want to scare nobody.

'Look,' I says, trying to get him to say something. 'Look, it's Mr Jackson digging. Bet you never thought you'd see the guvnor digging for you, eh?'

Our Pa still don't say nothing. The colour's coming back to his face but something's still missing from his eyes.

'Expect I owe you that pint, our Pa,' I say, desperate now. 'Expect there's plenty of men'll be buying you a pint today. I bet they'll be letting you back in the Duke of St Albans. The landlady might even let you kiss her.'

'Let him be, lad,' Mr Jackson says real soft. 'He's just been through an ordeal. It may take him some time to recover.'

We work without talking then. When at last our Pa's

uncovered, Mr Jackson checks for broken bones. Then he takes our Pa in his arms and hands him up to Joe. Joe puts him in a cart they use to haul stones, and two men pull him down the hill towards the gate. Mr Jackson and I climb out the grave, both of us muddy all over, and Mr Jackson starts to follow the cart. I stand there not sure what to do – the grave's not filled and it's our job to do it. But then two other diggers step up and take up the spades. They don't say nothing – they and Joe just start filling the rest of the grave.

I follow Mr Jackson and the cart down the path. When I catch up to him I want to say something to thank him, something that connects us so I'm not just another digger. I was close to him in Kitty Coleman's grave and I want to remind him of that. So I say the thing I know 'bout him and her, so he'll remember the connection and know how grateful I am to him for saving our Pa.

'I'm sorry 'bout the baby, sir,' I say. 'I bet she were, too. She weren't never the same after that, were she?'

He turns and looks at me sharp like. 'What baby?' he says.

Then I realise he didn't know. But it's too late to take the words back. So I tell him.

*May 1910*

# LAVINIA WATERHOUSE

The first thing I thought when I heard the bells tolling was that they might disturb Mama in her delicate condition. But then, Mama has never been so fond of this King as she was of his mother. His death is, of course, very sad, and I do feel for poor Queen Alexandra, but it is not like when Queen Victoria died.

I threw open the window to lean out. It should have been raining, or foggy, or misty, but of course it wasn't — it was a beautiful May morning, sunny and soft. The weather never does what it ought.

Bells seemed to be ringing everywhere. Their noise was so mournful that I crossed myself. Then I froze. Across the way Maude had opened her window too and was leaning out in her white nightgown. She was staring straight at me, and she seemed to be smiling. I almost stepped away from the window, but it would have seemed very rude since she had already seen me. Instead I stayed where I was, and I was rather proud of myself — I nodded at her. She nodded back.

We have not spoken in almost two years — not since Ivy May's funeral. It has been surprisingly easy to avoid her. We no longer go to the same school, and if I have passed her in the street I've simply turned my head and pretended not to see her. Sometimes at the cemetery when I've gone to visit Ivy May I've seen Maude at her mother's grave, and then I've crept away and gone for a walk till she's done.

Only once did we come face to face in the street. It was over a year ago now. I was with Mama and she with her grandmother and so it was impossible to avoid her. Maude's grandmother went on and on giving her condolences to Mama while Maude and I stood there gazing at our shoes, not a word passing between us. It was all terribly awkward. I did manage to glance up at her from time to time, and saw that she was wearing her hair up for everyday now, and had begun wearing a corset! I was so shocked I wanted to say something, but of course I couldn't. Afterwards I made Mama take me straight out to buy a corset.

I have never said much to Mama about falling out with Maude. She knows we fought, but not why – she would be mortified if she knew it was in part over her. I know she thinks Maude and I are being silly. Perhaps we are. I wouldn't admit it to Maude but I do miss her. I have not met anyone at the Sainte Union who comes close to being the kind of friend Maude was. In fact the girls there have been rather awful to me, I think because to be honest I am so much prettier than they. It can be a burden having a face like mine – though on balance I prefer to keep it.

I expect my nod at Maude means I have forgiven her.

I went down to breakfast, still in my dressing gown, with a suitably sad face for the King. Mama, however, seemed not to notice the bells at all. She is so big now that she cannot sit easily at the table, and so she was eating a plate of marmalade toast on the chaise longue while Papa read the paper to her. Even as he read out the news Mama was smiling to herself, with a hand resting on her stomach.

'Such sad news,' I said, depositing a kiss on each of their heads.

'Oh, hello, dear,' Mama said. 'Would you like to feel the baby kicking?'

Really, it was enough to make me flee the room. It is one thing for Mama to be pleased about the baby, especially at her age, and it is good that she has some colour in her cheeks. But she seems to have altogether forgot Ivy May.

Papa smiled at me, though, as if he understood, and for his sake I stayed and managed a bowl of porridge, though I did not feel much like eating.

When I went back upstairs to change, I stood in front of my wardrobe and debated for a long while about what to wear. I knew I should wear black for the King, but just looking at that old merino rag hanging there made me feel faint. Perhaps if I'd still had the lovely silk from Jay's I would have worn that, but I burned it a year after Ivy May's death, as one is not meant to keep mourning clothes — they might tempt Fate to make one need to use them again.

Besides, I wanted to wear my blue dress, which I love. It has a special significance — I have been wearing it as often as possible, especially leading up to Mama's imminent confinement. I want a baby brother. I know it's silly, but I thought wearing the blue would help. I don't want another sister — it would hurt too much, and remind me of how I failed Ivy May so miserably. I let go of her hand.

So I put on my blue dress. At least it is dark blue — dark enough that from a distance it could be taken for black.

What is sad about today is not simply that the King is

dead, but that his mother is truly gone now. If it were she who died I would not have thought twice about wearing black. I have begun to feel recently that I am the only one who still looks back to her as an example to us all. Even Mama is looking forward. I am getting tired of swimming against the tide.

# MAUDE COLEMAN

I lay in bed for a long time and tried to guess which bells belonged to which church: St Mary's Brookfield up one hill, St Michael's and St Joseph's up the hill in Highgate, our church, St Anne's, at the bottom. Each rang just one low bell, and although each was at a slightly different pitch and tolled ever so slightly more or less slowly, still they all sounded the same. I had not heard such a noise since Queen Victoria's death nine years ago.

I stuck my head out of the window and saw Lavinia crossing herself in her window. Usually when I caught a glimpse of her somewhere – in her garden or on the street – a jolt ran through me as if someone had shoved me from behind. But now it was so strange to see her make such a foreign gesture that I forgot to be upset at seeing her. She must have learned to cross herself at the Sainte Union. I thought of her years ago being frightened of going into the Dissenters' section of the cemetery where all the Catholics are buried, and smiled. It was funny how things change.

She saw me then, and, hesitating for a moment, she nodded to acknowledge my smile. I had not meant it as a smile at her, really, but once she nodded I felt I ought to nod too.

We turned away from our windows then, and I went to get dressed, hesitating over the dresses in my wardrobe. The black silk hung there still, but it would need altering to fit me now – I had filled out since last wearing it, and I was wearing a corset besides. I had worn black for almost a year following Mummy's death, and for the first time I had understood why we are meant to wear black. It is not just that the colour reflects a mourner's sombre mood, but also that one doesn't want to have to choose what to wear. For the longest time I would wake in the morning and be relieved that I did not have to decide among my dresses – the decision had been made for me. I had no desire to wear colour, or to be concerned about my appearance. It was only when I did want to wear colour again that I knew I was beginning to recover.

I wondered sometimes how Lavinia fared with such a long period of mourning for Ivy May – six months for a sister, though I expect she kept up with her mother and wore black for a year. I wondered now what she would wear for the King.

I looked at my dresses again. Then I saw Mummy's dove-grey dress among them and thought that perhaps I could manage that. It still surprises me that her dresses now fit me. Grandmother does not approve of me wearing them, but the stroke has left her unable to speak easily, and I have managed to ignore her dark looks.

I suppose she is thinking in part of Daddy, and I do try not to wear Mummy's dresses in front of him. I could see him now, smoking a cigarette out in the garden – something Mummy forbade him to do, as he always flicks the butts into the grass. I went downstairs in the grey dress and slipped out before he saw me.

On Swain's Lane the paperboys were crying out about the King's death, and some shops were already hung with black and purple banners. No one was painting their ironwork black, though, as they had done after the Queen's death. Some people were dressed in black, but others weren't. They stopped to speak to one another, not in the hushed tones of mourners, but jovially as they spoke of the King. I remembered that when the Queen died everything ground to a halt – no one went to work, schools were closed, shops shut. We ran short of bread and coal. Now, though, I sensed this would not happen – the baker would deliver his bread, the milkman his milk, the coal man his coal. It was a Saturday, and if I went over to the Heath children would still be flying kites.

I had been planning to return a book to the library, but when I got there it was shut, with a small notice announcing the King's death pasted to the door. Some still honoured the tradition. I glanced across the road at the cemetery gate, remembering the white banner from the library falling onto the funeral procession, and Mr Jackson, and Caroline Black. It seemed a long time ago, and yet I also felt as if I'd lost Mummy only yesterday.

I didn't want to go home, so instead I crossed the road, entered the gate, and began walking up the path towards the main part of the cemetery. Halfway up Simon's father was sitting on a flat tombstone and leaning against a Celtic cross. He had a hand on each knee and was gazing into the distance the way old men do by the seaside. His eyes flashed with the blue of the sky so that it was hard to tell what he was looking at. I wasn't sure that he saw me, but I stopped anyway. 'Hello.'

His eyes moved about but did not seem to fix upon me. 'Hello,' he said.

'It is a shame about the King, isn't it?' I said, feeling I ought to make conversation.

'Shame 'bout the King,' Simon's father repeated.

I had not seen him in a long while. Whenever I looked for Simon at work, his father did not seem to be digging with him, but was off getting a ladder or a wheelbarrow or a bit of rope. Once I had seen him propped up against a grave, asleep, but had thought he was sleeping off a night of drink.

'Do you know where Simon is?' I asked.

'Where Simon is.'

I put my hand on his shoulder and looked deep into his eyes. Although they were turned in my direction, they did not show any recognition. It was as if he were blind, though he could see. Something was wrong with him – he clearly would not push a spade into clay again. I wondered what had happened to him.

I squeezed his shoulder. 'Never mind. It's been lovely to see you.'

'Lovely to see you.'

Tears pricked my eyes and nose as I continued along the path.

I tried to stay away from our grave, and wandered for a time around the cemetery, looking at the crosses, columns, urns and angels, silent and shining in the sun. But somehow in the end I still found my way there.

She was already waiting for me. When I saw her I thought at first that she was wearing a black dress, but when I got closer I realised it was blue – which was what Mummy had worn so scandalously for Queen Victoria. I smiled at that, but when Lavinia asked why I was smiling, I knew better than to say.

# SIMON FIELD

They're sitting each on her own grave, like they used to. I ain't seen them together in a long time, though neither would ever tell me what the matter was with the other whenever I saw one alone. Too much happened in too little time for them girls.

They don't see me – I hide well.

They ain't quite themselves now – they don't have their arms linked, and they don't laugh the way they used to. They're sitting far apart and making polite talk. I hear Maude ask, 'How is your mother?'

Livy gets a funny look on her face. 'Mama is going to have a baby any day now.'

Maude looks so surprised I almost laugh and give myself away. 'That's wonderful! But I thought – I thought she was too old to have children. And – after Ivy May . . .'

'It seems not.'

'Are you pleased?'

'Or course,' Livy says. 'Life does go on, after all.'

'Yes.'

They both look at their graves, at Ivy May's and Kitty Coleman's names.

'And your grandmother – how is she?' Livy asks.

'She is still living with us. She had a stroke a few months ago and can't speak.'

'Oh dear.'

'It's just as well, really. It's much easier to be with her now.'

The two of 'em giggle as if Maude's said something naughty. I come out from behind a grave and scrape my feet in the pebbles on the path so they'll hear me. They both jump. 'Hello,' Maude says, and Livy says, 'Where have you been, naughty boy?' and that's like old times. I squat by our Granpa's grave across from them, pick up two pebbles from the path, and rub 'em 'tween my fingers.

'How did you know we were here?' Maude asks.

I shrug. 'I knew you'd both come. King's dead, ain't he?'

'Long live the King,' they say together, then smile at each other.

'Isn't it a pity?' Livy says. 'If Mama has a boy she shall have to name him George. I don't like that name as much as Edward. Teddy, I would have called him. Georgie isn't quite so nice.'

Maude laughs. 'I've missed your silly remarks.'

'Hush,' Livy says.

'Simon, I saw your father just now,' Maude says suddenly.

I let the pebbles drop back onto the path.

'What happened to him?' she asks real quiet.

'Accident.'

Maude don't say nothing.

'He were buried. We got him out, but . . .' I shrug again.

'I'm sorry,' Maude whispers.

'And I,' Livy adds.

'I got something to ask you,' I says to Livy.

She stares at me. Bet she's thinking 'bout that kiss down the grave, years ago. But that's not what I'm going to ask her.

'You know I marked all the graves here. Got all of 'em in the meadow, far's I know. 'Cept yours.' I jerk my head at the Waterhouse angel. 'You told me not to, all them years back, after the Queen died. So I didn't. But I want to now. For Ivy May. To remember she's there.'

'What, to be reminded she's just bones?' Livy says. 'That's horrid!'

'No, no, it ain't that. It's to remind you she's still there. Some of her rots, sure, but her bones'll be there for hundreds of years. Longer'n these stones, even, I'll bet. Longer'n my mark. That's what matters, not the grave and what you put on it.'

Maude looks at me funny, and I can see that all these years she ain't understood my skull 'n' crossbones either, for all her being smarter than Livy.

Livy don't say nothing for a minute. Then she says, 'All right.'

I get up and go behind the plinth with my pocket knife.

While I'm back there, scratching the mark, they start talking again.

'I don't care if Simon marks the angel,' Livy says. 'I've never felt the same about it since it fell. I'm always expecting it to fall again. And I can still see the break in the nose and neck.'

'I have never liked our grave,' Maude says. 'I look at it and none of it makes me think of Mummy, even though her name's on it. Did you know she wanted to be cremated?'

'What, and placed in the columbarium?' Livy sounds horrified.

'No, she wanted her ashes scattered where flowers grow. That's what she said. But Daddy wouldn't do it.'

'I should think not.'

'It's always felt wrong, burying her here, but there's nothing to be done. As you said, life goes on.'

I finish the mark and fold up my knife. I'm glad to have done it, like I finally scratched an itch on my back. I've owed Ivy May a long time. When I come out I nod at them. 'I has to get back to work. Joe'll be wondering where I am.' I'm quiet a minute. 'You'll be coming back to see me, both of you?'

'Of course,' they say.

Don't know why I asked that, 'cause I know the answer, and it ain't the one they gave. They're growing up and they don't play in the cemetery any more. Maude's got her hair up and looks more like her mother every day, and Livy's — well, Livy. She'll be married at eighteen, to a soldier, I expect.

I hold out my hand to Maude. She looks surprised but she takes it.

'Goodbye,' I say. She knows why I'm doing it, 'cause she knows the real answer too. Suddenly she steps up to me and kisses my dirty cheek. Livy jumps up and kisses the other one. They laugh, then they link arms and start down the path together towards the entrance.

I got an idea back there behind Ivy May's grave. Listening to Maude made me think about her ma's grave, and how our Pa got buried in it. I always thought maybe it were a sign she didn't want to be buried there. Sometimes I think Mr Jackson thought the same thing. The look on his face when her coffin were lowered into the grave was like a knife turning in his gut.

I go down to see Mr Jackson. He's in the lodge meeting with a family 'bout a burial, so I wait in the courtyard. A line of men are pushing wheelbarrows 'cross to the dumping ground. This place don't stop even for a king.

When Mr Jackson's showed his visitors out, I clear my throat. 'Can I have a quick word, guvnor?' I say.

'What is it, Simon?'

'Something I need to say inside. Away from everybody.' I nod at the wheelbarrows.

He looks at me surprised, but he lets me into the lodge and shuts the door. He sits behind his desk and starts straightening the ledger he's been writing in, recording the next burial — date and time and place and depth and monument.

He's been good to me, Mr Jackson. He don't never complain 'bout our Pa not digging. He even pays him same as ever, and gives me and Joe extra time to finish. Some of the other diggers ain't happy 'bout it, but Mr Jackson shuts 'em up. They looks at our Pa sometimes and I can see 'em shiver. 'Grace of God,' they whisper. 'There but for.' They don't talk to us much, me and Joe. Like we're cursed. Well, they'll have to live with me. I ain't going nowhere, as far as I can see. 'Cept if there's a war what Mr Jackson sometimes says there might be. They'll need diggers then.

'What did you want, Simon?' Mr Jackson says. He's nervous of what I might say, wondering if I got any more surprises to tell him. I still feel bad, giving that one up 'bout Kitty's baby.

It ain't easy to say it. 'I been up at the Coleman grave,' I says at last. 'Maude and Livy were there.'

Mr Jackson stops moving the ledger and lays his hands on the desk.

'Maude were saying how her mother wanted to be burn — cremated. And how she looks at the grave now and there ain't nothing there of her mother 'cept her name.'

'Is that what she said?'

'Yep. And I were thinking —'

'You were thinking too much.'

I almost don't go on 'cause he sounds so miserable. But something about Kitty Coleman keeps linking him and me.

'I think we should do something 'bout it,' I say.

Mr Jackson looks at the door like he's scared someone might come in. He gets up and locks the door. 'What do you mean?' he says.

So I tell him my idea.

He don't say nothing for a time. Just looks at his hands laying on the desk. Then he balls his hands into fists.

'It is the bones that pose the problem,' he says. 'We have to get the fire hot enough for long enough. Special coal, perhaps.' He stops.

I don't say nothing.

'It may take some time to organise.'

I nod. We got time. I know just when to do it — when everybody's looking somewhere else.

# GERTRUDE WATERHOUSE

When she came in I didn't say a word to Livy about the blue dress. I hadn't noticed her wearing it this morning. Though it did surprise me, I managed to hide it behind burbling about the baby. I hope at least that she wears black on the day of the King's funeral. They say it is to be set for a fortnight's time.

But then, perhaps it is just as well that Livy is wearing blue. I don't think just now that I could face the drama she brings to mourning. Dear Ivy May would have been appalled at how her sister has carried on over her, when she never did when Ivy May was alive.

I do miss her. That feeling never leaves, I have discovered, nor my guilt – though I have managed at last to forgive myself.

Perhaps I am being unfair on Livy. She has grown up quite a bit over this past year. And she said that she has made it up with Maude. I am glad. They need each other, those girls, whatever has happened in the past.

'Do you know, Mama,' Livy was saying just now, 'the Colemans have had electricity installed? Maude said it's wonderful. Really I think we should have it too.'

But I was not listening. I had felt something inside me that was no kick. It was beginning.

# ALBERT WATERHOUSE

I confess I'd had a fair few. What with toasting Trudy's health and the old King's passing and the new King's health, the pints did add up. And I was in there since mid-afternoon when Trudy started. By the time Richard came in I was more or less propping up the Bull and Last's bar.

He didn't seem to notice. Bought me a pint when he heard Trudy was abed, talked about the cricket and which games would be cancelled for the King.

Then he asked me something peculiar. Fact is, I still wonder whether or not he did say it or it was the pints talking in my ear. 'Maude wants to go to university,' he said.

'Come again?'

'She came to me today and said she wants to go to a boarding school that will prepare her for the exams to get into Cambridge. What do you think I should do?'

I almost laughed – Richard always has trouble with his womenfolk. But then, anything can happen with those Coleman women. I thought of Kitty Coleman holding my arm that time I took her home, and her ankles flashing slim and lovely under her skirt on her bicycle, and I couldn't laugh.

I wanted to cry. I studied the foam on my beer. 'Let her,' I said.

Just then our char ran in and told me I have a son. 'Thank God!' I shouted, and bought the whole pub a round.

# RICHARD COLEMAN

Maude sat with me in the garden tonight while I smoked a cigarette. Then Mrs Baker called for her and she went inside, leaving me alone. I looked at the smoke curling through my fingers and thought: I will miss her when she goes.

# DOROTHY BAKER

I shouldn't have waited so long to bring Miss Maude into it. But I wasn't to know, was I? I try to mind my business. And I couldn't say anything while her grandmother was running the house. That stroke has been the biggest blessing in disguise. I could see Miss Maude blossom once her grandmother's mouth was stopped.

I didn't say anything straight away after the stroke – it would've looked bad to go against a woman after something like that. But the other day a letter I'd meant for Jenny was returned, reading 'gone away'. Of course the letter had been slit and the coins stolen. I'd been sending her the odd shilling when I could spare it, trying to help her out. I knew they were close to the edge, her and her mother and Jack. Now it seemed they couldn't manage the rent.

Later when I was going over the week's menus with Miss Maude, I decided I had to say something. Perhaps I should have said it more casual, but that's not my way. We finished, and I shut the book and said, 'Something's wrong with Jenny.'

Miss Maude sat up straight. 'What's the matter?' We don't speak of Jenny, so it was a surprise to her.

'I've had a letter returned – she and her mum have moved.'

'That doesn't mean something's wrong. Perhaps they've moved someplace – nicer.'

'She would've told me. And she doesn't have the money for nicer.' I'd never told Miss Maude how bad it was. 'Fact is, Jenny's had a hard time of it ever since your grandmother let her go without a reference.'

'Without a reference?' Miss Maude repeated like she didn't understand.

'Without a reference she can't get another job as a maid. She's been working in a pub, and her mum takes in washing. They've hardly a shilling between them.'

Miss Maude was beginning to look horrified. She is still innocent of many of the ways of the world. I didn't dare tell her what working in a pub can lead to.

Then she surprised me. 'How can she raise a son on that?'

I hadn't been sure till then that she knew Jack was Jenny's son. But she said it calmly, as if she wasn't judging her.

I shrugged.

'We must find her,' Miss Maude said. 'That is the least we can do.'

'How? It's a big city – she could be anywhere. The neighbours would've given the postman a forwarding address if they knew it.'

'Simon will find her,' Miss Maude declared. 'He knows her. He'll find her.'

I was going to say something, but she was so trusting in the boy that I didn't have the heart to dash her hopes.

'Suppose we do find her,' I said. 'What do we do then? We can't have her back here, what with the new maid making a good job of it. It wouldn't be fair to her.'

'I shall write the new maid a reference myself.'

It's surprising how quick a girl can grow up when she's a mind to.

# SIMON FIELD

When Maude tells me to find Jenny, I don't ask why. Sometimes I don't need to know why. It ain't so hard to do — turns out she's been to see our Ma, who tells me where she is. When I go there her and her mum and Jack are in a tiny room with not a crumb of food 'tween 'em — Jenny spent all her money on what our Ma could do for her.

I take 'em to a caff and feed 'em — Maude's given me money for it. The boy and his Gran eat everything in sight, but Jenny just picks at her food. She's grey in the face.

'I don't feel well,' she says.

'That'll pass,' I say, which is what our Ma always says after a woman's been to her. A few years back Jenny wanted nothing to do with what our Ma does for women, but things is different for her now. She knows what it's like to have a child don't get enough to eat. That'll change anyone's mind about bringing another mouth into the world you can't feed.

I don't say nothing, though. Jenny don't need me to remind her how things change. I keep my mouth shut, and get her to have a little soup.

Guess I've caught her just in time.

# LAVINIA WATERHOUSE

Well. I don't know. Truly I don't know what to think. Maude has often said I must try to be more open-minded, and I suppose this is one of those moments when I should try. But it is very difficult. Now I have two more secrets to keep from her.

I have just come back from the cemetery, of course. Our lives seem to revolve around it. I had gone there on my own to visit our grave. I wanted to, just before the King's funeral. Mama, of course, couldn't come because she is still in bed, with little Georgie at her side. When I left they were both asleep, which is good as I didn't want to leave her alone otherwise. Elizabeth is there, though I don't trust her with Georgie – I'm sure she would drop him on his head. Papa is at work, though he said it has been very dull and quiet there this week, everyone with long faces and doing very little – waiting for the King to be laid to rest.

I could have asked Maude to go with me, but we spent all of yesterday together, queuing up Whitehall to see the King lying in state, and I was rather happy to be in my own company.

I went to our grave and placed a new posy for Ivy May,

and weeded a bit – around the Colemans' as well as ours, for it needed attention. The Colemans can be rather lax on that front. And then I just sat. It was a lovely, sunny, quiet afternoon. I could just feel the grass and flowers and trees around me growing. I thought about the new King – King George V. I even said it aloud a few times. It is easier to accept him now that I have a brother named for him.

Then I had the idea to tour the angels. It had been so long since I had seen them all. I began with ours, of course, and walked around counting. There are far more than thirty-one now, but I looked only for those old ones from my childhood. It was like greeting old friends. I reached thirty but for the life of me I couldn't find the thirty-first angel. I was deep in the cemetery, up by the northwest corner, still searching, when I heard the bell ring for closing. Then I remembered that I had forgot the sleeping angel, and hurried down the Egyptian Avenue to it. Only when I'd seen it, lying on its side asleep, wings neatly tucked, did I feel I could go.

I rushed down the path towards the entrance. It was really very late – no one was about, and I worried that the gates might already be locked. None the less, I ran into the meadow just for a moment to say goodbye to Ivy May.

And there I found Simon and Joe and Mr Jackson, beginning to pry up the granite slab on the Coleman grave! I was so shocked I just stood there, my mouth hanging open. For an awful moment I thought I had lost Maude too. Then Simon saw me and dropped his spade, and Joe and Mr Jackson stopped as well. They all looked so guilty that I knew something was wrong.

'What in heaven's name are you doing?' I cried.

Simon glanced at Mr Jackson, then said, 'Livy, come sit a minute.' He waved at the foot of my angel. I sat under it rather gingerly — I have never quite trusted it since it fell.

Simon explained everything. At first I could say nothing. But when I had got my breath back I said, 'It is my Christian duty to remind you that what you are doing is both illegal and immoral.'

'We know,' that naughty boy replied — he said it almost gleefully!

'It is what she wanted,' Mr Jackson said very quietly.

I gazed at him. I could have his job, and Simon's. If I told the police about this, I could ruin his life, and Simon's, and upset Maude and her father dreadfully. I could.

But that would not bring back Ivy May.

They were looking at me fearfully, as if they knew what I was considering.

'Are you going to tell Maude?' I asked.

'When the time is right,' Mr Jackson said.

I let them wait a little longer. It was very quiet in the cemetery, as if all the graves were waiting for me to reply.

'I shan't tell anyone,' I said at last.

'You sure, Livy?' Simon said.

'Don't you think I can keep a secret? I haven't told Maude about what happened to her mother, you know — about the baby. I did keep that secret.'

Mr Jackson started and turned red. I looked at him and, after years of leaving the puzzle unfinished in my mind, I at last allowed him to take his place next to Kitty in the story. To my great surprise I felt sorry for him.

Another secret. But I wouldn't tell. I left them to their gruesome task and ran home, trying not to think about it.

It was not so hard – once I'd got in and was holding my baby brother in my arms, I discovered it was quite easy to forget everything but his sweet face.

# MAUDE COLEMAN

It was long past midnight when Daddy and I came to the top of Parliament Hill. We had gone to the Hampstead Scientific Society's new observatory by Whitestone Pond to look at Halley's Comet, and were walking across the Heath on our way home.

It has been a disappointing viewing – the waxing moon was shining so brightly that the comet was rather indistinct, though its long curved tail was still spectacular. But Daddy loves the observatory – he campaigned so hard to have it built – and I did not want to spoil his evening there by complaining about the moon. I was one of the few ladies present, and kept very quiet.

Now, though, with the moon lower in the sky, the comet was more visible, and I felt more relaxed than I had been in the dome with its narrow slit of sky, crowded with men drinking brandy and smoking cigars. Lots of people were still out on the hill, looking at the comet. Someone was even playing 'A Little of What You Fancy' on an accordion, though no one danced – the King was being buried in a few hours' time, after all. It was strange that the comet should be in the sky the night before his funeral. It was the kind of thing Lavinia would make a great deal of, but I knew it was simply a coincidence, and coincidences can often be explained.

'Come, Maude, let's go home,' Daddy said, flicking a cigarette butt into the grass.

Something flared in the corner of my eye. I looked across at the next hill towards Highgate and saw a huge bonfire burning, lighting up the trees around it. Among the dancing branches I thought I saw the cemetery's cedar of Lebanon.

That fire was certainly no coincidence – someone had probably lit it for the King. I smiled. I love fire. I felt almost as if it had been lit for me as well.

Daddy disappeared down the hill into the darkness ahead of me, but I remained a little longer, my eyes flicking back and forth between the comet and the flames.

# SIMON FIELD

It takes a long time. We're at it all night. He were right 'bout the bones.

Afterwards as the sun's coming up we get some buckets and half fill 'em with sand. We mix the ashes into it and we sprinkle it all over the meadow. Mr Jackson has plans to let wildflowers grow there, like she wanted. That'll make a change from all them flowerbeds and raked paths.

I still got a little left in a bucket and I goes to our Granpa's rosebush and dump the rest there. That way I'll be sure of where some of her is, if ever Maude wants to know. 'Sides, bonemeal's good for roses.

# ACKNOWLEDGEMENTS

The Acknowledgements is the only section of a novel that reveals an author's 'normal' voice. As a result I always read them looking for clues that will shed light on writers and their working methods and lives, as well as their connections with the real world. I suspect some of them are in code. Alas, however, there are no hidden meanings in this one – just an everyday voice that wants to express gratitude for help in several forms.

Sometimes I wonder if Acknowledgements are even necessary, or if they break the illusion that books emerge fully formed from a writer's mind. But books don't come out of nowhere. Other books and other people contribute to them in all sorts of ways. I used many books in the making of this one. The most helpful were *The Victorian Celebration of Death* by James Steven Curl (Stroud: Sutton Publishing, 2000), *Death in the Victorian Family* by Pat Jalland (Oxford: Oxford University Press, 1996), *Death, Heaven and the Victorians* by John Morley (London: Studio Vista, 1971), and, my favourite, *On the Laying Out, Planting, and Managing of Cemeteries, and on the Improvement of Churchyards* by J. C. Loudon (1843; facsimile published Redhill, Surrey: Ivelet Books, 1981).

It is a novelist's privilege to make up what she likes, even when real people and places enter the story. The cemetery in this book is made up of a lot of fact and a fair bit of fiction – concrete details and flights of fancy interwoven, with no need to untangle them. While a real cemetery exists where this book takes place, I have not tried to recreate it completely accurately; rather it is a state of mind, peopled with fictional characters, with no resemblances intended.

Similarly, I have toyed with a few details in the suffragettes' history in order to bring them into the story. I have taken the liberty of putting words into Emmeline Pankhurst's mouth that she did not actually say, but I trust I have kept to the spirit of her numerous speeches. Moreover, Joan of Arc and Robin Hood did march in a procession, dressed as I have described, but it was not the Hyde Park demonstration. Gail Cameron at the Suffragette Fellowship Collection of the Museum of London was very helpful in providing me with useful resources.

Finally, thanks go to my quartet of minders – Carole Baron, Jonny Geller, Deborah Schneider, and Susan Watt – who remained steady when I wobbled.

# *The Virgin Blue*
## TRACY CHEVALIER

The compelling story of two women, born four centuries apart,
and the ancestral legacy that binds them.

Ella Turner does her best to fit into the small, close-knit community
of Lisle-sur-Tarn. She even changes her name back to Tournier, and
knocks the rust off her high school French. In vain. Isolated and
lonely, she is drawn to investigate her Tournier ancestry, which
leads to her encounter with the town's wolfish librarian.

Isabelle du Moulin, known as Le Rousse due to her fiery red hair,
is tormented and shunned in the village – suspected of witchcraft
and reviled for her association with the Virgin Mary. Falling pregnant,
she is forced to marry into the ruling family: the Tourniers.
Tormentor becomes husband, and a shocking fate awaits her.

Plagued by the colour blue, Ella is haunted by parallels with the past,
and by her recurring dream. Then one morning she wakes up to
discover that her hair is turning inexplicably red . . .

'Tracy Chevalier's first novel is a triumph. Excellent.'
*Time Out*

'An intriguing and poignant read.'
*Sunday Express*

'Such an achievement for a serious writer that you feel it
deserves an award.'
*Independent*

ISBN 0 00 710827 3

# *Girl with a Pearl Earring*
# TRACY CHEVALIER

In seventeenth century Delft, a prosperous town in Holland, life was orderly. Rich and poor, Catholic and Protestant, master and servant: all know their place.

So when Griet becomes a maid in the household of the painter Johannes Vermeer, she thinks she knows her role: housework, laundry, and the care of his six children. She even feels able to handle his shrewd mother-in-law, his restless, sensual wife and their jealous servant.

What no-one expects is that Griet's quiet manner, quick perceptions and fascination with her master's paintings will draw her inexorably into his world. As she becomes part of his work their growing intimacy spreads tension and deception in the ordered household and even – as the scandal seeps out – ripples in the town beyond.

Tracy Chevalier was inspired by the girl from one of Vermeer's most loved and mysterious paintings. She has created an extraordinary and moving novel on the corruption of innocence and the price of genius.

'A wonderful novel, mysterious, steeped in atmosphere, deeply revealing about the process of painting . . . truly magical.'
*Guardian*

'Chevalier is the master of the telling detail, the evocative image . . . this is a hugely affecting novel. The reader is drawn into the world of the painting, into the mood of the masterpiece. Moving, mysterious and at times almost unbearably poignant.'
*The Times*

'Ultimately absorbing . . . suspended in a particular moment, it transcends its time and place.'
*The New Yorker*

ISBN 0 00 723216 0

# *The Lady and the Unicorn*
# TRACY CHEVALIER

It was the commission of a lifetime.

Jean Le Viste, a fifteenth-century nobleman close to the King, hires
an artist to design six tapestries celebrating his rising status at Court.
Nicolas des Innocents overcomes his surprise at being offered this
commission when he catches sight of his patron's daughter, Claude.
His pursuit of her pulls him into the web of fragile relationships
between husband and wife, parents and children, lovers and servants.

It was a revolutionary design.

In Brussels, renowned weaver Georges de la Chapelle takes
on the biggest challenge of his career. Never before has he attempted
a work that puts so much at stake. Sucked into a world of temptation
and seduction, he and his family are consumed by the project and by
their dealings with the rogue painter from Paris.

The results changed all their lives.

'A beautifully written tale, I could not put it down . . . This is not just
a novel about the creation of a work of art, but a tale of ambition,
lust, betrayal and heartbreak . . . a compelling and enormously
enjoyable work.'
*Evening Standard*

'*The Lady and the Unicorn* will perhaps eclipse *Pearl Earring*.'
*Guardian*

ISBN 0 00 714091 6